THE DEAD WON'T SLEEP

Anna Smith has been a journalist for over twenty years and is a former chief reporter for the *Daily Record* in Glasgow. She has covered wars across the world as well as major investigations and news stories from Dunblane to Kosovo to 9/11. *The Dead Won't Sleep* is the first thriller in a series featuring crime journalist Rosie Gilmour.

THE DEAD WON'T SLEEP

ANNA SMITH

Quercus

First published in Great Britain in 2011 by Quercus
This paperback edition first published in 2011 by

Quercus
55 Baker Street
7th floor, South Block
London
W1U 8EW

A CIP catalogue record for this book is available from the British Library

ISBN 978 0 85738 492 8

10 9 8 7 6

Typeset by Ellipsis Digital Limited, Glasgow
Printed and bound in Great Britain by Clays Ltd, St Ives plc

For Franco – the legend – and that long
dusty road to Mongolia, with love. x

Only do not forget, If I wake up crying
it's because in my dreams I'm a lost child
hunting through the leaves of the night for your
hands.

Pablo Neruda, *100 Love Sonnets,* XXI

PROLOGUE

Ayrshire coast, September 1997

'She's dead! Christ's sake! Jack! Wake up for Christ's sake! The bird's dead. What the hell did you do to her?'

Somewhere in Jack's fogged head, he could hear the words drag him out of a drunken sleep. His head was thumping. He opened one eye and tried to focus on the figure towering over his bed.

'Wh . . . What? Who's dead? What are you talking about, Foxy?' Jack's voice was thick and groggy as he blinked and sniffed. He was in that shitty place between drunk and sober, his body shuddering from being woken before the booze had worn off. Then he was bolt upright on the bed, his head spinning, dizzy with the sudden exertion. The room swayed. Maybe it was the movement of the boat.

The look on Foxy's face made his stomach turn over.

Jack shook his head and leaned across the bed to see what was causing the worried look in Foxy's eyes. Foxy never looked worried.

When he saw her, his mouth went dry.

'Oh, fuck,' was all he could say.

Slumped on the floor at the side of the bed was a naked, waif-like blonde girl. Her pale blue eyes stared up at him with a look of surprise. Her lips were blue, and there was a shiny streak of dried saliva on her ghost-white silky cheek. One scrawny arm was raised above her head and the other draped over her skinny body. Her legs, long and slender, were slightly parted at the knees. In the cold light of day, she looked no more than fourteen or fifteen.

Dim recollections flashed through Jack's head, the images unfolding in a confused blur. The girl had laughed when he had joked about her fair, sparse pubic hair, asking her if she was really old enough to be doing this. She did look very young last night, but as he rolled her around the bed, her responses made him believe this little hooker had been around the course a few times. And anyway, by that time he wasn't much caring what age she was.

'Aw Jesus! Holy Christ, Foxy!' Jack leapt out of bed and pulled on his boxer shorts over his beer belly.

'I don't know! Christ! I mean . . . She was fine. She was all right.' He tried to remember everything they had done, in case he had been too rough. Jack liked rough, but he knew just how far you could push it. Rough enough to see the fear in their eyes, the pleading. It gave him control.

'It was just the usual stuff,' he said. 'Nothing crazy. Then we fell asleep. I mean . . . I was out of my face, Foxy. We all were. I didn't hurt her. Honest to Jesus I didn't. I swear on my kid's life.' Jack stumbled around the room, shoved his legs into a pair of trousers and pushed his beefy arms into a short-sleeved shirt.

The door of the cabin swung open and Bill stood in the doorway, dressed in his underpants. His eyes flicked around the room.

'Fuck's going on? What's all the noise?' He scratched his head. Then he saw the girl.

'Shit! What the hell happened?' He was across the tiny cabin in two strides.

All three of them stood looking at the limp body lying in front of them, as though if they kept on looking she would get up and laugh out loud at the expression on their faces. But she just lay there, staring up at them. Bill knelt down and felt her arm, then her neck. He pulled his hand back quickly.

'She's freezing. Christ! She's been dead for a few hours I'd say.' He stood away from her.

'What we going to do?' Jack looked at Foxy for answers. His mind flashed back to the night before. How they all took turns with the girl, and he ended up with her in his bed.

'I didn't harm her. Honest. You can see that yourself.' There were tears in Jack's eyes, and he felt a rising urge to throw up. The boat swayed and he rushed to the toilet. As he retched into the bowl, he could hear Foxy and Bill talking outside.

'We'll have to dump her.' Foxy's voice was controlled, the voice of reason. It was the tone he used when he had to remain calm in a crisis, when he was briefing his men on matters of great importance. It was the voice of the head of the CID.

Jack emerged from the toilet, his face crimson. He sniffed, and wiped tears from his face.

'Wrap her in that sheet,' Foxy said flatly, looking at both of them.

Jack and Bill followed the order, dragging the sheet from the bed. Jack lifted the girl by her shoulders, her arms flopping, as Bill lifted her legs and put the sheet under her. She was skin and bone. Her eyes continued to stare at them.

'Wait,' Foxy said, as they were about to cover her with the white sheet. He took a step towards them, reached out his hand and closed the girl's eyes. Nobody spoke. Then he picked up a mobile phone that was lying at her side, and flicked through the numbers.

Foxy led the way up to the deck, as Jack and Bill carried the girl's body up the steep steps.

'She's light as a feather,' Jack said, swallowing hard.

Outside on the deck, the early morning mist shrouded the land in the distance. In the pale, grey light you could just make out the craggy mound of Ailsa Craig pushing itself out of the water like a monumental silent witness. The air was damp, and in the chilly dawn there was no sound except the gentle lapping of the water against the side of the boat. Foxy motioned them to the edge of the deck, his rubber soles squeaking on the polished wood. He looked at the two of them and jerked his head towards the water.

Jack looked at Bill; they both stood there, paralysed.

'What? Like just throw her over?' Jack said.

'There's nothing anyone can do for her now, Jack,' Foxy replied. 'Nothing any one of us can do. And we sure as fuck can't call the cops.' Foxy looked out to sea, his face like flint. Then he threw the mobile as far as he could.

She hardly made a splash as she dropped down from the side of the boat. Jack watched her foot just before it disappeared beneath the water. Then nothing. All that remained was the white sheet, billowing in the swell.

CHAPTER ONE

Glasgow, February 1998

The mobile rang and shuddered at the same time in Rosie Gilmour's jacket pocket. She fished it out and glanced to see if she recognised the number. She didn't.

'Hallo.' Rosie's voice was sharp. She wasn't in the mood to talk to anyone. It had been a crap morning spent at the police press conference after the body of a girl had washed up on the beach at Troon three days ago. There hadn't been much left of her, but she'd been identified by dental records as the fourteen-year-old kid who had been reported missing from a Glasgow children's home nearly six months before. Rosie had worked on the story at the time. No matter how many times she waded through this kind of shit, it still got to her.

She pressed the phone hard to her ear, against the racket

of the Argyle Street traffic jam. She could hear the pinging sound of a callbox, but nobody was talking.

'Hallo,' she said again, her voice slightly more receptive. Better to be friendly. It could be anyone.

'Hallo.' The voice on the other side finally came through. Rosie thought she detected a slight slur. Christ, she thought. Some bastard's given my number out at the office.

'Is that Rosie Gilmour fae the *Post*? The reporter?' The voice was clearer now.

'Yeah. This is Rosie Gilmour. Who's this?' Her naturally suspicious mind surfaced. Either it was a junkie looking for payment for some story they had helped on, or some saddo wanting Rosie to sort out all her problems. Rosie wished people back at the newsroom wouldn't keep giving her mobile out to every misfit from here to Karachi.

'You don't know me, I don't want to give ma name. But I want to talk to you about that lassie that got washed up in the sea.'

The voice was definitely that of a junkie. Rosie had spent enough days with the flotsam on the streets that chic, trendy Glasgow turned its back on, to recognise the familiar slur of a gauching heroin addict. But it was what they said that was important, not how they said it.

'Yeah?' Rosie was interested. 'I'm involved in that story. I was at the press conference this morning. The cops are still doing tests, but it looks like she was an addict. Did you know her? Was she a friend?' Rosie's voice probed. She had to keep this girl on the phone.

Silence. Damn.

'Hallo,' Rosie said, 'are you still there? Hallo?' She cursed under her breath. Typical, dizzy bastard junkies. You never knew where you were with them.

Through the silence she could hear sniffs and sobs.

'Hold on . . . Hold on . . . Sorry. I'm upset. I can't stop greetin',' the girl sobbed.

'It's okay.' Rosie was relieved she was still there. 'Look, where are you? Why don't I come and meet you? We can have a wee chat.' Rosie's voice was consoling. She was good at this.

'Ah can't get ma name in the papers, but I know stuff. I know stuff that'll blow everything sky high. I know where Tracy was before she went missin'. I know. She was ma pal, she wisnae a junkie. No a right one. Just smoked heroin and took coke,' the voice said, between sniffs.

Rosie was hooked in. Even if this was the voice of some broken heroin addict wanting to tell her an unprovable, unpublishable story, she had to hear it. You win some you lose some – but more often than not you got a front page out of it. And even if you didn't, you never knew when you would need a handy contact in the gutter. The downside was that once you had made that contact and shown these people the slightest attention, they clung to you, got under your skin, and you just couldn't help lending a sympathetic ear, and, usually, a tap of a tenner.

The Strathclyde Police press conference that morning would have written off Tracy Eadie as just another dead junkie. The only difference was that she was fourteen years old and she was naked when she washed up on the beach at Troon. And, the headline grabber: she was from a children's home. That was the only reason it would get on the front page of the *Post* these days. Nobody even turned a hair now when a junkie was found up some close with a needle in their arm. Time was when it would be a splash and spread, with a parade of rent-a-quote experts wringing their hands at how awful life was in the lower depths. But now a dead junkie would barely make a few paragraphs in any newspaper. Rosie was disgusted by the shallow mindset of the tossers who set the criteria – the editors and executives, who too often replaced depressing, cutting-edge stories with showbiz crap. But that's how it was.

She had been on the story briefly when the kid went missing from the children's home, but, as usual, the news agenda moved on. There were rumours at the time that the kid had been working the Drag as a prostitute at night, but nobody had any concrete evidence. Junkies would tell you just about anything to get a few quid, so none of the claims that came into the *Post* at the time stood up. The cops and the social work department had insisted there was nothing to suggest she'd been working the streets. She was just another child from the system who went missing. She would turn up on a street some day, somewhere, homeless and drugged up.

'Tell you what.' Rosie spoke with more command than consolation now. 'Meet me at the Grass Cafe off London Road in twenty minutes. We'll talk then. No names, nobody needs to know who you are, just trust me. Okay? Don't worry, I'll look after you.' Rosie knew the last words would bring the junkie running to her. Being looked after might mean a few quid – enough for a tenner bag. If nothing else made her keep the date, that would. It made Rosie feel like a dodgy salesman, but it always did the trick.

'Right. Okay. I'll be there. How will I know you?'

'I've got black hair and I'm wearing a light raincoat,' Rosie said. 'But don't worry about me. What do you look like?'

'I've got on a blue rain jacket and jeans. Ma hair's blonde. Streaks.'

'I'll recognise you,' Rosie said, confident that she would look like any other haunted Belsen victim you saw in housing schemes across the city.

The line went dead.

CHAPTER TWO

Chief Superintendent Gavin Fox, head of CID at Strathclyde Police, pressed the intercom buzzer on the flashing telephone on his desk.

'Tell them to come in, Patsy.' His voice was friendly, benign. He hoped there were no telltale signs when he'd walked through the door of his office this morning on the eighth floor of Riverdale House. Patsy had been with him so long that she could detect if there was anything on his mind. She watched him like a hawk, but he didn't mind that. He even suspected she might have an inkling of some of the dirty little secrets in his life, but she was one of those women who just got on with her work and didn't ask questions – the way women used to be before they got too big for their bras and started all this women's lib shite. Now there were even women in the force telling some of the men what to do. Christ! Most of them were hairy-arsed lesbians, and he had no time for any of them. Women cops were fine, and there were times when a woman's touch came in handy on certain enquiries, but not on the front line. They couldn't be trusted, with their hormones diving all over the place and getting in the way of men's work.

Fox sat back in his chair and pushed away from his desk, turning his head to look out at the sun glistening on the River Clyde. He loved that sight. It always calmed him, watching the river flow as his mind charted a path down through the towns from Glasgow to the sea where he spent his sailing weekends on his beloved boat. But today, even the sight of the river gave his guts a little tweak. He took a deep breath and patted his stomach, toned from his rigorous fitness regime, as if to give it a warning to toughen up. He mustn't show any weakness in front of Jack or Bill. Holding his nerve was crucial, especially now. For the last six months, all three of them had lived in dread that the body they'd fed to the fish would wash up on the beach. From the moment the kid was reported missing from the children's home, there was a gut-wrenching inevitability that it was the girl they'd been with that night. You couldn't have made it up.

He had managed to contain his rising panic when he took the phone call three days ago on his way to work, telling him that a naked body had been washed up at

Troon. He was hoping there wouldn't be much of her left after six months in the water, and he was relieved when forensics said they were struggling to ID her, or find any cause of death. But within two days they knew from dental records who she was. Now, more than ever, he had to show Jack and Bill what he was made of.

'Chaps,' Fox said cheerily, as the door opened and Chief Inspector Jack Prentice and Superintendent Bill Mackie shuffled into the room. By the looks on their faces they were not bearing up.

'Sit down for Christ's sake,' Fox said. 'Look at the nick of the two of you. I've seen less guilty-looking men standing with a smoking gun in their hand. Christ almighty, gents, get a fucking grip!'

Fox was on his feet, moving from behind his desk to be closer to the pair. He was just plain Foxy now, and these were his mates of nearly thirty years. They had been together through it all, from lifting toerag housebreakers as beat cops and kicking seven shades of shit out of them in back alleys, to busting drug dealers and hired killers. They had lied for each other in the witness box to put lowlifes behind bars, and they'd never so much as turned a hair when some well-fed, port-jowled defence QC laid into them, trying to pick holes in their stories. Fuck them too! All they cared about was their fat legal aid fee to feed their champagne and cocaine lifestyle. Foxy and his mates knew what justice was and, if you wanted to take some bastard off the streets, you had to break some rules as well as legs along the way. Sure, they'd fucked up big-style now, but some cheap little junkie whore who happened to die on his boat was not about to bring them all down.

'Right, lads. How's it going?' Foxy said, rubbing his hands as he sat on his desk facing them.

Silence. He looked from one to the other, his eyes resting on Jack. He didn't look well.

'I'm shitting myself, Foxy,' Jack said. 'I don't mind telling you. From the moment we ditched that wee lassie over the edge of the boat I've hardly slept a wink. I knew she would turn up some day. I knew it. I feel like I'm constantly going to throw up.' Jack looked and sounded like a condemned man.

'Me too,' Bill said. 'My arse is twitching. But here's the deal . . .' He turned to Jack. 'Jack. You'd better buckle down here. The bottom line is that nobody has a single thing on any of us. I mean we're more or less above suspicion. It's only because *we* know what we did that we're worried. We'll just have to tough it out.' Bill sounded as though he was trying to convince himself. He'd been doing that better than Jack these past months.

'Exactly, Bill,' Foxy said. He pushed away the niggle in his stomach and kept his voice calm. 'And anyway,' he continued, spreading his hands out in front of him, 'we didn't actually do anything. The stupid wee bitch just died. I didn't lay a hand on her. Well, apart from the shag. I mean, none of us harmed her in any way. Under normal circumstances she would have been well paid and dropped off somewhere in the morning. We didn't kill her, she just upped and died on us. Wee fucking bitch!' He rubbed his chin and looked at the two of them. 'It must have been the coke. Perhaps she'd had a lot of stuff before she arrived at the boat.' He put his hands in his pockets and squared his shoulders. 'Look, lads, we've been through all of this back to front in the last few months. We'll deal with it. The bird's been in the water for six months. There's nothing on her for forensics.'

The door opened and Patsy came in carrying a tray with cups and teapot. She set it down on her boss's table and did not make eye contact with any of them, not even when Foxy thanked her.

He watched the door closing behind her before he continued.

'Bill,' he said, pouring the tea into cups, knowing they were noticing his steady hands. 'How did the press conference go this morning?'

'The usual, Foxy,' Bill said. 'The only real interest is because the bird was fourteen and she was naked. And because she was that missing lassie.' He looked away. 'There were obvious questions from the slavering hacks.

You know. Sexual assault. Rape. Murder. Big McCann from Ayr's handling it. They only gave the basic information out at the press conference. They said forensic tests were still ongoing. Somebody asked how long she'd been in the water, but they couldn't be accurate. I was there because the girl's from Glasgow and we're liaising, but I didn't say anything. Just sat in the background.'

'Fine,' Foxy said. 'They'll be sniffing around looking for a murder because of the other whore murder last year. But this is different. They'll never find anything. As you say, Bill, there's nothing to link her to the night she went missing. Nothing.' He was confident. 'So, Bill. Any questions about how she got there? Any imaginative theories from the hacks? You know how the bastards don't allow the facts to get in the way of a good story.' Foxy walked towards the window with his tea in his hand.

'No, not yet. We'll have to wait and see how the papers handle it, but these days nobody bothers with junkies. It's only because she was that missing kid, but we've suspected that since she washed up. We've lived with it. We'll just need to keep going.'

They both looked at Jack.

His face turned beetroot. 'I know, Foxy. It's my fault. We've already been through all that. How the fuck was I to know she was only fourteen and from a children's home?' Sweat had broken out on his forehead. 'But I was assured she was eighteen. One of her pals told me. One of the lassies we've used before. She said she knew her. What was I supposed to do? Ask for a passport?'

He looked pleadingly at Foxy.

'I mean this is the biggest nightmare of my life, Foxy. Honest to Christ. I'm at home with my wife and daughter and I can't concentrate on anything. Even at work, I feel as if I'm going around in a daze. That wee lassie. I mean we just fucking dumped her like a piece of meat.' Jack was on the verge of tears.

Foxy put his cup down on the desk and took a deep breath. He could see Jack was beginning to break already. If this was Jack when there was really nothing to worry about, he wouldn't like to see him if there was any heat on. Typical Jack. In the beginning, when they were just young cops together trying to make their mark, it was always Jack who was the weakest. A big bear of a man and the best pal anybody could ever have, but when backs were to the wall you could hear the sound of bottle crashing. The first time they got paid off by big Jake Cox, Jack had been panicking in case they were caught. It had taken a few payoffs and reassurances for Jack to get fully into how you could make the system work, and still manage to do your bit to clean up the streets. Over the years, he'd become more confident about it, as long as he knew his two mates would be at his side. They would never desert each other. They'd stick together – they knew too much not to – but now was definitely not the time for Jack to develop a serious conscience.

'Stop that now, Jack,' Foxy snapped at him. 'There's nothing to worry about. It's you and your fucking Catholic guilt. Okay, the lassie died. But she would have died anyway. Sooner or later. They all end up like that. She might not have been injecting heroin when we met her, but you can guarantee she would have been before the year was out. And she'd have been dead by twenty-one.'

He drank from his cup and set it down on the table.

'I mean we never abused her or anything. We didn't hurt her. We don't hurt any of these birds. It's just a bit of fun. Only this time it went wrong.' Foxy sat back down and looked straight at Jack and Bill, the way he always did when he was trying to convince them that everything would be fine.

'Listen, Jack. Bill.' He looked from one to the other. 'Now listen good. We're all in this together. We've just got to stay strong for a few weeks and this will all blow over. Let's keep our heads down and our chins up. 'Cos if we don't, it'll show and I don't want to think what could happen if any of this gets out.'

Foxy stood, a signal for Bill and Jack to leave. They got up and shook each other's hands. Foxy noticed that Jack's was like a wet dishcloth.

They went out of the room and Foxy walked over to the wall next to the window and looked at himself in the mirror. He was a handsome man for his fifty years. The dark hair, flecked with grey, gave him that distinguished look of a man you could trust. He looked at the framed photograph of himself on the wall, holding an award, surrounded by police chiefs and the Lord Provost. Yes. Gavin Fox had stood tall in his uniform, and he admired the photograph of him in his black tunic. He ran his hands over the picture, caressed the blue and red ribbons he wore that day over his breast pocket. Medals of distinction, honour. He just had a little weakness for women, but it was his secret. In twenty-five years of marriage, his wife had never suspected anything of his boat trips with the lads at the weekend. That's how it would stay, Foxy vowed to himself. That's how it must stay.

CHAPTER THREE

Few places depressed Rosie more than the East End of Glasgow. The smell of fat from greasy-spoon cafes hung in the air against the backdrop of cheap clothes shops, selling rubbish gear to kids and parents who existed in a world far removed from the designer stores in the city centre just a mile away.

For Rosie, the East End stank of poverty and failure. And every time she went there, a flood of buried childhood memories came rushing back to remind her of who she was and where she came from. Now she sat at the window, watching the drizzle cling to the grimy glass of the Grass Cafe, and closed her eyes to push away the image of the little girl trudging up the road in no hurry to go home. There was nothing to go home to. Her mum would be comatose on the couch as usual.

She could still call up that smell her mother had when

she used to grab Rosie and kiss her, once she'd roused her from drunken sleep. Stale booze and fags, mixed with the musty but potent smell of Worth perfume that had been on too long.

'Can I get you somethin'?' The voice broke into Rosie's gloomy reverie. She looked up at the skinny girl in the light blue overall, her hair tied up in a neat ponytail and her eyes bright and inquiring.

'Tea please. Just tea,' Rosie said, smiling at her.

The girl walked smartly back to the counter and ordered the tea from the woman behind the formica, working at the deep-fat fryers. They exchanged a few words then both glanced over at Rosie who looked away from them. They were probably wondering who she was. A copper? A social worker? Dressed in her raincoat and black suit, Rosie stood out from the other customers in the cafe. One woman sat eating chips and smoking a cigarette between mouthfuls. An old man with no teeth was trying to negotiate a fried-egg roll. Rosie felt a little sick as she watched him sucking the yolk. In the far corner a boy of no more than eighteen had made three attempts to pick up a mug of tea, but his hands trembled so much he couldn't put it to his lips. Another junkie. 'Glasgow's Miles Better'. Sure it was. Rosie smiled to herself thinking of the logo and the yellow, smiley-face icon that had been the city's image across the world. The thing was, despite all this crap and poverty and drugs, the city still had the balls to smile at itself.

The door opened and an emaciated young woman walked in, leading a little girl by the hand. She looked around, and her eyes rested on Rosie. Rosie hadn't expected a kid. She moved to get up and the girl came towards her.

'You Rosie?' she asked. The little girl by her side smiled at her.

'Yeah. Sit down, sit down. Thanks for coming.' Rosie had been down this road before with drug addicts, and you needed to be in control from the moment you met them. If you were a soft touch they would dip your bag the minute your back was turned.

Rosie said she was having some tea and asked if they wanted anything.

'Sorry,' Rosie said. 'I don't even know your name.'

'Mags,' the girl said. 'And this is my wee girl, Gemma. She's seven.'

'Hi, Gemma,' Rosie said, softening to the girl, who appeared well looked after for a junkie's kid. 'Do you want something to eat, Gemma?'

'Can I get chips?' the girl said, sitting on her hands, her big blue eyes looking from Rosie to her mum.

'Chips?' Rosie said. 'It's only half past ten in the morning. You can't eat chips at this time.'

There was a silence. Gemma's face fell. 'I like chips,' she murmured.

The waitress was at the table, watching the scene with her pencil and pad at the ready.

'One plate of chips please,' Rosie said. 'And . . . ?' She looked at Mags without saying her name in front of the waitress. Walls had ears around these places.

'A strawberry milkshake,' Mags said, pulling a pack of ten Embassy Regal from her pocket.

Rosie nodded to the waitress, who gave her a knowing look that said the milkshake was the typical junkie drink. The waitress looked as though she wondered what this well-dressed woman was doing in this company. Rosie ordered more tea for herself.

Mags lit up the cigarette and inhaled so deeply that Rosie wondered if the smoke was going to come out of her ears. Gemma sat staring at Rosie, who figured Mags must be around twenty-two. Her stick-thin figure made her look like a kid, and she wore a tight pink T-shirt, with a heart on the chest and a quote that said, 'love is in the air . . .' Rosie glanced at it and looked out of the window at the rain. Sure it was. The T-shirt came only halfway down Mags's midriff. There was no stomach, just a narrow waist and a silver ring in her navel. The pervert punters liked that skinny childlike frame, and Rosie knew they paid more if the girl was younger. But despite her skinny body, Mags's face showed the ravages of years of heroin. The pupils of her strikingly green eyes were tiny, indicating that she had recently had a hit, probably her first of the morning. At least she would be in coherent shape to talk.

'Well, Mags,' Rosie said softly. 'Tell me about Tracy Eadie. It's a terrible thing that happened, but the cops don't seem that bothered, to be honest with you. The only thing that's keeping them on the ball is that she was so young and from a children's home. That's what'll keep it in the papers.' Rosie knew that sounded a bit tactless, but she didn't see the point of pulling any punches. 'Is there anything you can tell me? Maybe I can do something. Maybe I can investigate.' Rosie leaned forward.

'Tracy's deed,' Gemma piped up, taking Rosie by surprise. 'It was on the news.'

'Shutit you,' Mags snapped. 'I told you. You can only come if you shut your mouth. I'll no tell you again.' Gemma put her head down, saying nothing. Rosie smiled at her, apologetically.

'Right,' Mags said, leaning towards Rosie. 'Right. I'm going to tell you somethin' about Tracy. You know the night before she went missin'? The night before she was never seen again? Well, I know where she was.'

She sniffed, her eyes darting around her.

'She was with the polis. The main man. Top detective. Head of the CID. On his boat.' Mags's eyes narrowed. She drew on her fag and swallowed the smoke.

Several little explosions went off in Rosie's head. Jesus. The boss man and a prostitute. A runaway from a children's home, no less. Gavin Fox? Christ. It was like all your birthdays coming in one miserable morning. Prove it, she could almost hear the editor say. No chance of ever proving it, she thought. She pictured the apoplectic newspaper lawyers who pored over everything she wrote in this new litigious world we lived in. You couldn't even imply that a man like Gavin Fox spoke to a prostitute the wrong way, far less that he spent the night with a teenage one. No chance.

Fox was Teflon man. There were plenty of rumours about his less than conventional ways, but nobody had a thing on him. He was squeaky clean, and he got results. People said he was on the take, but people had said that about detectives since the beginning of time. Proving it was a different matter.

'Aye,' Mags said. 'And he wasn't on his own. His other two mates were there an' all. They're high heid yins as well. Big guys. Top men.' She sat back. 'By the way, am I getting paid for this?'

Rosie's heart sank. She'd heard the fantasies of prostitutes before, and sometimes they gave Oscar-winning performances, but too often they lied through what was left of their teeth. She pushed the teacup away from her and moved as though she was getting up to leave. She went into her pocket, pulled out a ten-pound note and threw it onto the table.

'Right,' she said. 'I've heard enough. You phone me in tears about your dead pal, tell me a far-fetched story about a top policeman, then ask for money. Mags, do me a favour, pal. Away and find yourself some other eejit. Try the *Sun*. They'll maybe believe you.' Rosie stood up. If the girl was telling the truth she would stop her and withdraw the request for money. If she was lying, she would let Rosie go, still protesting that the story was true. There was always the chance that the girl would just let her go anyway, and even if the story was true, it was lost. Rosie took the chance.

'Wait,' Mags said, grabbing her arm. 'Wait. Right. I'm sorry. I don't mean I'm askin' for money. Sorry about that. Sit doon, please. Please.' She looked about to burst into tears. Gemma sat playing with her chips, watching her mum's anguish.

Rosie sat back down.

Gradually Mags spilled out the story. She had known a cop called Jack Prentice for years. He sometimes used her and other girls. Only the ones that were quite smart looking, not the proper stanks who could hardly stand up. He introduced her to his mates a few months ago.

They were both top policemen, but she only knew them as Bill and Foxy. She didn't know who Foxy was until she was watching the news one night and his face came on the telly. He was the head of the CID. Jack used to arrange for her to go on Foxy's boat overnight and she would have sex with the three of them. It was a yacht. It had sails. They always paid her well. It was Jack who paid her the money. And they used condoms, most of the time, but not for the blow-jobs.

Rosie glanced at Gemma but she was concentrating on the chips.

'Sometimes I took another girl, but she's dead now from an overdose,' Mags went on. She sucked on the straw of the milkshake. 'Then there was this night, about six months ago, I saw Jack was talking to wee Tracy Eadie. I knew her for about four or five months. She was in a children's home, because her da had been passin' her round his mates for money. Wanker. She was in that Woodbank place.' She put her arm around Gemma and pulled her close. Her voice became a whisper.

'Tracy was on heroin, just smokin' it, and started to work the Drag to pay for her habit. She was only twelve when she started takin' stuff, with the hash and the jellies. But she looked a bit older, wi' make-up an' that. Not old, like twenty or something.' She half smiled. 'She made good money because a lot of the men like young ones.

The next night, after Jack was talking to her, he was on the Drag and asked me could I find this girl Tracy, and if she was all right. I told him she was. He said to ask her if she would come to the boat. I said I would, and he gave me fifteen quid.'

Mags swallowed hard and looked beyond Rosie into the distance.

'I know she went on the boat. She told me she was goin' when I talked to her earlier on the night. I told her it would be okay and they were all right guys. I know she went with Jack because I saw her getting into his motor. I know he drove her to Ayr to go to the boat.' Tears came to her eyes. 'That's the last I saw her. She was on that boat with them. I know for a fact.'

'How do you know for a fact, Mags?'

Mags looked at her. 'She phoned me. She had a mobile some shoplifter gave her. She always had it. She phoned me from the boat later on that night. But I was wrecked and didn't have my phone on. She left a message though. She sounded out of her box. Coked up or something. Said she was feelin' sick. Said she wanted off the boat. And sayin' the names of the guys. That kind of stuff.'

Rosie sat forward. 'You got your mobile? Is the message still on it? Can I hear it?' She was trying not to sound as excited as she felt. If this message was on her mobile, it was dynamite.

'Nah,' Mags said. 'I've no got it with me. But I'll get you it. Honest. I'm no making it up. I'll get it, maybe tomorrow, but not now. I've got to graft.' She started sniffing. 'You see it was my fault. I shouldn't have let her go. She was only a wee lassie.'

Rosie took a deep breath. She lifted the cup to her lips, slugged a mouthful of tea, and put it back down on the saucer. She watched Mags, crying now. Gemma sat with her chin on her hand. She pushed the last couple of chips away and leaned across to put her arm in her mother's.

'You okay, Mum? Don't cry. Don't cry, Mum.'

Mags was telling the truth. Rosie was certain of it. She pictured the shockwaves if she was ever able to tell that story. But who was going to trust the story of this shambolic figure in front of her? Two hours from now, she would be stupefied by her next heroin hit and giving some anonymous punter hand-relief for a tenner in the passenger seat of his car. Who would believe her? Not McGuire, her editor, her biggest supporter. Not even him. But all of her instincts told her the story was true, and she would have to work out her next move. She wouldn't tell anyone at the *Post* yet. Too early. But if she could get the mobile with the message on it, that would be a different story.

'Look,' Rosie said. 'It's okay, Mags. I believe you're telling the truth, but you have to trust me. Don't talk to anyone and just trust me that I will get this story done. But it'll take time. We need to talk a lot more.' She touched her hand. 'Listen, can you get me the mobile now? I'll take you to wherever you want to go.'

Mags stopped crying. She shook her head. 'No. I can't. I've got to go just now.' She glanced at Gemma out of the corner of her eye. Gemma looked out of the window. 'I need to graft. I've no money for anythin'. Know what I mean?'

'We'll go somewhere. I'll get you sorted.' Rosie knew she was sounding too keen, so she added, 'It'll save you going to graft.' Christ. If McGuire could hear her offering to score heroin for a hooker, he would have to be scraped off the ceiling of his office.

Mags shook her head and started to get up.

'No. It's okay. I've got stuff to do. I've got to pay somebody else some money as well. They'll be looking for me. I need to go now.'

'Okay,' Rosie said, getting up. 'Can you meet me tomorrow? Glasgow Green at two? In the tearoom?'

'Aye,' Mags said as they walked to the door of the cafe.

Rosie touched the girl's shoulder. 'And Mags . . . Don't forget the mobile. I need to hear that message. It's important.'

'All right. I'll bring it.' Mags took Gemma's hand. 'Are you sure you'll be there?'

'Of course I'll be there. Now don't say a word to anybody,

especially any of the other girls. It could be dangerous for you. Understand?'

'Aye. Thanks.' Mags pulled Gemma's hand and they walked out and away. The little girl turned back and waved to Rosie.

'Thanks,' she said, 'see you tomorrow.'

Rosie watched them go off into the rain, down the dismal street, then she paid the waitress and left the cafe. She walked briskly, trying to shake off the ghosts that weighed on her shoulder.

CHAPTER FOUR

From the solid oak swing doors to the cobalt blue and white-tiled Victorian bathrooms, O'Brien's reeked of tradition and old-fashioned trust. For nearly a century, the movers and shakers had come here, some for business, some for pleasure. Many pushed their way through the doors simply to be seen. Others were there to rub shoulders with the celebrities or top lawyers and businessmen who gathered at the bar, or sat conspiratorially under stained-glass windows in leathered booths, striking deals as they sipped champagne. Young women waited in the wings, swooning at the thought of gaining access to the top drawer.

Discretion was everything at O'Brien's, and with a nod and a fistful of notes, the head waiter could procure anything your discerning palate desired – a boy, a girl, some cocaine for the lady. No problem, sir.

A busker playing his saxophone for small change in the narrow street next to the entrance served as a reminder that there was another world outside the plush green decor. Rosie always walked slowly when she neared O'Brien's so that she could hear the busker's lonely melodies drifting up through the grey city centre into the sky. She nodded and smiled as she approached the sax player, who raised his eyebrows and winked in recognition. Some big shot walking in front of her tossed a five-pound note into the sax player's case just before he went into O'Brien's. It lay there fluttering in the breeze among the coins. He nodded his thanks to the man, but kept on playing. Rosie gave the musician the thumbs-up and he almost smiled. They were old friends. More than that.

His name was TJ. The first time they'd met, Rosie had told him his name sounded like some cliché from the Cotton Club. TJ had laughed and said he *was* an old cliché. One evening he'd given her the lowdown on a wasted celebrity thrown out of O'Brien's after his cocaine-fuelled night ended in a punch-up. Since then, they'd started having a coffee now and again in the bookshop nearby, and from there the friendship had grown.

TJ never missed a trick, and he always called Rosie if he saw something interesting. Sometimes, Rosie even entertained the notion she was attracted to him. He was tall, with the swarthy looks that were high up her radar when it came to men. And he was older, distinguished looking with his lush dark hair greying at the sides. Late forties, maybe even fifty, with the kind of handsome face that would have made him a bit of a heart-throb in his youth, but now he looked more lived-in. Rosie always put the shutters up when she felt more than just a physical attraction to a man. It was to do with self-preservation. If you let the floodgates open, you had to live with the pain of loss.

But TJ had a way of looking at her that made her feel he could see out of the back of her head. And despite her resolve, now and again something did a little skip inside her when she saw him. He told her how he had served his time, steeped in drink and drugs in dens from Glasgow to New York, and that nothing, but nothing, ever surprised him. He even said it wasn't the money he busked for. He just did it because he liked to be out there, watching the world go by. In their frank encounters over coffee and, later, the occasional dinner, he had disarmed her with his easy philosophy of life. He said he had been to hell and back, but would never be drawn on the detail. TJ could cut through all the bullshit and Rosie found him easy to open up to. She smiled once more, catching his eye as she pushed open the doors of O'Brien's.

Inside, Rosie headed for the bar, walking past a group of men cluttered around an oak podium where a guy in a pinstripe suit was holding court as he poured from a bottle of champagne. She pulled herself up onto a stool and nodded to Gerry, the silver-haired barman from Donegal who had been serving at O'Brien's for twenty years. They used to say that Gerry knew where all the bodies were buried because he had eavesdropped on so many conversations over the years.

He smiled as he approached Rosie, polishing a glass with a towel.

'Ah, the delectable Miss Gilmour,' Gerry said, with mocking deference. 'How's every little bit of you? What'll it be?'

'That's two questions, Gerry,' Rosie said. 'The second one's a lot easier to answer. A G and T, please. And you can call me Rosie, seeing as you know most of my innermost secrets.' She smiled, enjoying the banter of her favourite barman.

'How're things, Rosie,' Gerry said, keeping a watchful eye on the bar as it began to fill up with early evening drinkers spilling out of their offices.

'Not too bad. You know. Just plodding along, keeping my head below the parapet.' Rosie said, giving her stock answer.

'I don't believe that for a minute,' Gerry winked. 'Your head's never been below the parapet in its life. C'mon. Whose life is about to be laid bare on the front page of the *Post*? Eh?' Gerry pulled a pint of strong lager on the nod of a customer.

'We'll see.' If only he knew. But then, knowing Gerry, he probably already did.

Rosie took a long gulp of the ice cool gin and tonic and relished the crisp taste. She caught sight of herself in the mirror behind the bar and screwed up her eyes to get a better view. She looked pale, with dark shadows beneath her eyes from the sleepless nights that sometimes plagued her. She resolved to get to bed before midnight for the first time in a month. Swallowing another mouthful of her gin and tonic, she also resolved to stop the booze for a month. Maybe next month . . . As she was about to order another drink, she saw Gerry glancing over her shoulder and back to her. She swivelled around and smiled.

'Hi, Don. Howsit going?' She took a tenner from her jacket pocket. 'Obviously you were waiting outside until I was about to order.'

'Timing is everything in showbusiness. You should know that, pal.'

Detective Sergeant Don Elliot sat up on the empty stool next to Rosie. He ordered a pint of lager and lit a cigarette, drawing deeply and blowing the smoke upwards away from Rosie. Somebody once told him that his craggy features made him look like Humphrey Bogart in *The Big Sleep*. He'd been trying to live up to it ever since.

'So what's happening, Rosie?' His eyes scanned her face. 'You look knackered. What's up?'

'Thanks a bunch,' Rosie said. 'You always know how to make a girl feel good.' She straightened up, rubbing her eyes. 'Nothing's up, I'm just a bit tired. Sometimes I don't sleep great.'

'That'll be your guilty conscience after all the people you've done over in that paper of yours.'

Rosie smiled. Don moved closer to her and put on his game face. 'Well, if you're ever lonely, and you've nothing to do in the middle of the night, you know where to find me.'

'I can always find something to do in the middle of the night.'

'One-in-a-bed sex romps don't count.'

'You should know. You're the expert.' Rosie enjoyed the harmless banter with Don. He'd been trying to get her into bed for the past five years. He said he enjoyed the challenge, and that one of these days he would sneak up on her when she was least expecting it. They both knew they were friends who used each other. Rosie was glad of his tip-offs on a big story, and Don was always ready to use her to drop some of his cronies in the shit. It suited his own agenda as he climbed the greasy pole at Strathclyde Police. Don always said it was a perfect set-up, even if he hadn't scored. Yet.

'So, Rosie.' Don swigged his beer. 'Been busy? I heard you were at the press conference for that wee Tracy bird. What's her name again?'

'Eadie.' Rosie shook her head. 'Yeah. Sad, Don. Desperate. She was only fourteen. Can you imagine? I mean what kind of fucking world do we live in that somebody dumps a wee lassie like that in the sea?'

'If I had my way, it's the parents of kids like that I'd ditch in the sea. They should have been fucking drowned at birth. The kid was already ruined by her pervy da, passing her around his paedo pals. That's how she ended up in the children's home in the first place. I'd cut his balls off and stuff them down his throat.'

'I know,' Rosie said, reflecting on the grim background that was revealed when the girl went missing, but they couldn't publish it at the *Post*. 'The thing is though, Don, if her father or anyone else had been prosecuted, then maybe more could have been done for the kid.' She shook her head. 'She must have felt totally abandoned in that home. Like it was her fault she was taken away from her family. I feel so sorry for these kids. Nobody ever picks up the pieces for a fucked-up childhood – except the kid. That's how it's always been.' She bit her lip. The alcohol was making her maudlin and there was no room for that. She put her drink down on the bar and pushed it away, aware that Don was staring at her.

He smiled. 'Always the bleeding heart, Rosie.' He touched her hair, and leaned forward. 'I know deep down you're not just the kick-in-the-door hackette they say you are.'

Rosie smiled back. 'Sure. I taught Mother Teresa everything she knows. Anyway, Don, what's the sketch on the kid? What are they thinking? Was she murdered and then dumped in the sea or what? She certainly didn't go for a swim.'

Don glanced around him quickly.

'Early days. There'll not be much left for forensics. And, of course, the fish will have cleaned her out.' He puffed on his cigarette. 'Hope you've not had any fish suppers in Ayrshire lately.'

'Very funny, Don. You're a sick bastard.'

He grinned. 'But, Rosie, there's something about this,' he whispered. 'Listen. I was talking to McGowan, and he said there's a few arses twitching over this.'

'What do you mean?' Rosie hoped she sounded casual. 'Because it's the second hooker to die this year, if you count the girl who was found up in that flat in Maryhill? Or because the cops failed to find a kid that was missing from a children's home until she washed up on the beach?'

'I dunno. Bill Mackie was taking an interest in it, and it's unusual for a Super from another division to become involved. I mean the lassie was found on the beach at Troon, so it's not Glasgow's patch.'

'So what do you think?' Rosie looked at his face for clues. She ordered another drink for them both and he paid.

Don finished his first pint and took a gulp of his second. She wasn't sure if he was edgy. He lit another cigarette.

'What's going on, Don? You can tell me.' She smiled. 'Sure it'll go no further.'

She knew he would tell her. He always did.

'Aye, sure. You're great at keeping secrets.' He rubbed his chin.

'C'mon, Don. I'm intrigued.' Maybe it would confirm that Mags was telling the truth.

Don took a deep breath.

'Right.' He looked around him. 'Listen, Rosie. You can't do anything with this. Not right now. Maybe not ever.'

Rosie nodded.

Don licked his lips. 'And anyway it might just be a rumour. Christ, it probably is, but I've heard that there's something dodgy about this girl. You know Bob Fletcher, the DI? He used to be in Central but he's moved to Internal Affairs now. You know him?'

She and Bob Fletcher went back a very long way, but she wasn't about to reveal that to Don.

'I know him,' she said, 'but I haven't talked to him in a long time. Long before he moved.'

'Well,' Don said. 'Bob's an old mate of mine. I had a

beer with him last night at a piss-up for one of our guys who's retiring next week. He hinted about cop involvement.'

He whispered the words 'cop involvement', but Rosie heard it all right. She tried to look surprised.

'What? Like she was with a polis? Surely not. They don't do that kind of thing.' Her voice was sarcastic.

'Aye.' Don nodded. 'And not just any polis, Rosie. Top men. The very top.' Don looked as though he was going to burst.

'No way. The Chief Constable?'

'No. Jesus, Rosie. Not that high up.'

'Who then?' She wanted it to come from him.

Don's eyes narrowed. 'Anybody ever tell you that you're a very foxy lady?' He smiled as he emphasised the word 'foxy'.

Rosie just mouthed the name Foxy back. Don nodded.

'Jesus H. Christ!' Rosie said. 'No wonder you can hear the sound of arses clanging shut. How do you know this?'

'Right. Listen, Rosie.' Don's expression was grave. 'There's always been a rumour that Foxy and a couple of others – don't know exactly who, but I've got my own ideas – apparently they use whores.'

'What!' She could get an Oscar for this.

'No kidding,' he said. 'I don't know for sure what the set-up is. Saunas and massage parlours, I'm told, but it's always been said that Foxy and a few of his cohorts are corrupt fuckers. Always have been. Anyway, that's what I've heard. That they've used whores all these years. Even that they got pay-offs from the sauna and massage parlour bosses. Brown envelopes picked up on a weekly basis and all the free rides they could manage.' Don was halfway through his pint. He shrugged. 'Can't understand it myself. A woman on a plate doesn't ring my bell.' He winked at Rosie. 'It's all about the chase for me.'

Rosie smiled. He was always flirting. She often wondered what he would do if she took him up on his offers. She ordered another for both of them. She was feeling quite high now.

'Yeah,' she said, 'but even so. Using whores is one thing, but this is about a fourteen-year-old kid from a children's home who's turned up dead. How could they be connected with that?'

Don shrugged, and lifted the glass to his lips. He took a sip and set it back down. 'I'm not saying they were connected with that. No way. But it's just that at the time the kid went missing, after a few days the whole search just dried up. It went cold and nobody seemed to be doing anything.'

'Maybe that's because nobody really gave a toss about a kid from that kind of background,' Rosie said, drinking her gin. 'You can bet your ass if she was from the posh, leafy suburbs and went missing, there would have been a blanket search still going on for her.'

Don shook his head. 'That's not really fair, Rosie. At the time, I remember there was a big team on it. Rumours that she'd been going out and working the Drag at night. It was the hookers who told cops. The thing is, I'm not sure that was even taken seriously. I remember that line being shot down very quickly. I still don't know if it was true or not. Maybe the kid was working as a prostitute. I think it was established that she had a drug habit.'

'Still doesn't give a reason why she ends up in the sea,' Rosie said, hoping he had more to say.

'You're right.' He smiled. 'Unless some cops who use whores got involved with her.'

'You should be writing detective thrillers, Don. Is that not the realm of fantasy?'

Don sniggered. 'Maybe it is. All I know is that there was no big interest in busting a gut to find this kid when she went missing, and now they're trying to play it down, saying she may have been depressed, suicidal and stuff. From the sexual abuse. Blaming the parents. I don't think anybody's even thinking murder. No injuries on the body and nothing to suggest she was strangled or anything. Suicide looks likely.'

'Yeah,' Rosie said. 'And I suppose she got the train from Glasgow, hired a rowing boat and rowed herself out to sea and then just jumped in?'

Don nodded. 'Therein lies the story.'

They sat in silence for a moment. Then howls of laughter from the champagne guys around the podium reminded them where they were.

'As you can see, my friend,' Rosie said, raising her glass. 'Life goes on.'

CHAPTER FIVE

Rosie could see it all from her balcony, three floors up at St George's Cross. The city shimmering in all its glory under a million lights. Mother Glasgow. She could nearly hear its heartbeat. If you stood long enough, you could witness all forms of human life on the streets below. Some of the faces on the buses would not have looked out of place in a Moscow bread queue: empty resigned expressions as they were transported away from the city to the sprawling housing schemes and another world.

Directly below, students headed for the happy hour pubs to gorge themselves with the remains of their student loans. Payback time wasn't even a concept – not in any aspect of their lives. Now and again Rosie would catch a glimpse of a drug deal being struck on the corner with a teenager in a baseball cap behind the wheel of a BMW. One time, during a sleepless night, she had stood on her balcony and watched amazed as a man pulled his girlfriend into a doorway and humped her there and then. And they say romance is dead, Rosie reflected ironically in the dark of the February evening. She drained her glass of red wine and stood hypnotised by the teeming rain.

Her thoughts drifted back to the early afternoon when she was sent by her news desk to speak to the family of the dead girl. It never got any easier, any less depressing.

She had told the taxi driver to keep the engine running when they pulled up at the block of flats in the Cranhill housing scheme. No curtains twitched in the windows of this block when strangers arrived outside. The heroin explosion of the last decade had ravaged schemes like this and created a lost generation, stumbling around like zombies towards their next fix. Most of the flats were boarded up with the aluminium sheets that had become the shameful backdrop to Glasgow's architecture in recent years – a stark contrast to the stunning carvings that tourists marvelled at on ancient city centre buildings. 'Let Glasgow Flourish', the city's motto, went way back and came from the very mouth of its patron Saint Mungo, who apparently performed four miracles there. He would have needed another one for these shithole flats that were a blot on every housing scheme across the city. This was the Glasgow of the Billy and the Tim, where lives were trashed on a daily basis, some even before they were born. And years of in-bred religious sectarianism and hate ensured it was the city where wearing the wrong coloured football jersey could get your throat cut on any given Saturday.

But there also *were* miracles. If you got to be a teenager without a drug habit you could just about walk on water. And if you were a miracle, you kept on walking and didn't look back. Bizarrely, Rosie always found that even in a whole block of these boarded-up flats, there was always one with a grimy window and a garishly coloured curtain half hanging off the rail. A kind of twisted lifestyle magazine image, labelling its occupants dysfunctional. The flat she was going to today was no different. The window was half open and Rosie thought she saw someone look out and then disappear when they saw the car arrive.

She took a deep breath and went into the entrance of the building. It stank of piss. Her feet scrunched on broken bottles as she picked her way through to the stairs. Used syringes were discarded on the steps. Another society party. It was a standard joke among journalists that it was always the top flat when you were following a miserable story like this one. Rosie climbed the stairs, glancing at the boarded-up doorways all the way to the fourth floor. A tiny shudder of fear ran through her, as it always did when she was alone in a set-up like this. She should have brought the taxi driver with her, but he didn't look like he wanted to be involved. He was jittery enough just sitting in the street with his engine running.

The door to the flat had no name plate, just the surname Eadie scrawled with a felt pen. The news desk had told her that a reporter had tried to get to the family at the time Tracy went missing, but nobody ever answered the door. The word from the cops was that they were real lowlifes. The bottom half of the door had been kicked in – recently, by the look of things. Rosie took a deep breath, trying to recover from the climb before knocking on the door. Knock, knock. Nothing. Again she knocked. The door opened and a squat guy who looked like he should be tethered to a heavy chain around his tree-trunk neck stood before her in his grubby vest and jeans.

'Fuck are you?' he growled. Rosie saw his fists clench by his sides and she swallowed hard. Her legs felt a little weak. Fists like that had no compunction when it came to punching women.

'I'm looking for the family of Tracy Eadie?' She stood her ground, entertained a fleeting fantasy of kicking him in the balls, but the thought only lasted a second.

'Ah said who the fuck are you? Whit d'ya want?' The colour rose in his shaven head.

'I'm from the *Post*. I wanted to talk to the family of Tracy Eadie. I know it's a difficult time . . . tragic time. But I was wondering if I could talk to her parents or family.'

Rosie reeled off her fairly standard opening gambit and hoped the funereal expression on her face would stop her getting a burst lip.

'Nobody wants to talk to anyone. Right. Now fuck off.' The ape-man rasped and stepped back.

Rosie had a rush of blood to her head and was on the offensive before she could stop herself.

'And who are you?' She knew her voice was too indignant for her own good. She braced herself.

'The fucking concierge! Now fuck off, ya useless fuck!'

The door slammed hard, and a couple of splinters from the damaged wood fell on the floor. Rosie turned to walk away. She sighed. This was not going to happen, but as she was on the second step, the door opened again. She turned around.

'Come in!' She heard the ape-man's voice, but when she got to the door there was nobody there. Just the long putrid hallway with its bare floorboards and graffiti on the wall.

Out of nowhere a Great Dane the size of a Shetland pony came bounding down the hall barking, and Rosie nearly passed out with shock.

'Holy fuck!' She couldn't help herself shouting. She was about to be mauled to death in a block of derelict flats. What a way to go.

'Dancer! Dancer! C'mere, ya daft bastard.' A tall skinny

boy of about sixteen came running down the hall and grabbed the dog round the neck.

'It's all right. He'll no touch ye. He's just a big pet,' the boy said, and grinned at her.

Rosie felt her legs shaking as she walked down the hall. 'Christ almighty,' she murmured under her breath.

Once inside the living room, the age-old thought rushed back into Rosie's mind. Why do they call it a living room? Living was a huge exaggeration of what was going on in here. There was a double bed in the middle of the floor and, lying on it, a fat woman with hair down to her waist, barely covered by the crumpled duvet. Rosie couldn't see her face but she could hear her retching into a basin.

The smell was overpowering. Rosie glanced around the room, looking for some window to open or a pocket of air she could dive into. Cans of super lager were scattered on the floor. A man lay slumped in a stupor on an armchair. He was bare-chested, and Rosie's trained eye noticed that his entire body was full of junkie's trackmarks. Beside the chair, a toddler in a grubby babygrow lay on a cushion fast asleep. Its hair was matted with food and its nose with caked snot. Rosie felt light-headed. The teenage boy holding the dog could see her shock and looked embarrassed. The ape-man just stood watching her. She thought she had better say something before she passed out.

'I'm Rosie Gilmour, from the *Post*. It's about Tracy. I take it this is where her parents live? Are any of you her parents?'

Rose was relieved to see that the woman had stopped vomiting. She watched as she sat up, her face flushed and her eyes bulging. She didn't speak.

'I'm her da,' the ape-man said, taking a packet of cigarettes from the mantelpiece and lighting one.

Rosie didn't know what she was going to say next, but it had better be quick because now she had the full attention of everyone, including the junkie who had just woken up and the dog whose nose was sniffing at her crotch. She pushed it away.

'Could I talk to you about Tracy? I'm trying to build up a picture of her early life and what happened to her. You know, with being in the children's home. I know it's a problem with kids in the homes. Running away. And drugs and prostitution.' It all came tumbling out as Rosie kept pushing the dog's nose away.

'She's been in that home for nearly a year,' the woman said. 'I'm her mammy. We had to put her in the home because she kept running away from school and stuff, poor wean. She's only a wean. Some bastard did this to our Tracy. They better get him. She's only a wean . . .' Her voice trailed off.

The ape-man stood staring.

'Why was she in the home? Just truancy? Is that it?' Rosie addressed the question to him.

He looked at her and his face flushed. He spat. 'It's they fuckin' social workers. They said she was gettin' interfered with. Even said I was letting ma pals dae it for money. Fuck me! Crap! No way! But they took her and put her in the home. Now she's deed. Bastards!' His eyes were full of hatred. Rosie looked at him, feeling she knew exactly what he was. Everything Mags had told her had been true. He had been passing his daughter around. She tried to hide her contempt. Just get on with the business at hand.

'Would you have a picture of Tracy? We're going to have a go at the social work department, and a picture would be a help. So we can tell the story properly. Like how come she was going out at night in the first place? How come the home didn't know what she was doing? They should know stuff like that.' Rosie kept her head.

The boy went into a bedroom and returned with a picture of a bright blonde teenager in school uniform. She was smiling, showing striking white teeth. But there was something in her pale blue eyes that said she had already seen too much. Rosie took the picture and put it in her pocket.

'I'll make sure you get it back.' She looked at the mother, who was staring straight ahead, while the ape-man was looking at the floor.

'She's beautiful,' he mumbled.

Nobody else spoke. Then the silence was broken by the dog jumping on Rosie and wrapping its paws around her.

'Christ almighty! Get him off!' She pushed the slavering dog away.

'Dancer! Down, Dancer! Down!' The boy dragged him away, smiling. 'I think he fancies you,' he laughed.

'I'm really more of a Border collie woman, to be honest,' Rosie replied, and tried to smile as she backed out of the room and walked away. She had almost broken into a run when she got into the hallway.

The sound of the phone ringing brought Rosie back to the balcony. She went inside and glanced around, trying to identify where the mobile ring was coming from. Eventually she found it in the kitchen.

'Hallo?' The sound of a callbox. 'Hallo. Is that Rosie?' It was Mags.

'Yeah. Hi, Mags, are you all right? Why are you using a callbox, Mags? Where's your mobile?'

There was a sound of sniffing.

'I need to talk to you. I'm getting hassle from the polis. They're panicking about Tracy, an' I got a slap from one of them tonight. I'm still seeing you tomorrow, Rosie?'

'Sure. Glasgow Green. Don't worry, Mags. Don't go out tonight to the Drag. Stay at home.'

'I've got to go.' Mags sounded anxious. 'I've no stuff. I need to pay my debts, Rosie. I owe the dealers. I'll get chibbed if I don't pay them.'

Rosie sighed. 'See you tomorrow, Mags, and don't forget to bring the mobile with you . . . You watch yourself now.'

The phone clicked off.

CHAPTER SIX

The ice cubes cracked as the whisky drenched them in the heavy crystal glass. Jack liked that sound. He watched as he poured, and noticed that his hand was trembling. He poured a little more, just to calm his nerves. He had just come home after giving that junkie whore Mags Gillick a bit of a duffing up to make sure she kept her mouth shut. Christ! He could have choked the life out of her. Now, in the tiled kitchen of the suburban detached house he and his wife Myra had lived in for thirty years, he was trying to keep calm. He had to get a grip of himself. This should be his sanctuary. Nobody could touch him here.

Jack took a deep breath and swallowed some of the whisky. It felt good. He could hear Myra reading the newspaper in the room next door and shook his head in frustration. Why does she always have to read the fucking headlines out? Every night, the same routine. They sat after dinner and Myra settled down with the newspaper, reading aloud the headlines of any story she found interesting, assuming that Jack would be fascinated as well. As if he couldn't fucking read. If only she knew that the routine almost drove him to distraction, even though he grunted interested noises with each new story. Stupid little things like that really pissed Jack off these days. Especially during the last few months, and even more so in recent days when he was so tense he felt his head might explode . . . 'GIRL WASHED UP ON BEACH WAS MISSING TROUBLED TEEN PROSTITUTE.'

Jack froze as Myra read out the headline. Why doesn't she shut her mouth, he thought, taking a huge swallow of his drink. He poured another slug into the glass and walked into the lounge, feeling the whisky burn all the way down to his stomach. It had been just about bearable when Alison was living in the house with them before she went to university in Edinburgh. At least he and Alison could have their little private smiles to each other when Myra started reading the headlines. They understood each other. But since she left he felt trapped alone with Myra, and he was beginning to despise her.

'What's that, darlin'?' He tried to sound distracted.

'The girl on the beach at Troon. Apparently she was only a wee lassie and was in one of those care homes. My God! It says here she was on the game. And drugs. Christ!

She was only fourteen. Isn't that terrible, Jack?' Myra never took her eyes off the newspaper so at least she couldn't see the anxiety in her husband's eyes.

'Yeah,' Jack grunted. 'Terrible. It's all drugs now, Myra. Drugs. I heard the lads talking about the case today. There's a big investigation into it. Papers are all over it. You know. Because she's so young. And because she was missing.' Jack spoke matter-of-factly. The whisky was helping.

'Do you think she was murdered, Jack?' Myra asked, dropping the newspaper down and looking at him.

'Don't know.' Jack hoped his face showed nothing. 'I heard them say it doesn't look like murder. No sign of injuries.'

'What about rape?' Myra persisted.

'Don't know, darlin'. Looks like she was in the water for weeks, so there might not be any evidence of that.' Jack hoped it didn't sound like a prayer.

Later, in bed, Jack woke up and felt the cold sweat breaking out all over his body. It had been like that in the beginning, after they dumped her, but it had gone away after a while. In the last few nights it had come back with a vengeance, and when the anxiety started like boiling water being poured down his back, he just had to ride the feeling until it stopped, leaving him soaking. At least Myra was such a deep sleeper she didn't notice he was lying awake, willing the first light of dawn to spread across the sky. At least then he could get up, get dressed for work and get out of here. He wiped sweat from his forehead. He was dripping.

Jack could still see the terrified look on Mags's face when he got hold of her earlier on. Foxy had told him to make sure he gave the bitch the message that her face better stay shut. So Jack waited until he knew exactly where Mags would be, then he drove out and got her. He waited for about five minutes when there was no sign of her and he guessed she must have picked up a punter. That wouldn't take long. While he waited, he wondered how the hell it had come to this. It had all started with some harmless fun with the hookers a few years ago. Cops always knew you could get a blow-job for free if you made sure the lassies weren't arrested. It was easy, and good fun. Nobody got hurt, and now and again they gave the girls a few quid for their efforts. Some of the birds were all right; not the ones who could hardly stand up in the doorway, the ones who still had half a brain and some flesh on them. They were fine for using.

It was Foxy's idea to start bringing the half decent ones to the boat, and Jack had the job of finding them. There were others too, for mates of Foxy's. Jack was never told who they were, but he just did what he was asked and organised the girls. He didn't want to ask too many questions around Foxy in case he fell out of the inner sanctum that had always been him, Bill and Foxy. He was pleased that Foxy kept it that way, even as he rose through the ranks to become head of the CID. Close mates were everything, Foxy had said. Like brothers, except that you could choose them.

When Mags had eventually turned up last evening, she was standing at the low wall at the edge of the River Clyde, where Jack appeared out of nowhere.

'Fuck sake!' She was startled, when he grabbed her arm. 'I nearly shat myself. Fuck sake, Jack.'

Jack said nothing but pulled her into the shadows and against the wall.

'You better make sure you keep your trap shut, Mags,' Jack said, grabbing her hair and pulling her head back. The lights from the street hit her eyes and Jack could see she was high as a kite.

'I will, Jack. I will,' she said. 'Fuck, Jack. You're hurting me.'

Her fear made him instantly hard and he pushed himself against her and pulled up her tiny leather skirt. Then he pushed her higher up against the wall and jerked her head around so she could see the inky river flowing below.

'You're going in there if you open your mouth about Tracy. Got it, bitch?' Jack pulled her hair tight.

'I won't. Oh fuck, Jack. No way. I never even liked her. Don't hurt me.'

With her free hand, she reached down between his legs and grabbed him, trying to open the zip of his trousers. 'Come on. Just do it, Jack. You know you want to. I'll never tell anyone. Never.'

Jack had turned her head back to face him. He looked at her scrawny neck, at her pale eyes ringed with heavy black make-up, and pushed her head downwards until she was kneeling, pulling at his trousers until she had him in her mouth. He groaned, while she did the only thing she was good for.

He watched the traffic move across the other side of the water, and the lights in the flats overlooking the river where people lived within the rules. He had been in a different world for so long, he could scarcely remember anything else.

Now, in his bed, the memory of the sordid encounter made Jack feel horny again. He turned his wife over to see if there was a flicker of interest, but she just let out a snore and pulled away from him.

CHAPTER SEVEN

Rosie had been waiting nearly twenty minutes and still no Mags. After her second cup of coffee in the cafe on Glasgow Green, she decided to take a walk around outside. It was freezing, the ground still hard and white with the frost from the morning, but at least it wasn't raining. Something about the rain in this neck of the woods, with all the other forms of misery you saw of an afternoon, really put you in a black depression. But the watery sun was up there somewhere in the greyness, and Rosie was enjoying the walk and the sharp cold air. She was far enough away from the long stretch of road at the edge of the Green, where the hookers at the cheapest end of the market off London Road hung around during the day. Some of them were so out of their box on heroin they could barely stand up. But still the cars cruised the length of the road and back again, picking up one, sometimes two, girls at a time and dropping them off minutes later. Enough for one more hit, and the junkie boyfriends who pimped their girls would emerge from the shadows to take the cash.

Inside the tourist shop at the People's Palace, just a short walk away, were books on Scottish life and history. Robust tales of strong, hard-working people who were the heart and soul of this great city. Rosie wondered who would tell the stories of the tragic girls who littered the streets – their miserable tales of self-destruction. Nobody wanted to hear those stories any more. But the police and some hookers, now that was a story worth telling.

As she stood waiting for Mags, Rosie was building up her own little guilt trip. She was using these girls too. Using them to get the scoop that every hack would kill for. But it was more than that for Rosie. Every one of the girls who hawked their bodies on these corners had been like Tracy Eadie at one time. Just a teenage kid staring out of a school snapshot, full of hopes and dreams. This story really would matter the day after it became chip-shop paper. This one might make a difference. She had to believe that . . .

It was Gemma she saw first, wrapped up in her red duffel coat, skipping alongside her mother, and looking for all the world like a normal, happy kid. She waved, and Rosie waved back. As they approached, Rosie saw that Mags looked even rougher than she had the day before. She was wearing the same clothes, the skimpy T-shirt leaving her naked midriff freezing in the chill.

'Hi,' Rosie smiled. 'How you doing, Mags?' She nodded to Gemma who smiled up at her with big, blue eyes. Rosie ruffled her hair.

'I'm shattered,' Mags said. 'Totally fucked, man.'

Rosie glanced at Gemma who didn't flinch at her mum's language. She suggested they go inside for a coffee, and she gave Gemma money to go to the shop to buy sweets and a colouring book of Glasgow Green – the way it was in fairytales. Once the child was gone, she and Mags sat at a table near the window in the warmth of the Winter Gardens. The huge greenhouse building was filled with tropical plants from all over the world, and it was warm more to suit the plants than the customers. Tourists loved the Winter Gardens, but Rosie always felt a little claustrophobic among the giant plants that reminded her of *The Day of the Triffids*.

To Rosie's surprise, Mags asked for tea this time, not a milkshake. But her hands were shaking so much that she spilled it when she tried to put it to her lips.

'Fuckin' hell.' Mags wiped the table with a napkin. 'I'm frazzled. Haven't had a hit since six this morning. I can't stay long, I need to get sorted.' She sniffed. Junkies always had a permanent cold.

'Okay,' Rosie said. 'Talk to me, Mags.'

Rosie reached into her pocket and brought out her dictaphone. She put it on the table and switched it on. She didn't need to show Mags she was recording her, as the tape would still have picked up their voices from her pocket. But she wanted to be straight with the girl from the start. She was desperate to ask if she had the mobile phone with her, but decided it was better to get the story on tape first.

'You're fuckin' jokin'.' Mags's reaction to the tape was predictable. 'A tape recorder? No way, man. I'll get fuckin' done in.'

Rosie assured her that they would probably never use it. It was just for the lawyers, and if it ever came to the crunch and the story was told, the cops might fold if they knew the paper had a tape to back things up. Nonetheless, Rosie was resigned to doing without the tape, when, to her surprise, Mags decided to go along with it.

'I got a dig last night,' Mags said, sniffing and swallowing. 'From one of the cops. Don't know if you know him. Jack Prentice? I think that's his name. He's high up.'

Rosie tried not to react. She knew too well who DCI Prentice was. A bad bastard, according to Don. But him and Foxy came through the ranks together. That was why he'd been promoted to where he was. Used to be in the old vice squad.

'He got me last night,' Mags said. 'When I was out workin'.'

'Yeah?' Rosie was intrigued that Prentice was arrogant enough to actually go out and duff up a hooker at a time like this. 'What did he do?'

'What did he do?' Mags almost laughed at the question. 'He fuckin' threatened to drown me, that's what. Had me nearly hangin' over the wall into the Clyde. Said I'd get dumped in there if I opened my mouth about Tracy. I had to give him a blow-job to get him off me.'

Rosie looked at Mags's face. She wasn't much more than a kid. Mags managed to lift the cup this time. She was able to take a gulp of tea, then put it back down and lit a cigarette.

'I'm tellin' the truth, Rosie,' she said. 'I can show you where it was. Where it happened. I've gave Prentice more blow-jobs than I've had hot dinners.' She laughed. 'I shouldn't say that, because that's no right. I haven't had a hot dinner in about six months.' She laughed a phlegmy laugh and broke into a hacking cough.

Rosie shook her head and smiled at Mags's black humour.

'Mags.' She leaned across the table. 'Why don't you start right now, and tell me everything. I know you don't have a lot of time, but tell me how this all came about. You know, with the cops, and with Tracy Eadie.' She sensed Mags was feeling anxious and knew she needed some heroin.

'We can go and get you fixed up in a little while if you want,' Rosie said. 'I've got my car. I'll take you, then we can go and talk some more. What do you think?' Rosie knew Mags would agree, because there might be a few quid in it for her. If someone paid for her next hit, she wouldn't have to go shoplifting in the afternoon.

Mags looked at the tape recorder, then at Rosie. She drank another mouthful of tea and shifted in her seat.

'Listen, Rosie,' she said. 'I'm rattlin', man. Can we go and get fixed up first? I'll be easier after that.'

Rosie looked at her. Mags's leg was going like a piston, and the cigarette trembled in her nicotine-stained fingers.

'No worries.' Rosie put the tape recorder back in her pocket. 'Let's go. Just tell me where.' She stood up. 'But in and straight out, Mags. All right?'

'I know.'

Rosie stayed in the car, Gemma in the back, anxiously watching the tenement close that Mags had just vanished into. She knew she shouldn't be doing this. If McGuire found out she was out on her own, taking a junkie prostitute to score, he would hit the roof. After last year, when she nearly got herself killed in Northern Ireland by going off alone to a dangerous enclave for a meet with an IRA dissident, McGuire demanded to be kept posted about where she was at all times, if the story was at all dodgy.

And this was certainly dodgy. She had driven to the red sandstone tenement a couple of streets off London Road where Mags said she could get herself sorted for the next few hours. Rosie was a little ashamed that she had even slipped her ten pounds to do it, but she kept assuring herself that it was a means to an end.

She turned round. Gemma was quietly colouring in the book, with bright green trees and birds flying around the sky. Not a hooker in sight in her little world. Rosie looked out of the window and watched the procession of junkies going in and out of the close. Waifs of girls and skinny boys with sunken eyes and hollow cheeks. They walked that bouncing walk that junkies do, their legs rubbery. They gibbered to each other as they made their way to wherever they were going, to get enough money to make their way back for more smack. Eventually Mags came out, sniffing and wiping her nose. She very quickly slipped into the car.

'Let's get out of here,' she said. 'I hate this place.'

Rosie watched as Mags leaned her head back, relaxed and calm. 'What did you do?' She whispered, so that Gemma wouldn't hear.

'I just smoked some smack,' Mags said. 'Just enough for a while. I've no jagged in about two years. I'm on a methadone programme, but it's never enough. I'll get somethin' later. Let's go into town.' Her voice was slow.

They had to do a detour across the city because of road-works, and drove past St George's Cross, stopping at the traffic lights outside Rosie's flat.

'Do you live in a big house, Rosie?' Gemma asked, suddenly sticking her head out of the window.

'No,' Rosie smiled. 'Not big.' She pointed to the building. 'Actually, I live up there.'

'Have you got a balcony?'

'Yeah,' Rosie said, realising she'd blundered by even hinting at where she lived when she had a hooker in the car. But Mags was looking out of the other window into the middle distance, not remotely interested.

They drove back down to Argyle Street and stopped outside a cafe under the Heileman's Umbrella. They got out just as a train was thundering overhead. Gemma gasped, grabbing hold of Rosie's hand.

'It's just the train, Gemma,' Rosie reassured her, squeezing her hand.

'What if it falls off?' Gemma said. 'What if it falls off the rails,' she said, pointing up.

'It won't,' Rosie said. 'It won't fall off the rails,' and felt the squeeze of the little fingers wrap around her hand.

In the cafe they ordered chips for Gemma and white rolls with sausage for themselves. Mags didn't eat hers; she ordered a strawberry milkshake.

'I need sweet things,' she explained to Rosie, as though

she was apologising. 'It's what you need.'

It was quiet in the cafe at that time of day and Rosie got Mags to start talking. She switched on the tape recorder, and watched the girl's face as she told the story – in amazing detail for someone who must be out of her face most of the day. She asked her how she could remember so much.

'I dunno. Sometimes you can really remember the most stupid details, yet other times you don't know what day it is.' She took sips from her milkshake and stroked the kid's hair as she spoke.

Mags told her that she and another prostitute named Margo used to get pulled up by the cops nearly every night, and then one of them started asking for hand relief. Before the week was up they were doing a few cops most nights. Prentice was one of them and he was a real bastard sometimes, but he could also be quite nice as well. One time he gave Mags a tenner and dropped her off at her house.

It was a couple of months later that Prentice pulled her again and asked her if she wanted to go on a trip on his mate's boat. She went, and took her pal Margo with her. There were three of them altogether, but she didn't twig the other two were cops straight away as they were all doing cocaine in front of her. They had a good stash. She smiled and said that alone should have told her they were cops, because they always had the best dope. They all got out of their faces and the girls had sex with the three of them. Margo did two of them at once. She was nuts. The one with the dark hair, called Foxy, paid Mags and Margo an extra twenty quid to do a lesbian act, which they did from time to time for other punters anyway, so it was no big deal. It was only after the third time on the boat that they found out they were all cops. Even then, they didn't know who Foxy was until, as she had said before, she saw him on the telly. She said the other guy's name was Bill. He was a top man as well.

Rosie could barely believe her ears. How in the name of Christ would she ever be able to get this past the lawyers?

Mags stopped for a moment as Gemma shoved her book in front of her to show her the picture she'd been colouring in. She stroked the child's hair again. 'Brilliant, doll. That's brilliant.'

'So,' Rosie said, gently. 'Tell me about Tracy, Mags. How did all that come about.'

Mags started talking again. She said that Margo died of an overdose after jagging heroin for the first time in over a year. Mags didn't go on the boat for a few weeks after that, but one night Prentice came to her again and asked who that wee girl was along the road standing in the doorway. Mags knew she was called Tracy and that she lived in a children's home. She thought she was about fourteen, but she had seen her picking up punters night after night. And she'd told her that she was just turned sixteen. Some of the girls didn't like young birds, because they were in big demand, but Mags had been friendly to her. Prentice gave her twenty quid and asked if he could get the girl to go on the boat. Just by herself this time. Mags didn't think anything of it, because even though she had never been on her own with them, she wouldn't have been worried if she had to go by herself. They were cops. It had always felt safe enough.

She didn't tell him how young she thought Tracy was, or that she was from a children's home.

When she told Tracy that she might get at least fifty quid and a bit of coke, she was up for it. That was the last time she saw her, getting into the car with Prentice months ago.

Mags went quiet and stared beyond Rosie and out into the street. Her cheeks were wet. 'It's my fault,' she said. 'If I didn't get her into that, she would still be here. I should have said to Prentice she was only fourteen and maybe he wouldn't have risked it. I shouldn't have let her go on her own.' She shook her head. 'But I was that desperate for the money I didn't care.'

Rosie handed her a flimsy napkin. She didn't know what to say. She knew that sooner or later Tracy would have ended up like the rest of them. In a flat somewhere, surrounded by filth and squalor, jagging up or smoking.

But at least she was at peace now, away from the horrors that took her into that world in the first place.

'So,' Mags said, 'that's the story. Well most of it.'

'What do you mean most of it?' Rosie finished her coffee.

Mags fidgeted around and lit up a cigarette. 'Well, the word is that it's no just cops,' she said. 'Since Tracy died, I've heard the children's home where she stayed was dodgy. Funny stuff goin' on.'

Rosie leaned forward, making sure the tape was still running.

'What do you mean, other people? What home?'

'Woodbank. I don't know exactly what goes on. Maybe it's just shite.' Mags shrugged. 'But I heard it was judges and lawyers and people like that. I heard that the guy at the children's home gives them boys and wee lassies.'

'You can't be serious, Mags. Kids? Jesus.' Rosie's disbelief was obvious.

'I dunno.' Mags looked at Rosie. 'I only know what I did and who I was with. And I know Tracy. But I don't know about anybody else for sure. But I heard that they get boys from the train station sometimes and they take them to some house in the country. It's all posh people. Judges and stuff.'

'Who told you this? Can I meet them?'

'No.' Mags shook her head emphatically. 'I can't trust none of the other girls. I can't trust nobody. I could only trust Margo, and she's dead. I only knew Tracy a bit, and now she's dead. I bring anyone else into this, then they might talk an' I'll be dead meat too.'

Rosie knew the chance of her ever using what Mags had just told her and getting it into the paper, was highly unlikely. One thing at a time, she decided. She needed to hear Tracy's message on the mobile.

'Okay,' Rosie said. 'Have a think about it. Right now the first thing is to work on the Tracy story.' She stretched over and touched Mags's hand. 'What about the mobile? Have you got it with you?'

Mags went into her pocket and brought it out. Rosie watched as she punched in some numbers and stuck the phone to her ear. She listened to it, then nodded to Rosie.

'That's it,' she said, calling it up again. 'There's some noise in the background, but you can hear Tracy's voice.' She handed over the phone.

Rosie immediately squeezed the tape recorder between her ear and the mobile to make sure it was recording, just in case she didn't get a second chance to listen to it. Mags watched her. Rosie concentrated as she listened, and a chill ran through her.

'Mags . . . It's me. Tracy . . . Are you there, Mags?' The voice was clearer than Rosie had expected. 'Fuck sake, Mags, where the fuck are you? It's Tracy. Listen, I'm out ma box, I feel funny. Loadsa coke. I feel sick. I'm in the toilet, Mags . . .

Mags. Can you hear me? I feel sick. I want off of this fucking boat. These guys are mental. They're all blootered and coked up. That big Jack guy that brought me doon here in his motor, he's all right. But that Fox guy, the one whose boat it is? He told me to shut it when I said I wanted to go back, said I could swim . . . Bastard. They're fuckin' polis, Mags. Mags . . . Can you hear me? . . . I feel sick, Mags, I want outa here . . .' The voice trembled and trailed off.

'See?' Mags said. 'She was tryin' to get me, tryin' to talk to me, and my fuckin' phone was switched off. I was out ma face that night. She needed me, Rosie. It was me who got her on that boat, and she wanted to get off, because maybe she'd took too much stuff. Maybe she was dyin' or somethin'. And I wasn't even at the other end of the fuckin' phone. Shit.' Tears spilled out of her eyes.

'You couldn't have done anything anyway, Mags,' Rosie said, consoling. 'She was on a boat, miles away. There's no way you could have got to her.'

Mags nodded. 'I know. But maybe I could at least have calmed her down or somethin'. At least talked to her. Poor wee lassie.' She bit her lip and looked away.

Rosie still held the phone. 'Can I take this with me, Mags? Just for a couple of hours? I'll get it back to you tonight or tomorrow, but I want to let the editor hear it, and get the number checked. It's better if I have the actual phone.'

Mags looked edgy.

'No. No way, Rosie. Sorry. No way.' She shook her head. 'I'm no bein' a fanny or anything, but I need my mobile for the day. I've got somebody phonin' me. Guy I owe money to, and if I don't take his call then he'll just come and find me and kick the shit out of me.' She put her hand out. 'Sorry. I need it back, Rosie. I'll get it back to you. Anyway, you've taped it haven't you.'

Rosie didn't see the point in telling her that a taped conversation recorded from a phone meant nothing. She needed the phone, and she would get technical people onto it, voice experts, anyone who could prove that message came from that number. Anything that would give an indication of where the call was made. Pity there were no other voices in the background, nothing that could link it with Fox and the others, but it was still good. She knew the problems with ID when a mobile wasn't a contract phone, but she was desperate for technical people to see just what they could find. The phone could be crucial, but she knew Mags wouldn't part with it. Not today. She conceded, and handed it back.

'Okay. Tomorrow then, Mags?'

Mags nodded, and Rosie leaned across and touched her wrist.

'Listen, Mags. The important thing is for you to keep quiet about this. Never – and I mean *never* – tell anyone you spoke to me. You understand that, don't you, Mags?'

'Aye, I know.' She rolled her eyes to the ceiling. 'I'm not as fuckin' daft as I look. I've got three certificates you know, from school. I did exams. I was goin' to be a fuckin' schoolteacher.' She smiled widely at the thought.

'Really?' It wasn't the first time Rosie'd met junkies who didn't fit the usual profile. 'What happened?'

Mags was quiet for a moment. Gemma looked from her mum to Rosie, and back again.

'My ma died and my da just got drunk all the time.' She stared ahead, remembering. 'It was miserable in the house. I was cryin' all the time, so I started goin' up to my pal's house and we were all smoking some hash. Then one night, I tried smack. It was brilliant. Like a blanket. Like my ma had come back and cuddled me. But it's not like that now. It doesn't feel like a cuddle any more. It's just cold all the time. Cold inside.' She put her arm around Gemma. 'I'm going to get better though. For her.'

Gemma smiled up at her mum, and Rosie felt like crying. She looked at Gemma and she could see herself all those years ago. She squeezed Mags's hand.

'I'm sure you will.' She swallowed.

Rosie's phone rang in her pocket. She lifted it out. It was McGuire on his mobile.

'Where the fuck are you, Gilmour?' His voice was sharp but Rosie was used to it.

'Oh, hallo, Mick. I'm with somebody. I had to spend most of the day with them. I'll be back in twenty minutes. Then I'll tell you all about it.'

'It better be good,' McGuire said. 'You've disappeared off the radar screen. The whole point of these fucking fancy mobile phones is that people can keep in touch. Especially you.'

'I'm on my way.' Rosie pressed the button, cutting him off.

She told Mags she had to go, and asked her to phone her that night, just to let her know she was all right. As she left, Rosie gave a couple of pound notes to Gemma for sweets and the kid thanked her with a beaming smile.

CHAPTER EIGHT

On the ground floor of the *Post*, Rosie shot into the lift just before the doors closed. She could see by the looks on the faces of the telesales girls from upstairs that they were in a hurry. They were carrying a box of cakes and biscuits as well as steaming coffee in plastic cups. Rosie squeezed in and nodded to them, and they all stood in silence watching the little light flash on as it hit each floor. What was it about lifts that rendered people speechless?

When the lift was almost at the editorial floor, the girls started chattering. One of them addressed a middle-aged woman next to her.

'So what about your anal fissures, Shona?' she asked. 'Are they any better?' The other passengers in the lift looked at each other in disbelief.

Shona flicked her eyes upwards and shrugged. 'Same,' she replied. 'Still agony, bleeding every time I–'

'Thanks for that, Shona,' one of the younger girls said, cutting her off. 'I was looking forward to that strawberry tart.' The girls giggled, and the lift pinged for editorial.

'Enjoy,' Rosie said, getting out at her floor.

On her desk was a note saying, 'See editor', but before she could pick it up, her phone rang. It was Marion, McGuire's secretary, who had spotted her coming onto the editorial floor.

'You've to come straight through. The boss is waiting for you.'

'Should I bring some Chardonnay? Or is it already chilling.'

'Chilling's not the word,' Marion said.

Rosie hung up her coat and went straight across to McGuire's office. She wasn't going to tell the news editor, Marty Lamont, what Mags had just told her. She didn't trust him. He'd only been in the job five weeks, and the pair of them had already clashed. Lamont had flexed his muscles in the first week and sent Rosie to follow a trivial story that a junior reporter could easily have covered. She did it, though, without question, but when she came back in, she took him to one side and told him in no uncertain terms never to pull a stunt like that again. Some fat-arsed news editor, who couldn't report himself missing when he was a hack on the streets, was not about to push her around. Things had been a little frosty since.

She walked past Marion and knocked on McGuire's half-open door, then walked in before he could tell her to enter.

'Come in,' McGuire said from behind the newspaper, his tone sarcastic. He crumpled the paper and looked at her over narrow reading specs. His heavy, black eyebrows and slicked-back hair made him look like some city finance dealer.

'Where in the name of Christ have you been, Rosie?' He motioned her to sit down and leaned back, resting his shiny black Oxford shoes on the desk. He checked that the crease on his blue pinstripe trousers was perfect. As if it was ever anything else.

'It's a long story, Mick,' Rosie said as she sat down, and rubbed her hands across her face. 'But it's mega. In fact it's so mega, I'm scared to repeat it.' She smiled. McGuire had his hands folded behind his head. He took one hand to remove his glasses and look directly into Rosie's eyes.

'Well? Go on.' He raised his finger to point at her. 'But before you start, I'm not happy that you pissed off all day and didn't even phone. You know the rules.'

'Sorry. Won't happen again.' She smiled at McGuire, because they both knew it would. But Rosie was confident that he liked her enough for her to get away with just about anything – so long as she kept delivering the goods.

There was no easy way into the story, so Rosie just spilled it out, painting the picture for him and watching him reacting to it, just the way she had done. She would trust McGuire with her life, and she knew this was right up his street. He was a ballsy, instinctive editor, and he always relished laying one on the establishment. But Rosie knew that, even as she spoke, he would also be considering the political implications of a such an explosive story.

McGuire punctuated her story with exclamations of 'Fuck me!' and 'Jesus wept!' and she decided not to tell him anything of what Mags had said about the children's home. No point in getting him overexcited at this stage. She was still trying to take it all in herself, and would wait until she had done a bit of digging. When she got to the end of her story, McGuire was silent. He lifted his feet off the desk and got up to pace around the room. Rosie's eyes followed him as he walked up and down, his hands dug into his trouser pockets.

'So, right. Let's see what we've got here. We have the word of a hooker.' McGuire turned to Rosie, scratching his chin. 'A junked-up hooker. That should give the lawyers a good dose of the trots.'

'I think it's true, Mick,' Rosie said. 'I believe she's telling the truth.' She needed him to be on her side on this, but she knew the lawyers would tell him not to touch it with a barge pole, and she felt her confidence weakening a little already.

'She might well be telling the truth.' McGuire ran his hand across his thick black hair. He surveyed the award-winning front pages that were framed and mounted on the wall. 'Poor bastard probably is. But you can't go around saying the head of the CID is humping junkie girls on his boat. Underage hookers, no less. We'd be printing fivers instead of papers.' He turned to Rosie, saying, 'You know that, don't you?' and went back behind his desk.

He said he could nearly hear the collective screams of panic when the managing editor and the rest of the hierarchy got to know about this – in the unlikely event they could ever run the story.

Rosie's spirits sank. She thought of Mags, and that innocent snapshot of Tracy before the heroin had swallowed her up. She had hoped for better than this. The sound of Tracy's voice on the tape still rang in her ears. She reached into her pocket and brought it out.

'Look, Mick,' she said, rewinding the tape. 'Listen to this. Tracy made a call to the girl Mags from the boat. Something happened at some stage of the night, and Tracy phoned Mags in a bit of a state. Mags didn't get the call because she was, well, the usual junkie stuff, out of her box. But the kid left a message. Mags let me hear it today and I taped it. Listen. It's her voice.'

She put the volume up as loud as it would go, sat it on

McGuire's desk, and played the message. His eyes narrowed as he listened.

'Play it again.'

She played it again, and then a third time.

'You got the mobile?'

Rosie looked at him and sighed. 'No, Mick. If I had the mobile, you would have been listening to it on the mobile. Mags wouldn't part with the phone today. Said she needed it for something, and she'll give it to me tomorrow. But I taped this from the mobile.'

McGuire nodded. They were both well aware of the difficulties.

He folded his arms. 'It's great to have the voice on tape, Rosie, but unless we get the mobile and get some techno guys into it, we can't prove anything. Lawyers will know we can't prove that the voice on the tape is the kid's, plus, we can't prove where it came from. If we had the mobile, well, maybe we could. Need the mobile.'

'I'll get it tomorrow, Mick,' she promised, trying to hide her disappointment, and hearing Tracy's voice played over and over in her mind.

'This is going to be a nightmare to get in the paper. A nightmare,' McGuire said.

'I know.'

'But I'll tell you one thing, Gilmour.' McGuire looked straight at her. 'We'll have a good fucking try.' He banged his fist on the desk. 'What's your next move?' He had that twinkle in his eye. Rosie had seen it before. He was in.

She told him they were still doing tests on the body, but there were no signs of injuries or struggle.

'I talked to my man in Forensics,' she said, 'and he told me the post mortem didn't tell them that much. About six months in the water, so there was a lot of decomposition. Obviously there'd be no bodily fluids and no DNA of other parties. Her brain was gone, and there wasn't much fatty tissue left on the body at all. Probably wasn't much in the first place. With no brain, they wouldn't even be able to run tests for drug addiction. Not that it mattered anyway. My man said it would be impossible to prove conclusively the cause of death.'

'Which would suit the cops perfectly.'

'Exactly,' Rosie said. 'You can guarantee they'll be saying it was most likely suicide – kid depressed from the earlier abuse and stuff. It gives them an out. People stop looking after someone says suicide.'

'But we know different,' McGuire smiled.

'That we do, sir.'

She suggested that, initially they run the story, having a go at the social work department since this kid was in their care . . . just see what it flushed out. You never know, perhaps someone would ring in with decent information. Stranger things have happened. On the day after that was published, they could run a follow-up story hinting that Tracy may have been with some very important people.

'That way, we don't implicate anyone.' Rosie clenched and unclenched her fist. 'All we do is get their arses twitching. They'll know that we know more, and they'll be panicking, wondering what is going to spill out next.'

McGuire agreed. He said they shouldn't tell anyone else at the moment, not even Lamont.

'I know he's not exactly your best mate,' he said, with a smirk.

'He's an arsehole,' Rosie said, deadpan.

'He's organised. Methodical,' McGuire offered.

'So was Adolf Eichmann,' Rosie said.

McGuire half smiled. 'Anyway, you don't have to deal with him, so forget about him. You only answer to me.' He sat back in his chair, hands behind his head again. He looked slightly puzzled.

'So tell me this, Rosie.' He looked at her. 'Because this is a problem for me.'

She held her breath, wondering what he was going to say.

'What I can't get is, why would high-ranking detectives be using cheap hookers like this?' He screwed up his eyes. 'I just . . . I just can't see why. Do you get my drift, Rosie? These guys have been around the block. They're well paid. If they want a quick shag, there have to be other ways.

There are bars where they could pick up a woman for a bit of uncomplicated rumpy.'

Rosie shook her head. 'They're all married, Mick. It's not that easy. They'll have lives, families. And the thing is, they're all ex-vice squad, so they grew up messing around with the prostitutes. It's one of the perks of the job, if you want to put it that way.'

'Christ.' McGuire shook his head. 'Perks? With some syphilated shagbox?'

'That's not the point, Mick. With these guys it's all about using the power they've got. Basically, they do it because, well, because they can. They probably always have done. One of my good contacts told me that Fox and his mates were getting paid off by the sauna bosses. One massage parlour in particular. I know a crook who says Prentice used to pick up the wedge of cash every week in a brown envelope. Plus, they got girls to use.' She could see McGuire was engrossed. She continued.

'I believe that. These guys might have risen up the ranks in the police, but the bottom line is they haven't evolved as human beings. You know what I mean? They're still the same redneck bruisers they always were when they were young coppers, kicking the shit out of delinquents and then getting a blow-job on the way home to the wife.' Rosie looked at McGuire, who had a wry smile.

'I do like it when you talk dirty, Gilmour.'

Rosie smiled. 'C'mon. You know what I mean, Mick. Cops. The police force. It attracts good guys, the old-fashioned Elliot Ness heroes from the movies who want to make the world safe and all that shit, but the very nature of the job means it also attracts bullies. And crooks. That's always been the way. Bent coppers go back to the beginning of time, it's part of the culture. The kind of mentality that uses people for sex is part of any institution where there is power. From the clergy to politicians. The list goes on.'

'Oh, Christ,' McGuire said. 'We're on our soapbox now, right? Okay, Rosie, I get the picture. But you realise they will obviously deny it on a stack of Bibles, so I'm not going anywhere near this unless we can really nail it down.' His face was stern. 'Watch my lips, Gilmour. Nail it down.'

'I will. You know I will.'

McGuire asked about Mags and about her heroin habit. Rosie told him about the girl's background, and about the child. He seemed sympathetic.

'Right,' he said. 'Fine. Let's get on with it. Just be careful with that girl. And don't be doing anything daft like giving her money for heroin.'

Rosie was on her feet now, trying not to look at him. But she knew that McGuire was probably aware she had already done that. She smiled as she turned and walked out of the room. As she passed Marion, she winked. 'He's a pussycat,' she whispered.

Back at her desk, Rosie sat down and started typing. Over the top of her screen she could see Lamont watching, and allowed herself a wry smile. She went into the toilet where Annie Dawson, one of their bright young reporters was at the wash basin, slapping cold water onto her flushed face. She had clearly been crying.

'What's the matter, Annie? What's wrong, kid?'

She sniffed. 'Oh, Rosie. I just got the most awful bollocking from Lamont, in front of everybody. I just don't know if I can do this job any more. I just can't do anything right.'

Rosie put her arms around her, patted her back. 'Oh, come on, Annie, don't be silly. You know you've been doing really well. The subs say your copy's great. You're going to be a big star in the future. You'll see.'

Annie tried to compose herself. 'But every time Lamont gets the chance he puts the boot in. This time it was because I didn't get a picture from the family of the kid who drowned in the swimming pool. But nobody got one. None of the papers.'

Rosie bit her lip. She had once been where Annie was now – trying to punch above her weight, years ago, when a newsroom floor was a bear-pit of bullies and machismo, and few female reporters ever shone. It had changed a lot in recent years, but arseholes like Lamont still lived in the dark ages.

'Listen, Annie,' she said. 'Forget that bastard. He's going nowhere fast. He's getting found out quite quickly. The only thing he can do is shout at people. Someone like you, with raw talent, will see a tosser like him off the premises in a few years. Don't let him get to you. You can't let him win. Now, come on. Fix your face, then get back out there and get on with your work. You're better than him. Okay?'

Annie blew her nose. 'Thanks, Rosie. Thanks. I really appreciate it.'

Rosie jerked her head in the direction of the door.

CHAPTER NINE

In the cafe next door to O'Brien's, Rosie could see through the steamed-up windows that TJ was sitting alone in a booth. The steady drizzle must have forced him inside off the street. She was glad, because after the kind of day she'd had it would be good to offload some of it on her old friend.

TJ hadn't seen her come in. He sat with his sax alongside him on the fake leather seat, sipping from a glass of milky coffee, lost in his own world, behind a cloud of smoke. He looked up when she came towards him, and his face broke into a smile.

'Rosie.' He stubbed out his cigarette. 'Sit down. Take the weight off your intrepid feet.'

She slipped off her raincoat and slid into the seat opposite him. A waitress appeared at her side and she ordered a coffee, the same as TJ's. He ordered another for himself.

'So.' His dark eyes studied Rosie's face. 'How are things in the big wide world, darlin'?'

'You tell me,' she said. 'You see it all from where you stand and play your sax every day.'

'Ah! But all I get is a glimpse, I don't get right in about it like you. I don't get to make it all happen. And I don't get to turn all the bad bastards over from time to time.' He grinned. 'I just play the background music.'

Rosie sat back. If she let him talk, she knew he would be off on one of his monologues of life that he always delivered so well. She could listen to him all day, loved his accent, Glasgow, with a slight transatlantic drawl from years of world travel. It was a very peculiar kind of friendship. One that had grown intense but, unusually for Rosie, hadn't ended up in bed. Maybe that would have ruined it, and she was afraid to take the chance.

The way she had led her life, brief encounters were much more manageable. After about nine months, she usually got bored with a relationship and moved on. She'd always had a penchant for foreign men, something to do with the short-termism of it. You came, you saw, you conquered – you got a flight back home. And nobody got to hurt you. At least that was the theory. But along the way, now and again, someone crashed through all the barriers and the control was lost. Her most recent had been a perfect storm. If fate hadn't been so cruel, it wouldn't have thrown two raging forces like them together. It ended in tears – hers – and nearly two years on, he was still under her skin. But Rosie was accomplished at managing that kind of stuff, and she had vowed never to go down that road again. Control was more important. That way she could focus completely on her job, because if a female reporter didn't do that in the harsh environment of a daily newspaper, you would be delivering flowers while the guys got in with the big story. Falling in love was for another time. Maybe never.

TJ was different. He was her friend, and as long as they stayed that way, there was no reason to walk away. But there was some serious chemistry between them, no question. She knew TJ knew that too, but he seemed as reluctant as she to take it any further. Being with him took away the loneliness for Rosie. The relationship was a kind of shelter for both of them.

Sometimes, when they ended up drinking a bottle of wine over dinner in some bistro, Rosie barely had to speak. TJ just told her story after story. He had been everywhere, done it all. The drink. The drugs. The women. And, through time, she had shared many – but not all – of her own stories with him.

'So howsit goin'?' he asked.

'It's been a crazy day, TJ.' Rosie sipped her coffee,

enjoying the warmth. 'Fasten your seatbelt and I'll tell you.'

She began, and he lit up another cigarette, drawing deeply on it. Occasionally he offered a puff to Rosie, even though she'd given up smoking two years before. She only smoked when she was half drunk. She told him the full story – about the kids and the judges – just the way Mags had told her. She knew she could trust him. When she'd finished, TJ leaned forward and lightly touched her arm.

'You're going to have to watch yourself, Rosie.' His eyes narrowed. 'These bastards stop at nothing. If you think Foxy and co. are going to stand by and let this happen then you'd be very naive. They'll never allow a story like that to come out.' He sat back. 'Of course, you'll write it. Do a brilliant job, as usual. It'll go all the way to your management. But it *will* get stopped. I'll guarantee you that.'

Rosie knew he was talking sense. If it came to the crunch, the managing director and everyone would be brought in to try to quash the story.

'Nobody in the establishment will want a story like that to come out,' TJ went on. 'It's too destabilising. The very faith in the people who make all the rules is at stake here. You've no chance, darlin'. Sorry. I know that's not what you want to hear.'

She looked at TJ. Right at that moment, she felt like bursting into tears. It had been a highly emotional couple of days and she was dog-tired now that the adrenalin was waning and she was beginning to relax. Stop being a stupid woman, she told herself. She was conscious that TJ was studying her with that knowing look he sometimes had.

'Don't be so defeatist,' she snapped. 'We have to give it a go. We can't just lie down and let it be.'

'And what happens once you've ruffled everyone up? And the lawyers knock back the story? You're a marked woman. You'll be driving home one night and get a pull from the cops and, lo and behold, there'll be a stash of coke in your glove compartment. Make no mistake about it, Rosie, these bastards will get you. Or they'll pay some of their gangster mates to do you over.' He stubbed out his cigarette.

They sat in silence for a minute, Rosie mulling over what he had said. It wouldn't be the first time she had upset the police and waited for some unpleasant consequences. But you had to take risks. She decided she'd had enough of TJ's advice.

'I think I'll hit the trail.' She slipped out of the booth and picked up her coat, avoiding eye contact.

'Sorry, darlin'.' TJ sighed. 'I just don't want you to get hurt.' He smiled to lift the mood. 'I mean who else would listen to the stories of an old rocker at the fag-end of his life?'

'Fag-end, my arse,' Rosie said, as TJ got out of the booth.

He put his arms around her and hugged her close. She could smell the smoke and that other smell he had that she liked. She didn't know what it was, but it always made her feel safe.

'Go home,' TJ said. 'Have a bath. Listen to some whales moaning, or monastic chants. Or better still, come home with me and we'll smoke a joint.'

'No thanks, pal. A joint is probably the last thing I need.'

As she walked away, TJ shouted after her.

'I've got some great whale music.'

Rosie didn't turn around, but gave him the two-fingered salute that she knew he would expect.

CHAPTER TEN

Rosie slipped into the pew at St Gregory's and sat in the heavy silence of the empty Catholic church. Early morning mass had just finished, and the smell of incense still hung in the air. All Souls' Day. They must have had Benediction. She looked up at the statue of the Sacred Heart with its outstretched arms, and swallowed hard. Tears came, the way they always did when she sat here on this day every year. She had long since questioned and ditched the dogma that the dead were really all souls waiting for the rest of us on the other side, but still she kept coming here. In her heart, she had nowhere else to go. Here, despite the choking sadness that overtook her, when she sat in the empty church she could still feel her mother's presence. Wherever she looked, from the metal railings in front of the marble altar to the dark confessional boxes, Rosie could picture herself when she was six years old, sitting with her mother who was still beautiful and happy then. She could see herself – in the little blue velvet cape she wore over her white First Communion dress – walking slowly back from the altar, hands joined, and stealing a glimpse at her mother's beaming face among the rest of the parents. She had been great then.

Rosie thought of Gemma, of how watchful the kid was of Mags, as though she'd seen her fall apart too often. She remembered the feeling all too well. How you covered things up, invented little stories to make yourself feel equal to the rest of the kids in school. Of course she had a daddy, she told them. He was away in the Merchant Navy, but when he came back he was bringing presents and stuff from all over the world. From Africa and China. When they whispered and laughed, because their mothers had told them different, Rosie walked away and sat by herself. She didn't need them anyway. She had her own little world. And when her mum was sober enough to do things, sometimes they would get all dressed up and take the blue train from Glasgow to the beach at Helensburgh and spend the day just walking, soaking up the atmosphere. Fish teas in the cafe, then home for the best sleeps ever . . .

The vestry door opened and the grey-haired old priest came in. He nodded at Rosie, genuflected at the altar, and came over to where she sat.

'Hallo, Father,' Rosie said, composing herself.

Father Dunnachie studied her face. He had known Rosie most of her young life, and her mother too, ever since he had arrived at St Gregory's from Donegal many years ago as a newly ordained curate. He had been moved around various churches during his lifetime, before coming back to St Gregory's, where he was now semi-retired.

'Thought I might find you here,' he said, touching her shoulder. He sat down beside her. 'All Souls' Day. You never miss it, Rosie.' He turned to her and smiled.

Rosie knew the smile had a hint of sarcasm because it was the only day of the year she turned up at church. They sat in silence for a moment, then the priest spoke again. 'I've some news for you, Rosie. I'm almost certain we've located the plot where your mother was buried. I'll know for sure in the next few days.'

'Really, Father? That's great. I thought it would be just about impossible.'

She didn't really know why she was doing this, but something inside of her was driving her on. When her mother died in such tragic circumstances, Rosie was removed from the house by the welfare. It was all a blur at the time, but she remembered the first few nights in the freezing children's home, crying herself to sleep. She recalled the confusion and anguish of stumbling from one day to the next, watching from the draughty window sill every night for someone to come up the long driveway and take her home. Nobody did. Not for a long time. Not until her mother's sister came up from where she had been living in Manchester, and took her to join her family in the Glasgow east-end tenement flat they called home. Nobody ever mentioned her mother's name again. It was as though she'd never existed.

Rosie had had no concept of funerals or cemeteries, or even what they did to her mother after that day she found her. She had heard the words pauper's burial, but they were whispered in shame. It had haunted her all her life but, like everything else, she had kept it to herself, buried inside along with the other emotions she kept in check. But over the past few months, the need to find out where her mother was buried had almost become overwhelming. She'd come to St Gregory's one morning after mass and approached the priest, and told him who she was. She was grateful he had remembered her. He told her that, from what he had gathered, her mother was buried in an unmarked grave in a cemetery that was closed down now. It would be hard to find it, but he promised to help. I just want somewhere I can visit, Father, Rosie had told him, and he nodded his understanding.

Somehow, Rosie told herself, if she could find the grave, put up a headstone or something, then she would feel less alone, less abandoned. If she could go there and talk to her mother from time to time, perhaps the nightmares would go away . . .

'I've had the records trawled through,' Father Dunnachie continued, 'and I've come up with a few names of people who were buried in the same month of that year. Unmarked.' He was careful not to say pauper's grave, but they both knew what he meant. He told her to come back in a couple of weeks, when he hoped to have the exact spot.

'Thanks, Father.' She got up to leave.

'Are you well, Rosie?' he said. 'I mean, in yourself. You're looking a wee bit pale.'

Rosie swallowed. Get a grip, woman, she thought, and said, 'I'm fine, Father, just working long hours. A big story.'

His eyes flicked skywards. 'That newspaper of yours. Sure it's all scandal.' She didn't want to get him started on the Page Three girls.

'Of course, Father, but some of the scandals need to be exposed. This one does.'

'Good luck to you, Rosie.'

She turned and walked up the aisle, knowing he was watching her all the way. Outside in the crisp sunshine she breathed in the fresh air. She felt better than she'd felt for weeks. She smiled. Maybe someone really *was* watching over her.

CHAPTER ELEVEN

Only the damned and the desperate were still working the Drag at this time of the morning. When you were this deep in the gutter you only had one choice: keep working until you made enough to get some gear on the way home. The last thing you wanted was to wake up frazzled and not have a hit. In her short skirt, Mags's thighs felt raw in the biting wind, and the freezing sleet slapped her face. Just one more punter, she told herself, then home to the wean. Gemma had been sound asleep when she'd left her alone, locked in the flat. It wasn't ideal, but she was always home before the child woke up.

Another car approached and drove on. She stepped forward, but the guy inside took a look at her then drove away. Pervert. So many of them came only to window-shop – fantasising about it was all they needed to get their rocks off. She spotted a guy across the street lighting a cigarette and could see from the match's flame that he was looking at her. He crossed the road towards her, and approached slowly.

'Awright?' He looked like a punter.

'Yeah,' Mags said 'You all right?'

'Aye.' He glanced around him. 'Busy night?'

He was definitely a punter.

'Not bad.' Mags could hear her teeth chattering. 'Looking for business?'

He looked her up and down, then nodded his head. She told him it was forty pounds for full sex and twenty for oral. He grimaced at the price. Mags couldn't afford to let him go.

'I'll do hand relief for a tenner,' she said. 'Call it a closing down sale.'

The punter didn't crack. He mumbled that oral would be fine.

Mags told him to follow her. She walked round the corner into the deserted alley where she could see the street at the other side. A bin had blown over in the wind and rubbish was strewn along the cobblestones. It swirled around them as they picked their way in the darkness. He followed her to the small car park at the side of the warehouse where she had already been twice tonight. She stood against the wall as he took a step towards her. She could barely see him in the dark, but heard him breathing fast as she reached down and ran her hand across the front of his jeans. He was bursting out of them already, so this shouldn't take long. She unzipped him and put her cold hand inside where it was warm and smooth. He gave a short moan as she moved her hand up and down him so he would come quicker and she wouldn't have to spend so much time blowing him. Mags knelt down and put her mouth around him, and he groaned, grabbing her hair and pushing her head against him. It was over in less than a minute and he let out a loud gasp. Mag spat and stood up, wiping her mouth on a scrap of tissue from her pocket. For a single moment their eyes met and Mags was thinking he had a weird, dark look about him. She would be glad to get rid of this one. He didn't speak, but went into his pocket and Mags heard the rustle of notes. But when his hand came out again, there was a flicking noise, and even in the dark she could see the gleam of a blade.

It happened so fast, the blade was across her throat while she was still staring at him in disbelief. Before she slumped she put her hand up to her neck and felt the warm blood gushing out between her fingers. Then her knees went weak and, as she slid down the wall, she heard the sound of her mobile phone slipping out of her pocket and clattering onto the ground. He watched as she lay on the ground, not struggling, but just repeating the same name. 'Gemma,' she whispered. 'Gemma.'

Rosie could hear the phone ringing, the way it always did when she had that dream. It was the same dream that had haunted her since childhood, from that day she came home from school and found her. She had stood there in a daze, the phone ringing on the hall table just a few feet away, but she couldn't move from the spot to answer it.

Now she heard it ringing again, the sound growing louder and louder as she felt herself being dragged out of the nightmare. She blinked in the darkness of her bedroom and heard the rain battering at the windows. She leaned across the bed and picked up the phone, checking the time on the radio alarm. It was ten past six. This could only be bad news.

'Hallo?' She cleared her throat.

'Rosie?' She recognised the voice of her cop contact Don. 'Rosie, it's me. Sorry, but it's important.'

'Don? What's the matter?'

'I thought you'd want to know. An early shout. There's a prostitute been found with her throat cut, just off the Drag.'

Rosie's heart jumped in her chest. Please don't let it be Mags.

'Any name? Do they know who she is?' She was wide

awake now and could hear her voice shaking. She tried to compose herself. Although she trusted Don, she didn't want him to know just how much she knew. Not yet anyway.

'Some bird called Mags.' He was matter-of-fact. 'Don't know her second name. Oh, hold on . . .' She could hear him rustling paper. 'It's Gillin, or Gillick, or something. I was out there with the night shift. She's a wee skinny blonde thing. Poor wee bastard. Imagine some fucker cutting her throat.'

Rosie felt sick. Her head swam and she sank back onto the pillow.

'You there, Rosie?'

'Yeah.' She managed to answer. She saw Mags in the cafe, laughing and coughing. She saw her stroking Gemma's hair. Gemma. What about Gemma?

'Do we know where she's from, Don? Any relatives I can go see?' She wanted to make sure it was Mags.

'No,' Don said. 'But wait till you hear. Uniform went round to her address and there's this wee lassie lying sleeping on the couch. She's only about eight or something. Social work are round there now. The bird must have left her in there all night by herself. These fucking junkies. Honest to Christ.'

'Can I go round and get an early look at the place?' Rosie was already thinking of the story, and how she would put it together. Don wouldn't be suspicious if she simply wanted to go to the house and the scene of the crime.

'Yeah, suppose so. But just watch what you're doing because you'll be there even before the evening paper hacks. It's not half six yet.'

'I'll be careful. Don't worry, I just want some early colour. I mean, that's the second hooker who ends up dead in a week. This story is getting bigger.' She wondered if Don would take the bait.

'Don't know, Rosie, but what I *can* tell you is that there have been some pretty heavy calls made to the DI this morning. I was up at the crime scene and Jack Prentice turned up. I mean, what's he doing there at this time of the morning? It's not even his gaff.'

Rosie said nothing. She thought about Mags' mobile and the last message from Tracy. It would be gone forever now.

'You still there?'

'Yeah. Sorry, Don, I'm just getting up. I'll talk to you later.'

She walked into the bathroom in a daze and turned on the shower full blast. She stood watching as the steam filled the room, then stepped inside and let the warm water rush over her face and body. The tears came, slowly at first, spilling out of her eyes. And then she heard herself sobbing as she stood with the water beating onto her back. She thought of how scared Mags would have been in that single moment when she knew what was happening to her, what utter terror she must have felt. Then Rosie stopped crying and turned on the cold shower, wincing as it hit her warm body. They had done it. They must have. It was too much of a coincidence.

Suddenly she felt very, very scared.

CHAPTER TWELVE

A handful of locals had already gathered in the street outside Mags's house. In the darkness they were like shadows, the blue light from the police car flashing momentarily on their faces. Now you see them, now you don't. They wore the tired, grey faces of people who had seen it all before. Rosie walked towards three or four women standing together watching Mags's front door. Tragedy in places like this always brought people out of their homes and onto the street, some to criticise and pontificate, others relieved that – this time – death had not come to their doorstep.

Behind the torn curtains of Mags's ground floor flat, Rosie could see a stark bare bulb light up the living room. Inside, she could make out a policewoman and another woman looking downwards. They must be talking to Gemma, she thought.

One of the street women turned to Rosie. 'Fuckin' ridiculous. That wee thing left by herself and her mammy out whorin' it. Fuckin' scandalous.' The other women, their arms folded against the cold, nodded in agreement.

One of them turned to Rosie and looked her up and down. 'You fae the social?' She lit a cigarette and sucked in the smoke.

'No,' Rosie said, knowing that wouldn't be enough information for them.

'Did you know Mags?' asked another woman, eyeing her suspiciously.

Rosie looked all three of them in the eye in turn. They could easily turn on her if they knew she was a journalist. They needed somebody to blame at a time like this.

'I was Mags's friend. I met her some time ago and I liked her a lot. She was a good person. Just the drugs were the problem. I think she was trying to come off them.'

'Aye. Usual shite.' The first woman shook her head. 'They're all tryin' to come off them, but they never do. If they're not smacked up, they're half-jaked on methadone. The end result's always the same. They end up in a fuckin' box and it's the weans that are left.'

Across the street, the front door opened and a burly policeman emerged, carrying Gemma in his arms. She was wearing her red duffel coat over her pyjamas. One of her slippers fell off onto the path and a policewoman picked it up and pushed her foot back into it. Gemma's chalk-white face looked smaller somehow, pinched and tired. No spark at all. She glanced around, confused, as though she was expecting to see her mum there. The policeman put her into the back of the panda car and she knelt up on the seat, looking out of the rear window. Just as the car was about to draw away, she spotted Rosie and her eyes lit up. She rapped the back window excitedly and Rosie gave her a discreet wave. Everyone turned around to look at her, including the two detectives standing by the car. The car pulled away and Rosie could see that now there were tears in Gemma's eyes as she banged on the window. Rosie bit her lip because she understood how Gemma felt right now. She had been there. Alone, wondering where she was going, crying for her mother.

'I suppose that'll be her in care,' one of the women said. 'Just like half the weans around here. God help her.'

'Where'll they take her?' Rosie asked.

'Christ knows. They might get her foster parents or she might be kept in that Woodbank. Let's just hope she gets fostered because, the way I hear it, some of the lassies from there are already out working the Drag and some of them aren't even teenagers. Beasts. Men are beasts.'

The other women nodded, and Rosie knew she'd better say something.

'Yeah. Terrible.' She pulled up her collar. They were watching her to see if she was going to say anything more interesting, but she turned and walked away. She could feel their eyes on her back, but the longer she was there, the more chance the detectives would come sniffing around her.

By the time she arrived back at the newspaper office, Rosie had some idea in her head of the story she would write for tomorrow's paper. She'd talk to McGuire about it. It would be out by now that Mags had been murdered – the second dead prostitute in a week. Even though the cops had not come out and confirmed the kid had worked the Drag, there were enough other people saying it for the newspapers to have already started dripping the line. There would be a press conference later in the afternoon. No doubt, the question on every reporter's lips would be, is there a serial killer on the loose who is targeting street girls? The papers loved a serial killer. The cops would have the answers ready for that one. They would take the opportunity to re-emphasise that there was nothing to suggest that the first girl was murdered, nor were the deaths connected. But Rosie knew better.

When she reached her desk she found a note telling her to see the editor.

'You look like shit.' Bob Reynolds, the crime reporter,

who sat opposite her, watched as she took her notebook from her bag.

'Thank you, Oscar Wilde,' Rosie said. 'At least I know I can look better. You'll be an ugly bastard all your life.'

Terms of endearment on the editorial floor. The two of them actually got on well and had worked together on some major stories. But Bob was the crime reporter, and he always tried to pull rank if the major story Rosie was involved in had a criminal connection. She usually let him lead the way, but then had to rewrite the copy because McGuire always said that Reynolds couldn't write home for money, especially after the pub doors had opened.

Rosie liked Reynolds, but she trusted him about as far as she could throw his six-foot frame. He was like a caricature from an old black and white movie: furtive, dark, talking out of the side of his mouth like he was always giving you some inside track. But he was very close to the cops, and Rosie knew that he would protect them at all times. She knew she couldn't even let him get so much as a faint whiff of the story she was working on.

'Another bird dead,' Reynolds said. 'You were out at the house. How come? One of my copper mates saw you.'

Rosie was caught off guard. She would have to have some kind of story as to why she was out on a murder story before the crime man had been there.

'Oh, a contact of mine.' She recovered quickly. 'From the prostitutes' rights group. One of them phoned me saying that they knew the girl and that she had been found dead. Murdered.'

'How did they get to know so early?' Reynolds persisted. Rosie knew he didn't believe her.

'Don't know. I suppose the cops must have phoned to see if they knew anything about her. She used to go to the Drop-In Centre, for condoms and stuff. Somebody connected to there phoned me really early this morning, so I thought I would go out and have a quick recce. There might be some colour piece to be done.'

Rosie was relieved when her phone rang. It was McGuire's secretary.

'You've to come through,' she said.

She didn't even bother to tell Reynolds where she was going, but she could feel him watching her as she walked across the vast editorial floor, which was beginning to fill up with reporters now that it was after nine. In a couple of hours every desk would be occupied, and the whole place would be alive and bustling, phones ringing and banter between the journalists growing, as the newspaper marched towards its deadline.

Rosie headed through the open door of the glass partition in the far corner where Marion sat at her desk outside McGuire's office, guarding him from disgruntled executives or meddling bean counters from the finance department. Rosie nodded to Marion and walked into the office.

'Well!' McGuire took off his reading glasses as Rosie came in. 'Shut the door and sit down.'

She sat on the red leather sofa and opened her notebook.

'Fuckin' hell, Gilmour.' He was excited. He rubbed his hands. 'This is beginning to warm up. Two stiffs in a week. Christ!'

'I'm sure the families of the prostitutes don't see it that way, but I take your point.' Her voice was sarcastic. She knew McGuire would expect her to say that. He liked to wind her up, always telling her she was just a bleeding heart and would never be hard enough to be an editor like him. Not that she ever wanted to be. She liked to lie straight in her bed.

He grinned. 'So. What now?' He put his feet up on the desk. 'Speak to me. I want to work out how I'm going to handle this before Lamont and the rest troop in for conference at eleven.'

Rosie told him that, first and foremost, she felt Reynolds had to be allowed to write the main story. She would go to the press conference with him and do all the atmosphere and colour of the day. They had already agreed earlier that he should be nowhere near the big picture. McGuire also knew that Reynolds was too close for comfort to the cops.

They would run the story straight as a murder and see what came out at the press conference. Rosie was to do a separate piece on prostitutes and, now that three had been murdered in a year, questioning what police were doing – if anything – to protect them. The woolly-headed liberals would love that, McGuire told her. The story of Tracy's death and the prostitute connection would be separate, but Rosie would pursue the social work department with questions, asking why they had not done their job and protected her.

When they had finished the discussion, McGuire wanted to talk about the real story. Rosie told him how she had been phoned at six by her cop mate.

'The contact who phoned me this morning said that Jack Prentice was up at the murder scene very early on,' Rosie told him. 'That's not normal. It's not his patch. I think there's more to it.'

'What like?' He sat forward. 'You don't think they bumped her off? Fuck me, Gilmour!'

Rosie got up from the sofa. 'I'm absolutely certain they bumped her off.'

She paced around in front of his desk. 'Listen, Mick. I got a call from Mags two nights ago. I told you that yesterday. She got duffed up by Prentice and she gave him a blow-job. She was worried that something was going to happen to her, really worried.'

'So what do you think? Are you saying they hired someone to cut her throat?'

'You can hire anybody in this city to cut anybody's throat if the money's right. You know that,' Rosie said. 'Yes. I think they got somebody to get rid of her. Problem is, I don't know if they did this because of Tracy, or because they knew she talked to me.' She spread her hands. 'Well, actually nobody did know she talked to me – apart from you.'

'Well I sure as fuck didn't tell anyone!'

'I know. Christ!' Rosie shook her head. 'I know you didn't. But I think somehow they found out. What about Reynolds? Does he know anything?'

'No, for Christ's sake, he knows fuck all. Sometimes he doesn't even know what fucking day it is. Drunken fucker.'

'Well.' Rosie took a deep breath. 'The only thing I can think of is that Mags blabbed to another hooker when she was smacked up, and she's passed the information back to the cops. Some of them would do anything for a few quid. It wouldn't have mattered that it was the garbled ramblings of a junked-up hooker. All it would need to reach the top ears is that Mags had blabbed to a reporter.'

McGuire took his feet from the desk and stood up. 'Shit, Gilmour,' he said. 'That puts you in a bit of danger, does it not?'

'No. They might not know it's me.' Then she remembered being seen by the detectives out at Mags's house this morning. She told McGuire. He looked concerned.

'Tell you what. Why don't we move you out of your flat for a couple of weeks. You know, just in case.'

'Where to?' She didn't want to move. 'I hate hotels.'

McGuire was already moving to buzz Marion. 'We'll rent you a flat. And we'll get you a minder. I don't want you getting a bullet in your back, it would ruin my chance of becoming chairman.' He laughed and Rosie laughed with him. But it was nervy laughter, and they both knew it.

McGuire called Marion in and told her to find Rosie a flat in town for the next month. Somewhere nice, but not too expensive. He knew he didn't have to tell her to keep it quiet. She was the very soul of discretion. That was how he had managed to keep two women on the go for the past five years.

CHAPTER THIRTEEN

Foxy pushed his chair back and sat with his feet on the window sill, his hands clasped behind his head. When Patsy brought his coffee in, he looked a picture of power and confidence.

'You know, you should relax more,' she said to him.

He smiled. She was one of the few people who got away with talking to him like that. But Patsy had been with him all through the ranks and he took more snash from her than anybody. She knew about his women. She also knew that his trips on the boat at the weekends had as much to do with sailing as a bunch of guys on a so-called golfing holiday to Magaluf.

'How can I relax when my quest in life is to make this city safe?' He smiled, and sipped his coffee.

When Patsy closed the door, Foxy took a deep breath and ran his hand over his chin.

'What a fucking mess,' he whispered. 'What a right fucking mess.'

As he waited for the arrival of Jack and Bill, he went over in his mind the conversation he had just had on the telephone. He had called Jake Cox, the thug boss of Glasgow's underworld, known and feared across the city and beyond, as the Big Man. For the best part of twenty-five years, Jake and Foxy had been what you could call mates – a kind of working relationship as Jake built up his empire. It was a perfect arrangement. They didn't step on each other's toes and both of them reaped the rewards. Often, in return for being allowed plenty of leeway, Big Jake delivered for Foxy, be it a murder inquiry or a robbery. If some little toerag in his regime had stepped out line, they were delivered to the cops and they were fitted up. Simple as that. Or if that didn't suit Foxy's wishes, they turned up dead.

One of the biggest turns Jake had done for Foxy was when the police instituted a high-profile gun amnesty, announcing in the press that anyone who handed in a weapon would not be prosecuted. When it kicked off, Foxy had gone on television, waxing lyrical about how this would take guns out of the community, make the streets safer. Only a trickle of weapons had been handed in at first, but after the meet with Big Jake, suddenly there were guns being found everywhere, by police acting on anonymous tip-offs. Foxy was Wyatt Earp and this was Dodge City. Shotguns, rifles and handguns started turning up in graveyards, behind shops, in derelict warehouses. Foxy was making a breakthrough. Another civic lunch celebrated his success, another promotion followed.

But Gavin Fox wasn't just a bent cop. He was a bent cop with a philosophy. He convinced himself that he was making a real contribution to fighting crime. He justified his way of life, because he knew you could never ever truly win the fight against drugs or beat the kingpins of the underworld. But, as a cop you could at least ensure a level of control. Everybody got their cut because everybody, deep down, was a little bit crooked, a little bit greedy. He knew how to make it work. With his success at catching criminals at street level, he rose through the ranks, and when he got to the top, he could still keep a handle on the street. It worked both ways, for him and for Jake. As long as he delivered the goods, he survived – with the fat salary and the large pension. And Big Jake was the ultimate untouchable.

In return for all his collaboration, Jake was allowed to build up his millions, raking in a fortune from robberies and drug deals. It worked, just so long as every now and again somebody took a fall. Just so long as that somebody was never Jake or Foxy. Big Jake had wined and dined Foxy and the others. He had even been sailing with them a couple of weekends on the boat, providing the hookers and the coke. It had always worked perfectly. Until now.

Too late, Foxy realised that he had made a mistake in calling Jake to tell him about the problem with the whore they'd dumped from the boat, and his worry it might get out. He had got a call back from Jake yesterday to say that this bird Mags had blabbed to another hooker that cops were involved with Tracy, and she could blow it all sky high. Foxy told Jake she would have to be kept quiet, but the last thing he wanted was for her to have her throat cut.

'Christ almighty,' he had said to Jake. 'How the fuck did that happen? I only meant her to get a wee warning. Now I've got to pretend to solve a fucking murder. I've got the fucking press all over us like a rash.'

'Don't be fucking daft, Foxy.' Jake had laughed. 'They'll no remember it this time next week. She was just a wee slag like the other one. Nobody's even got a smell of what's happening here.'

Foxy was quiet for a moment, but his stomach was twitching. 'Just the same, Jake, I didn't want her killed. That takes us into a different ball game here. I'm not happy. I'm not happy at all, Jake.'

There was a moment's silence. Foxy was in no doubt who was running the show here, and it wasn't him.

'Okay.' Jake's voice was consoling. 'Maybe my man was a

bit heavy handed, but it'll blow over. Before you know it, we'll be sailing doon the watter with a decent bottle of champers and some Charley on the side.' He laughed his rasping breathless laugh, and Foxy could see his big face, leathery from years of sunning himself on the Costa del Sol.

Jake was still chuckling as he said goodbye, and hung up the phone, opening the drawer of his desk where Mags's mobile phone lay after it had been given to him by the hitman he'd hired to kill her.

'Fucking psycho,' muttered Foxy.

As soon as Jack and Bill walked in, Foxy knew things were unravelling fast. Jack looked like a ghost. Black circles shadowed the heavy bags under his eyes. You could see the clamminess on his pasty face. Foxy had never known him like this before. Bill looked his usual self though, and threw Foxy a glance in acknowledgement that all was not well with Jack.

'Sit down, boys.' Foxy was up to greet them. 'Christ, Jack, you all right?' Foxy squeezed his arm. 'You look like you're about to peg it. Calm down, man, for fuck's sake.'

Jack's face started to crumple, and Foxy and Bill looked at each other in disbelief. Foxy swallowed hard. This was the very last thing he needed. Jack had his head in his hands. He was shaking and Foxy realised to his horror that he was crying.

'I'm sorry, Foxy. Oh shit, I'm so sorry. I just . . . I'm just fucking going to pieces. I'm sorry.'

Bill reached across and touched his arm.

'Come on now, Jack,' he said. 'You'll be all right. We're all together. Come on now, we're your mates. We're all fine.'

Bill grimaced at Foxy, now standing over them with his arms folded. Foxy pulled up a chair and sat down next to Jack. He put his arm around him and pulled a handkerchief out of his pocket and gave it to him.

'It's all right, Jack, get it out. It's the tension. It's been tough for us. Tough six months. Last few days even tougher. But it's going to be all right, Jack, you'll see. Just need to dig deep.'

Jack tried to sit up straight, and took his hands away from his face. He blew his nose and sniffed.

'Sorry guys,' he said, weakly. He turned to Foxy. 'It's just that sometimes I think I'm cracking up. I can't sleep or anything.'

Foxy patted his shoulder. 'Not at all, Jack. But listen, pal, we've been to hell and back, us three. We don't crack up. We'll be out the other end of this in a few weeks and then it'll be business as usual. You'll see. We're in charge here.'

Jack shook his head, and his face reddened.

'But, Foxy,' he said. 'That wee bird Mags . . . her throat cut . . . I mean, what's happening? That wasn't us, was it? You didn't get that done, did you, Foxy?'

Foxy stood up and looked from Bill to Jack. He knew he would have to tell them.

'It was the Big Man,' he said, shaking his head. 'Fucking hell. I told him about the problem, but I didn't expect anything like this. Nobody was more surprised than me, I can tell you, lads.'

'Holy Christ,' Bill said. 'What a psycho Big Jake is. You think a few slaps would have done a wee lassie like that, but he had to go the full hog. Who did it?'

'Don't know. He said something about a guy from Newcastle that they use sometimes. I don't even want to know. I've made it clear to him that I'm well pissed off, but you know what he's like.' He shook his head. 'Anyway, it's done now, so just forget about it. It didn't happen.'

'The press conference is this afternoon,' Jack said. 'The shit'll hit the fan.'

'No it won't.' Foxy was firm, looking Jack in the eye. 'Just keep the ball on the ground. I've already spoken to McIntosh, who's running the inquiry, and said I want to be kept informed of every cough and spit. This is a high-profile case now, and that might actually work in our favour. We'll throw the press a few lines. They'll be wanting a serial killer, so I've told McIntosh not to deny this as a possible line of enquiry . . . keep it vague because we don't know. That'll get 'em going. And the good thing is that the wee Tracy bird story will be way down their agenda now, because there is no evidence to suggest she was murdered. I know how these sewer rats work.'

'But do you think Mags actually spoke to any reporter?' Bill said. 'Or was she just trying to be smart in front of the other hooker?

Foxy leaned on the edge of his desk. 'The answer to that is I just don't know. Hard to say.'

'I'll talk to Reynolds,' Bill said. 'In case it's him or anybody in his office.'

'If it was Reynolds we'd know about it.' Foxy went back behind his desk. 'Anyway' – he shuffled some papers – 'let's keep all this in perspective. We can't be starting to panic over who this daft wee whore spoke to or not. Let's just sit tight and see how it pans out. Most important thing is that we keep it together. Right, Jack?'

Jack got up and took a deep breath. 'Right, Foxy. I'll be all right. I feel better already.'

'Maybe you just needed a good greet,' Bill said, sniggering. 'Maybe you're pre-menstrual or something.'

They all just about managed a laugh, and for the briefest moment they were back on the boat, just like the good old days.

CHAPTER FOURTEEN

Rosie struggled to pull up the zip of the hold-all she had packed to take to the flat. It was always the same. No matter how carefully you packed, there was never enough room, wherever you were going. Eventually it was done and she slung it over her shoulder and walked out of her bedroom and into the living room. She did one final check that all the plugs were out and switches off before turning on the alarm and getting out of the flat in the statutory thirty seconds.

She breathed an exhausted sigh when she got into the lift. She was tired. Proper sleep hadn't come for the best part of the week. And the dream kept coming back, the way it always did when she was under pressure. She had woken up twice with her eyes wet; she had been crying in her sleep. She was always glad when the morning came. Tonight when she got to the flat she would soak in a hot bath and then collapse into bed. She knew that when she was done in like this, she'd sleep for twelve straight hours. She couldn't wait.

She went down the stairs and across the hall towards the shared entrance to the flats. When she pressed the security button to release the heavy wooden door and stepped outside, she did a double take. It looked like Mags's little girl, Gemma, sitting on the steps. When the girl looked around and smiled at her, Rosie knew she wasn't hallucinating. She stood staring at her, confused, wondering if anyone was with her. Rosie's stomach turned over. Jesus!

'Gemma?' she said, as if she was making sure.

'Hiya, Rosie.' Gemma stood up, looking sheepish. Her face was red from crying, and she seemed about to burst into tears.

'Gemma.' Rosie still could not quite believe it. 'What are you doing here? I mean, how did you get here? What's going on?'

Gemma took a step towards her. Rosie could see her little eyes were tired, red-rimmed.

'I ran away. Can I come and stay with you?' Then she took a deep breath, and the words came out in a huge, heaving sob. 'They said my mammy's in heaven an' she's not coming back.' She threw herself at Rosie and wrapped her arms around her waist.

Rosie looked around nervously. She put a tentative hand on the girl's head and patted her. Christ! This could not be happening!

'Sssh, now.' She suddenly fought back the urge to cry as well. 'There now, Gemma . . . It'll be all right . . . You'll see.'

'But I've got no mammy now,' Gemma sobbed, her body shuddering.

Rosie didn't know what to say to her. Nothing in her chequered life had prepared her for a moment like this, but she had to get out of the street just in case, as McGuire suspected, someone was watching her. She took the child's hand and pulled her towards her car parked close by.

'Quick.' She opened the back door of the car. 'Inside. We'll have a wee talk, Gemma. Just calm down, pet. You'll be fine.' Rosie had no idea what she was going to do.

She drove a couple of streets away and pulled into the side of the road, switching off the engine. She turned around to face Gemma, who smiled back at her, sniffing, her chest still quivering from the sobs.

'Tell me what happened, Gemma.' Rosie hoped she sounded calm and collected, though her heart was going like an engine.

Gemma told her that the woman, who Rosie guessed was her social worker, had told her that her mum had been hurt and was in heaven now. But she was going to be cared for at the home, and soon she would probably find foster parents who would take great care of her. The woman told her about other little girls and boys who were now living in smashing houses and had bikes and everything. Some of them even went to Spain for their holidays. But Gemma said she didn't want to stay there. She didn't like any of the people. And she had wet the bed two nights in a row. At that she started crying again.

'That's okay.' Rosie leaned over and held her hand. It felt small and warm. 'Sometimes that happens, Gemma.' She wiped her tears with her hand. 'It's because of everything that's gone on with you. Once you get settled you'll be fine, I promise. You will, darling.'

'Can I not stay with you?' Gemma's watery blue eyes questioned. 'That's why I ran away. I like you, and my mammy says you're brilliant.'

Rosie bit her lip and swallowed. 'How did you find where I lived? You've never been here.'

'Aye,' Gemma said, pleased with herself. 'Remember when we drove past that day and you pointed at it? The balcony? I liked the balcony.' She smiled. 'I just came round the back and sat on the steps. I was gonnae wait till somebody came out, then run in and look for you. I saw it in a film once.'

Rosie smiled and shook her head. By now, people at the

home would know Gemma was missing. She'd have to take her back. Her mind raced with a dozen possible scenarios. There'd be a search for her. Police. The whole shooting match. And here was she, sitting with the runaway kid of a murder victim in the car. She could be done for abduction. But she couldn't simply take her back because the police would be involved by now and she'd be interviewed. She'd be linked to the victim. They'd put two and two together and know she was the one Mags had talked to. Panic began to rise in her.

'Gemma.' Rosie took a deep breath. She spoke calmly. 'Gemma: you know you can't stay with me. It doesn't work that way. The welfare people, the social workers, they have to take care of you now. I mean, even if I had time, I couldn't just let you stay with me. Have you any idea how many people will be looking for you by now? Police will be everywhere. You have to go back, pet. You really have to.'

'But please,' Gemma begged. 'Please let me stay with you. I won't eat much. I just like chips. I won't make a noise. I won't wet the bed. I promise.'

Rosie sighed. Her phone rang. It was McGuire.

'Howsit goin', Gilmour?' his voice was cheery. 'Are you settled in?'

Rosie almost laughed. If only he knew. But she couldn't tell him right now. She had to work out what to do first.

'Not quite. I'll be going there in a little while. I'll give you a ring later. Need to go now, I've set the alarm on the house.' She hung up. She needed to talk to someone, but not McGuire. Not right now. She phoned TJ's mobile, checking her watch at the same time to see if he was out busking yet. He answered immediately.

'Hey, Rosie. How goes it?'

'Things could be better.'

'Has nobody shot you yet?'

'Not yet.' She swallowed. 'TJ, listen. I need to see you right now. I need your help.'

He told her he was on his way to his busking pitch outside O'Brien's, but he could leave that for a while. She arranged to pick him up at the top of Buchanan Street.

'You all right?' TJ said. 'You sound a bit edgy.'

'I passed edgy about ten minutes ago,' Rosie said, and hung up.

She pulled into the side of the road when she saw TJ standing in a shop doorway, and gave the horn one quick toot. He caught sight of her and walked towards the car. Rosie felt relief as she watched him, moving towards her with his casual, confident stride, his black saxophone box slung over his shoulder. Just knowing that TJ was around gave her a sense that things would work out. Though she chided herself for her weakness in relying on him, she was always glad when she did, because he had never let her down.

'Sorry, TJ,' she said as he got in the car.

'No problem, darlin', what wouldn't I do for you?' He glanced in the back seat at Gemma, who smiled at him.

'Who's this? Are you collecting weans now?'

Rosie took a deep breath and told him what had happened. Every now and again, TJ kept glancing over his shoulder to Gemma, who was sitting upright and looking anxiously from one to the other.

'Jesus,' TJ said when Rosie finished. 'Oh sweet Jesus, Rosie. This is definitely a new one on me.' He laughed. 'Tell me, pal, do you actually plan these things just to test me out?'

Rosie recalled how TJ had pulled her out of more than one hole the last two years. No questions asked. No obligations.

'I wish it was a game,' Rosie said. 'I wish. But what are we going to do, TJ?'

'What do you mean me *we*, Kemo Sabe?' He laughed. He ran his hands through his greying hair and stared out of the windscreen. Everyone was quiet, then Gemma piped up.

'Is that your man, Rosie?'

Rosie and TJ glanced at each other.

'This is TJ,' Rosie said. 'He's my best friend.' She felt TJ staring at her.

'I've no got a best friend,' Gemma said. 'Used to have.

Her name's Linda. She went to live with her granny 'cos her ma's in the jail.'

Another silence.

'What we going to do?' Rosie whispered to TJ.

'We'll have to take her back,' TJ said. 'Even if we leave her close to the home, you know, at the bottom of the road or something.' He raised his eyebrows. 'You can't keep her, Rosie. You can't just keep somebody's kid.'

'I know, I know . . .' She turned to Gemma and took her hand.

'Listen, Gemma. Now you have to listen to me and try to understand.' Rosie rubbed the back of the little girl's hand.

Gemma nodded slowly.

'Darlin', it is very important that you go back to the home. If anyone knows you were here with me I would get into a lot of trouble, so I don't want you to tell anybody. Okay?'

Gemma nodded again, her eyes filling with tears.

'Now . . . Once you go back to the home, I'll make arrangements to come and see you at least twice a week. I'll even ask the social workers if I can get you out for an evening. Maybe we'll go to the pictures?'

The child looked less downcast.

'Maybe I can stay in your house for a night? Maybe we could sit on the balcony?'

Rosie looked from Gemma to TJ, who shrugged and looked out of the window.

'We'll see,' Rosie said. 'I promise you, Gemma. No matter what, I'll come and visit.'

'Promise? You won't forget?'

'I won't,' Rosie said, feeling her voice crack, remembering what it was like to be forgotten. 'Never. I promise.'

Gemma sat back in the seat and both Rosie and TJ turned around to look at her. TJ brushed his hand across Rosie's and shook his head, half smiling. 'Let's go,' he said. 'Come on. Before we all end up in the pokey.'

CHAPTER FIFTEEN

The combination of red wine, stress and exhaustion was fatal for Rosie. She was already quite drunk and they were only halfway through the meal. She was at that stage where she talked non-stop, and TJ was listening intently, asking questions now and again, that would set her off on a rambling, colourful explanation.

She would probably regret this, but right now she felt good. TJ had insisted on taking her to the small Italian bistro downstairs from his flat in the city centre. She told him she was too tired to go anywhere except her bed after the day she'd had, but TJ convinced her she was more in need of some company and a few hard drinks than a rest. Eventually she agreed, and when the bistro's owner, Giovanni, welcomed them at the bar with a hug, and a gin and tonic that barely touched the sides, she was soon feeling a whole lot better.

Two hours earlier they had driven Gemma within about fifty yards of the children's home and dropped her off.

'I can't believe I'm doing this,' Rosie had said. 'You couldn't make this up.'

It was his plan, and he told her just to do it and keep quiet. It was the only way. Gemma had promised to go straight to the door. She would say she'd gone for a walk and got a bit lost. She'd only been missing for just over an hour, and unless the children's home was run like a prison camp, they probably wouldn't even have missed her. They had watched from the car as she walked along the street towards the big, grey sandstone building. She pushed open the door, giving them a furtive wave before she went inside. They waited for about five minutes, keeping an eye on the door to see if there was any activity, but there wasn't. They left then, telling themselves there was nothing more they could do.

'I feel wrecked already.' Rosie rubbed her eyes as TJ filled up her glass with red wine. 'You shouldn't have allowed me to drink when I'm this tired.'

'Nonsense. You've hardly had a couple of glasses.' He downed his drink and gave her a devilish look. 'Hey. Let's get hammered. You've no work tomorrow, and you've already cost me a full night's busking by dragging me into your kidnapping scam.'

Her eyes flicked across his face, the sallow skin and

dark features that TJ had said was the Black Irish in him. His father had been from Donegal and his mother was from Glasgow. But he always joked that his ancestors were sailors from the Spanish Armada, who jumped ship when they saw the beautiful Irish girls. The romance got lost somewhere between the Irish sea and the rat-infested Glasgow tenement he grew up in.

'You never tell me all of your story, TJ.' Rosie was always fascinated by his tales of growing up, and how he just walked away from Glasgow one November morning when he was twenty-two and didn't come back for twenty years. He'd lived in New York, trekked across Europe, and for a couple of years lived in Cuba.

'What're you talking about? I've told you loads of stories. What's to tell?' He smiled, running a finger around the rim of his wine glass.

Rosie sipped her wine, watching him order coffee for both of them when Giovanni came to the table, then said, 'Yeah, but I can never really get inside your head. I mean, you're out there busking, and you say you don't need to do it for the money. What's that all about? Don't you ever wonder, after all the travelling and restless stuff, what's going to happen? When will it stop?'

She blinked, knowing she was beginning to sound a bit drunk. 'Sorry,' she said, 'I don't mean to decipher your life. But you know, TJ, I just wonder about you sometimes.'

He leaned forward, lit a cigarette and blew the smoke out slowly.

'It's okay.' He looked her in the eye. 'So what if I keep travelling? Why stop? Why stay in one place? Who made that rule? I'm happier when I'm moving. It's when I stop that I feel unhappy.'

Rosie took his cigarette from between his fingers and had a drag of it, then gave it back.

'Are you unhappy now?'

He smiled. 'Yeah. Because you keep smoking my fags, Gilmour. Can you not buy your own?'

'I don't smoke. You know that.' She took his again, had another draw, and handed it back to him.

'Aye. Not much, you don't.'

'You never answered my question.'

'Do you hacks never take a day off?' He smiled and ran his fingers through his hair. 'No. Right now, right at this moment, I'm not unhappy. I like being with you, Gilmour.' He looked at her, then away. 'You're nuts, but you're not predictable. Once you get predictable, we'll not be having these touching little interludes.' He clinked his glass with hers.

Rosie grinned back. 'Well that's good to know. Good that we'll be mates till the bitter end.'

TJ raised his glass and they clinked again.

He called Giovanni for the bill, and insisted on paying it despite Rosie's protests.

'I've got a great idea,' TJ said as they stood up. 'Let's go to the salsa dancing and drink tequila just for the sheer badness of it.'

Rosie laughed. 'Can you salsa?' She put on her jacket.

'Can I *salsa*?' He knotted his scarf around his neck. 'Did I not live in Havana for nearly two years? I'm talking snake hips here, darlin'.' He shimmied as he shoved his arms into his jacket.

Giovanni walked them to the door and kissed Rosie on both cheeks, then did the same to TJ.

'I love you, Giovanni,' TJ said. 'I want to have your babies. They'd be beautiful.'

Giovanni laughed, his big belly shaking under his apron, and slapped TJ on the back as they went out into the freezing night.

The salsa bar was dark. Rosie could barely make out the faces of the people at the tables next to her. TJ told her that the darkness was all part of the ploy to make it more like the smoke-filled basement bars in Havana he'd more or less lived in, where everything seemed mysterious and sexy in the candlelight. On the dance floor, couples gyrated to the music. Some of them actually knew what they were doing and snaked their hips towards each other in a sexy sway to the sultry music. Others were women out on a girlie night, just getting bladdered. Fat bellies and backsides swivelled in no coherent direction. Rosie looked at her watch and knew she should be asleep. But what the hell? She was having fun. TJ brought two tequilas and a couple of slices of lemon to the table.

'Why are we drinking tequila?' Rosie asked. 'Isn't that Mexican? Should it not be rum?'

TJ shrugged. 'Yes, of course, but tequila's much more fun. More instant.' He sat down and clinked his tiny glass with hers. 'Right. Come on then.' They both swallowed in one. Rosie could feel the shot burning all the way down and stuffed the lemon into her mouth to take the taste away.

'Tastes like toilet cleaner.'

'Really? I've never tasted toilet cleaner. You hacks really know how to live.'

He lit a cigarette and offered it to Rosie. She could still feel the drink burning her stomach and took a long draw from his cigarette. A waitress passed by and TJ ordered two more tequilas. Rosie protested, but she didn't mean it. Just go with the flow ... see what happens after a few more of these ... tomorrow was another day ... But if she kept this up, it would be a sore one.

Two shots later, TJ was holding her hand and touching her arm. A little tingle ran through her.

'Next year,' TJ said, looking her in the eye, 'assuming we're still friends and you haven't been shot, I'll take you to Cuba. You'd love it. I could show you stuff there. It'd be a real blast.'

'It's a deal.' Rosie clinked his glass. 'In fact, why wait till next year? Let's go tomorrow. Get the hell out of here.' They both laughed. But her stomach took a funny little leap. Did he want more than friendship? She hoped not, and she hoped she didn't either. But right there and then, she would have gone to Cuba with him. Just kept on going and never come back. That would really be living on the edge. Jesus, it must be the tequila! She waved to the waitress and ordered two more.

'That's it, Rosie. Just go with it,' TJ laughed, and clapped his hands.

This was getting crazy. The music changed, and in a minute the dance floor was full. TJ stood up and put his hands out towards her.

'Come on, Gilmour. I love this song. I used to play it on my sax in a bar in downtown Havana. Come on.'

'I can't dance like that.' Rosie got up. 'I'll make an eejit of myself.'

'Bollocks. I'll show you.' He took her hand and weaved his way through the chairs to the dance floor. He held her hand and showed her a few steps. Rosie was a little unsteady, and he moved closer and pulled her towards him.

'Just move to the sway of my body.' He held her close. 'That's it. Just get my rhythm and keep on going. It's a bit like dry humping.'

Rosie was giggling. This was good. They swayed and danced on the crowded floor, TJ swirling like an old pro. And when the music stopped, they were locked somewhere between a dance and an embrace, their cheeks touching. He turned her face towards him and kissed her full on the lips. Not exploratory. Hard and decisive. She felt his tongue flick into her mouth and she kissed him back. It didn't last long, but it was long enough. When they pulled back Rosie could feel his breath on hers as she looked into his eyes.

'Let's go home,' TJ whispered, and gripped her hand tightly as they left the dance floor.

She followed him as he lifted their jackets, and they walked out of the club in silence.

His flat was only a couple of blocks away, and they didn't speak until they got to the front door. Rosie was lost for words, but she could hear her heartbeat. She should stop this now, but she couldn't. What if it ruined everything? She knew what was going to happen, but she couldn't think beyond that.

'You okay?' TJ pushed open the main door of the flats.

Rosie nodded and they went inside the dark hall, towards the staircase leading to TJ's flat on the first floor. He took her hand as they walked up the stone stair and Rosie could feel her heart pounding in her chest. She didn't feel so drunk now. TJ stopped on the stairway. He turned to her and pulled her towards him. He was breathing fast as his lips ran over her face and neck, and she could feel him hard against her. He touched her breasts and she put her arms around him. He started tugging at her jeans. Jesus!

They weren't even going to make it to the flat, but she didn't want him to stop.

He was breathless. 'Come on. Let's go in.' He took her hand and they climbed the stairs to his flat and opened the door.

He slammed the door shut and they fell against the wall. Rosie kicked off her shoes and shrugged off her jacket. TJ was on his knees on the hallway, pulling at Rosie's jeans until they were down round her ankles and she kicked them away. Through the open door, while he was easing her pants down her thighs, Rosie could see the living room bathed in alternating flickers of light and darkness as the neon flashing from the bar across the street shone through the window. It was like a dirty movie.

'Jesus . . .' She closed her eyes as TJ buried his head between her legs . . .

Later, much later, Rosie opened one eye to see the morning light coming through the bay window. The sky was pale and grey. Her head was pounding. She turned slowly to where TJ was sleeping softly on the pillow next to her, and she watched his peaceful face for a moment. Then she closed her eyes, recalling the sheer craziness of last night. Christ. She'd done drunken benders before, and sure enough they'd ended like this. But the self-loathing that usually kicked in just made your hangover ten times worse, so she hadn't been down this road for a long time. Christ almighty, this was her mate. This was worse than crazy. She turned on her side and rubbed her eyes. They were wet, and suddenly she remembered the dream again.

'You okay, Gilmour?' TJ stirred beside her. 'You were crying in your sleep.'

He reached across for her hand, but didn't open his eyes.

Rosie turned on her back and stared at the ceiling. 'Sometimes I do that.' She was embarrassed. 'I wake up and my face is wet. It's just some dream. I cry in the night.'

TJ turned to face her and propped himself up on one elbow.

'Want to tell me about it?' His fingers traced a line across her forehead and her cheek.

She took a deep breath and sighed. She had never told anybody before about the dream. It would mean explaining everything – her whole life. All the shit and misery she had tried so hard to put behind her, but that kept coming back to her in that dream. If only she could make it go away.

'I see something in my dream, TJ,' she found herself saying. 'Something from my childhood. A lot of bad things happened. My moth–' Tears welled up and Rosie turned on her side. She could feel his hand on her back, gently caressing her spine.

'Sssh,' he whispered, and moved closer to her. 'It's okay. Talk to me.' He leaned close so that his head was next to hers. 'I love you.' His voice was soft in her ear. 'You know that, don't you, Rosie?' His lips brushed against her shoulder. 'I'm sorry if that doesn't fit into your very ordered life, but I just wanted you to know.'

Rosie swallowed back her tears. She tried hard to get a grip of herself. Because more than anything at that moment, she wanted to turn around and tell TJ that she loved him too. That even if last night had never happened, she loved him. That she hoped last night wouldn't change them, now that they had been together like this. And she wanted to tell him that more than anything she was terrified of losing him.

He put his arm around her and gently pulled her onto her back. He wiped her tears with his hand and smiled.

'Talk to me, Rosie. Come on.'

CHAPTER SIXTEEN

Rosie had slept for twelve hours straight. When she awoke in the bright yellow bedroom of the flat that was her temporary home, she felt refreshed. She had spent all day yesterday recovering from the night before, and she smiled now, remembering how attentive TJ had been before she had left his flat in the morning. She hadn't expected that level of devotion. Nobody in her life had ever been like that, except one man a long time ago. And he had broken her heart. She couldn't help herself bringing down the shutters. She could see that TJ knew, and he was wise enough to take a step back. When she said she wanted to go home, he drove her in his rickety old car to the flat, and kissed her gently on the lips before she left. No questions. No judgement.

Now, in the plush but sterile minimalist West End flat, Rosie suddenly felt more alone than she had in a long time. She'd enjoyed the clutter of TJ's messy flat and the jazz music blaring on the stereo before she'd even got out of bed. She must be going off her head, she told herself.

To break the silence and escape the navel gazing, she flicked on the television and watched some politician being filleted by a silver-haired presenter. Without showering, she got up and pulled on a tracksuit and went down to the newsagent's for the Sunday papers. When she had arrived yesterday, to her surprise the fridge was already stocked with orange juice, milk and enough to keep her going. Marion was more than just an invaluable PA to McGuire, she'd been a lifesaver to Rosie. She'd bailed her out of scrapes in war-torn lands when she needed a flight, a hotel or fast cash. And they were kindred spirits, who'd a few stories to exchange at drunken office parties about the ones that got away, and the ones they were glad they let go.

After breakfast, and a long hot shower, Rosie was ready to face the world. She had made up her mind that she would go to the children's home and look in on Gemma. TJ had told her to think twice about going down this road because she could leave herself wide open for questions, but she'd made a promise to the child. To the peaceful toll of Sunday morning church bells, she drove away from the leafy, West End avenues where people lived well-heeled lives behind big oak doors to the run-down East End. It was a different world, not just the buildings and the sense of decay, but the people who walked the streets. You could see the poverty from their clothes, their demeanour. You didn't have to go into a tenement to see their struggle.

At Woodbank Children's Home, barely any noise came from the yard where a few children played. Some kids were kicking a football, others sat on the swings, but there was none of the usual din you heard in a schoolyard. No squeals or giggles. Rosie watched from her car, planning what she would tell whoever she had to deal with at the reception. She assumed that on a Sunday there would only be a skeleton staff and they may not have too much objection to a friend of Gemma's mother calling in.

She needn't have worried. The fat woman behind the reception was barely awake when Rosie went up to the counter and asked if it was possible to see Gemma Gillick. The woman sighed and chewed gum as she pulled a clipboard from below the desk and scanned a list of names.

'Oh, aye. She's still here.' Then she looked up at Rosie for the first time.

'Are you a relative?'

'A friend. Of her mother's.'

The fat woman looked her up and down, then nodded. She didn't even ask for her name or a signature.

'She's in the wee cafe with another girl.' She half smiled. 'She's got a new pal. It's just along the corridor, then into the left.' She pointed, then sat back and scratched her belly.

Rosie couldn't believe how easy it was.

'Thanks,' she said, walking away. 'I won't be long.'

In the cafe, rows of white formica tables were empty, apart from two girls sitting at the end. Gemma was drinking from a can of Coke and the other girl, older, was swishing something around in a plastic beaker. Gemma's eyes lit up.

'Rosie!' Gemma jumped out of her chair and sprinted across the wooden floor. 'Rosie! You came!' She threw her arms around Rosie's waist and hugged her. Rosie patted her head, glancing around self-consciously.

The other girl, who had bright red hair swept up in a ponytail, watched from the table.

'This is my pal, Trina. She's ten. Her ma's in the jail. But she's coming back for her one day.'

Gemma took Rosie's hand and pulled her in the direction of the table. Trina sat up straight, her face breaking into a smile. There was a sprinkling of big freckles on her cheeks.

'Hiya,' she said.

'Hallo, Trina.' Rosie smiled. 'I'm Rosie. A friend of Gemma's mum.'

Trina looked at her, then at Gemma, approvingly. 'Aye,'

Trina said. 'Gemma said she had a pal that lived in a big flat with a balcony. But I thought she was talkin' shite.'

Rosie tried to keep a straight face.

'Have you got a balcony? Is it true?' The girl looked from Gemma to Rosie, and said, 'I know somebody who threw their baby off a balcony. She's in jail now. She's nuts.' She blinked rapidly, two or three times.

'Really?' Rosie studied her face. Striking green eyes. They blinked again, rapidly.

'Trina knows loadsa people.' Gemma nodded proudly, sitting closer to her new friend. 'She knows a lot of stuff. And she's my best pal in here. She blinks. But she's all right.'

'Good for you,' Rosie smiled. 'Good for both of you.'

Rosie asked Gemma how she was settling in. It wasn't too bad now that she'd met Trina, she said, but she'd wet the bed the night before last. Trina nodded as if she understood her friend's worries. Rosie was struck by the dark circles under Trina's blinking eyes.

The girls both talked excitedly about the kind of food they ate in the home, and about some of the other children. Rosie laughed as Gemma said she might get a boyfriend soon. They were so innocent. She could picture how they would be in a few years time, and her heart sank.

'And sometimes we get sweets from the caretaker. He's

all right. He takes people out for the day. Just the good kids. I'm going soon.' Gemma chattered on.

'What do you mean, "out for the day"?' Rosie said, the alarm going off in her head as she remembered what Mags had said in the cafe about judges and lawyers being involved with kids at a children's home.

'Not for the day,' Trina said. 'Just sometimes for the afternoon. And once I went and didn't come back till night time.' She blinked and looked away.

'Who comes and takes you out?' Rosie pretended to share their enthusiasm. Silence. Gemma looked at Trina. She looked around the room furtively, then leaned towards Rosie.

'You're not supposed to say anything about it,' Trina said. 'It's not sore or anything. And they give you sweets and ice cream.'

Rosie felt a wave of sick apprehension.

'You can tell me, Trina.' Rosie knew she could be in court in a heartbeat for even beginning to question a child like this, but she couldn't help it. 'I'm Gemma's pal. We talk a lot about stuff.' Rosie moved her chair closer to the table.

Trina sat back and swigged from the beaker until it was empty. She belched and both girls giggled.

'I don't like the big fat guy,' Trina said. 'He's all sweaty. But he gave me five pounds. I've hid it in a wee box in my locker. It's mine.'

Rosie's heart beat faster. 'Where does this happen, Trina?'

'In the big house.' Trina looked out of the window, then back at Rosie. 'It's like them films. Like a palace or something. Miles away, past the woods and stuff. There's big gardens and trees all cut in funny shapes.'

'Whose house?'

'The judge,' Trina said, as if she was surprised that Rosie didn't know.

Rosie's stomach turned over. For the next five minutes she gently teased the story out of Trina. Gemma looked on fascinated, saying she was hoping to go on one of the trips soon. They didn't happen every week, just about once a month. It was all organised by Paddy, the caretaker of the home, and usually when things were quiet. You had to be careful not to tell anyone or you would have to stay here for the rest of your life. That's what Paddy said.

There were only about five or six got chosen and it was quite good fun. They all played games when they went into the big room with the huge crimson curtains. Then sometimes a man would take one of them away. He touched them a bit between their legs, just rubbing them, and it wasn't sore. Sometimes you sat on their lap and you could feel something sticking into your back, and the man made funny grunting noises. It was all part of the game, but Trina said one boy started crying when a man told him to put his hand inside his trousers and feel him. That nearly wasted it for everyone. Paddy said you had to do what you were told or else it would all be finished, and there'd be no more trips, no more money and no sweets.

Rosie was trying not to show anything in her expression, and she was inwardly cursing herself for not bringing a tape recorder with her. But even if she had it on record, she knew it would incriminate her as much as anyone else. Here she was, sitting in a children's home with two minors, listening to a story of sexual abuse. And one of them involved some judge or other. She knew that it broke just about every rule of child protection law, and she would get the book thrown at her.

Trina couldn't tell her much more than that one of the men was called the judge, and she described the journey to the house. It seemed to be away from Glasgow towards Edinburgh, and Rosie got the impression it was somewhere deep in the countryside. Maybe Lanarkshire. When she got back to the office she would try to find out who the judge was. McGuire would need to be given sweet tea when she told him this.

'Okay,' she said, eventually. 'Listen, Gemma. I'm going to ask in the next couple of days if I can take you out for the afternoon, and maybe Trina could come too. Would you like that, Trina?'

'Aye. Brill.' Gemma nudged Trina who smiled broadly, still blinking.

'Right. I'll ask someone in charge for permission, but you're not to say anything yet. Okay?' She looked at Trina. 'And I don't think you should be saying anything about what you told me just now. That wouldn't be good.'

'I know.' Trina seemed happy to have shared her secret.

Rosie got up and Gemma hugged her. 'Will we go out soon?' she said, looking up at her.

'We'll see. I'll try. Now you be good.' She blew her a kiss and gave Trina a wave as she turned to walk away.

'Can we sit on your balcony?' Trina shouted after her. 'Maybe with a pizza? Maybe even get a video or something?'

Rosie turned to look at the two wide-eyed children.

'Sure,' she said, swallowing. She remembered her own childhood, the waiting and hoping someone would come. 'Sure.'

CHAPTER SEVENTEEN

Jack honked the horn impatiently for the second time as he sat in his driveway waiting for Myra and Alison to come out. He felt as though he was going to explode, and he had to grip the steering wheel to keep a hold of himself. That was happening all the time now. The least little mishap set him off. He was losing it. Big time. The other day at work he almost freaked out in the lift because it wasn't getting to the third floor quickly enough. How was he ever going to get his life back with all this bearing down on him? In bed at night he lay awake, panic raging through him, sweating and shaking while his wife slept. He couldn't even begin to respond to her if she touched him, and she had already accused him of having an affair because he showed no interest in her, though she only ever wanted sex if she was in the mood – and that wasn't very often.

At work, he was biting everyone's head off, and even when Bill coaxed him to go out for a drink to let off some steam, he refused. It had been building up slowly over the past six months, but now every day it was getting worse. Only the phone calls from Foxy kept him going. Foxy's consoling voice, promising him everything would turn out fine. One day at a time, Foxy had told him. But right now, hour by hour was bad enough.

'Hurry up for fuck's sake,' he murmured as the door of his house opened, and Myra came out followed by Alison.

'Look at the face on him, Alison,' his wife said as she opened the passenger seat door. 'Face like fizz at every turn.'

Alison smiled at her father and he tried his best to soften his expression. He loved her more than anything in the world, but if he could have, he would have been a million miles away from his wife years ago. He despised her. He even blamed her for the prostitutes. If she wasn't such a routine, boring bitch who only wanted sex every Thursday after her aerobics class, maybe things would have been different. It wasn't that he was kinky, but Myra wouldn't even discuss doing anything remotely different, far less experiment. She'd never given him a blow-job in his life, and was horrified when he tried to push her head down one night when she'd had a few drinks and was looking frisky. That was five years ago, and he hadn't tried it again.

Alison was different. She was everything to him. They had a kind of secret affinity with each other, as if Alison knew the pressure Myra put on him and how unhappy he was. He adored her. She had made him proud the way she had studied at school and made it to university with flying colours. She was going to be a doctor, and Jack felt that would raise him to a different status altogether. A daughter who was a doctor. And him just a boy from the back closes of Maryhill.

Now he was driving her to the station so she could catch the train back to university in Edinburgh after spending the weekend at home. Recently, even she had seen how tetchy he was and had asked him if everything was all right. Fine, he'd told her. He was just working on a difficult inquiry. She was not to worry. And Alison had accepted it.

'So what's the plan tonight, Alison?' Jack tried to sound cheery. 'Out with your flatmates? Mind, you've a lot of studying to do.' He knew he didn't need to remind her, but he wanted to. Myra sat beside him, leafing through a magazine, seemingly uninterested in the conversation.

'Just out for a couple of hours, Dad. There's a quiz night at the local boozer.'

'Just be careful. That's all.' He smiled in the rear-view mirror and she grinned back.

'Listen to him,' his wife piped up. 'You'd think he sat in playing dominoes every night. Sure, you're never home.

If it's not that bloody boat with the boys, then it's some other policeman's farewell drunken party night. Who are you to lecture?'

Jack looked at her and looked away. He wasn't going to be drawn into this argument because right now he didn't know if he could keep his temper. He pushed away the vision in his head of stopping the car and slapping his wife hard. Christ! How he would love to do that.

At the station they all got out of the car, and Jack hauled Alison's bag from the boot. He watched as she hugged her mum. Myra patted her daughter's back, but didn't hold her close. Jack knew that Alison's biggest hug was always reserved for him.

'Come on then, my darlin'.' He swept her up and held her tight. 'Jesus, Alison.' He felt his chest tight with sudden emotion. 'I miss you when you're through there. I really do.' He hugged her hard and buried his head in her hair.

'I know, Dad.' She squeezed him. 'I miss you too, but before you know it I'll be running the show at the Royal Infirmary in Glasgow.' She released herself from the hug and looked into his face.

'Are you sure you're all right, Dad?' Alison scanned his face. 'You look done in. Really tired.'

'Just work, pet.' Jack sniffed. He felt like crying. If she only knew the kind of man her daddy really was she'd be repelled. It would destroy her.

'I'm fine, Alison.' Jack held her hand. 'Just you get back to uni now, and work hard. See you next weekend.' He let her go and she walked away, turning to wave before disappearing into the crowd.

Several hours later, Jack sat in his car in the Cathkin Braes, staring into the middle distance. The sun had never really broken through the cloud, and now the darkness was coming down, spreading across the landscape. He had driven here because it was one of the spots that had always been so much a part of his life, and it was where he felt he could see things more clearly. Sometimes he would just come here and sit, and in the silence he could see images of his entire life. He knew who he was when he sat here. And even the view was great. You could look down and see the whole of Glasgow, from the East End right up to Partick in the distance. Over a million lives were being led out there. Over a million stories, every one different. None like his.

He remembered coming out here with Myra when they were young and in love. It was here they had their first sexual encounter, in the back of his car. Now he smiled at the thought of it. How different things had become between them in recent years. She was so buttoned up, so grasping, and so demanding – she wanted the best of everything in the house. Jack couldn't keep up with her.

Every time he got a promotion, she'd spent his salary increase almost before it went into the bank. And she never questioned where any extra money came from if he handed her a few quid to go and buy herself a new outfit or something for the house. Every week, his cut of the pay-off from the sauna boss went into her pocket. He hated her now.

Jack remembered the good old days with Foxy and Bill, when they were coppers on the beat. How they used to bring young neds up here and give them a good kicking. They couldn't stand the way these punks used to thumb their noses at them while they robbed and slashed their way through the housing schemes. It was here, too, that they had made deals down the years with the Big Man. He would pay them off in wads of twenty- and fifty-pound notes for work they had done, for blind eyes that had been turned. Then there was the gun amnesty that made Strathclyde Police the envy of the rest of Britain. Gangsters had agreed to hand in their guns. Every other day, more shotguns and pistols were discovered after tip-offs to the cops. Mostly it was to Foxy and Bill, and it brought them huge accolades in the force and beyond. Nobody but them and Jack knew it was all organised with the Big Man. They scratched his back and he scratched theirs.

But if he was really honest with himself, it had all got out of hand in the last two or three years. Since Foxy had been made head of the CID, the whole game had got out of control.

Hookers on the boat and the odd bit of cocaine had been fine. They'd used whores all their lives and it was one of the perks of the job, but they'd been doing it more and more recently. Then, after the girl had died on the boat, something died inside him. It wasn't just that she died, it was the fact that they threw her over the side. He kept thinking of Alison and how she was at that age. His conscience had never bothered him all the time he was using the prostitutes, but dumping a wee lassie into the sea like that haunted him. He had actually considered going to Special Branch and spilling the beans, but he knew he couldn't do that, they wouldn't believe him. And the way he had been behaving these past few months, they would have said he was ready for the laughing academy. He might even have got locked up. Then when the bird Mags was killed, Jack knew there was no way out.

But now, for the first time in a very long while, he felt clear in his mind. He was glad he'd written the letter to Alison. He knew she would be devastated that the father she knew and loved was very different from the one he had just written about. In time, he hoped she would understand. But he had to confess, and to pray for her forgiveness. It had been a very long letter, eight pages, confessing what Foxy, Bill and he had done over the years. Everything about the pay-offs from Big Jake and the sauna boss; the prostitutes, the boat, the drugs; the fit-ups, naming names of some of the men they had framed on murders and armed robberies. He spared her the fact that he too went with prostitutes. He couldn't bear to write that, he was too much of a coward. But he knew she would assume he must have done. He wrote details of the night with Tracy, from the moment he picked her up in Glasgow until they threw her into the water. He confessed it was Big Jake who was behind Mags Gillick's murder. He said how he couldn't go on any longer with all this on his conscience. He couldn't live with the guilt, so he would die with it. This was about telling the truth.

When he stuck the letter in the post box he hoped she would do something with it. He included a photograph he'd taken of Big Jake on Fox's boat. It was time for retribution, for punishment for the lives they had led. They didn't deserve to get away with it, and he was ready to take his punishment. He would burn in hell. He sat back and switched on the engine of his car. He adjusted the hosepipe he had attached from the exhaust pipe, and pushed his seat back so that he was in a relaxed position.

It didn't take long. He barely noticed it happening. He felt sleepy. With his eyes half shut he looked out once more, and saw the whole of Glasgow begin to flicker under the street lamps. Night was coming. It was over. He was glad.

The following morning, as Rosie plonked herself down in her seat at the *Post*, the phone rang. She recognised Don's voice.

'Jack Prentice is dead. He's done himself in. Found in his car in the Cathkin Braes. Hosepipe.'

Rosie didn't answer, and the phone clicked off.

CHAPTER EIGHTEEN

'The shit has hit the fan,' Rosie said, going into McGuire's office and closing the door.

He looked up from his desk, then sat back, motioning with his hand for her to sit down. 'Talk to me.'

Rosie's insides were churning. She took a deep breath and sat down on the sofa to compose herself.

'Jack Prentice has killed himself,' she said. 'I've just had a call. And I've checked it out through another source. Hosepipe job. Up in Cathkin Braes.'

'Fuck me!' McGuire said. 'Not very imaginative. Typical plod.' He spread his hands out as though waiting for Rosie to toss him an idea. 'What next? Did he leave a note?'

'Christ knows. Too early for that. It just happened last night, late.'

Rosie's head had been spinning since the phone call from Don a few minutes ago. She had been trying to have a plan of action before going in to see McGuire, but she couldn't get her head around it. Prentice was dead. Mags was dead. It was clearer than ever now that Mags was telling the truth, and that Gavin Fox and the other two were in it up to their necks. Not that she had ever been in any doubt. But since she'd visited the children's home and listened to the disturbing story Trina had told her, she had been preoccupied by that all weekend. That was an even bigger story, one that would rock the country, and when the time came she would bust her gut to expose these people.

She told McGuire there would no doubt be an attempt by the cops to play down Prentice's suicide, and that Reynolds would be better handling the story. It would be straightforward. They would say that Prentice had been suffering from depression for some time, and would give Reynolds enough evidence to back that up. There wasn't a snowball in hell's chance of anyone connecting his death to the other stuff.

'I think we should just tell the story,' Rosie said. 'We can simply say that it comes at a time when police are probing the deaths of two prostitutes in the past week, and one unsolved hooker murder last year. It doesn't suggest any involvement and it's a valid enough thing to say. But it'll rattle Fox's cage, and anything we can do to noise him up is good.'

'Yeah.' McGuire was on his feet, already visualising the story in the paper. 'And make sure we've got a picture of Prentice for tomorrow's paper. You never know. There must be a few hookers who know him. One of them might pop up and back the Mags story.' He grinned. 'Not that half a dozen junkie hookers telling the same story would stop the lawyers twitching, but it would help.'

'Sure,' Rosie said. 'Reynolds will organise a picture. Might even get Prentice in his Freemason apron.'

'Now that would be just dandy,' McGuire laughed, and went back behind his desk. He gave Rosie a look that said it was time to go, but she decided that now was as good a time as any to tell him what Trina had told her.

'Listen, Mick,' she said. 'There's been another development that I think you should know about. It's really over-the-top stuff, but if it's true, then Christ knows how we'll handle it.'

McGuire looked at his watch.

'I've got a meeting shortly, before conference.'

'This is important, Mick,' Rosie insisted.

He leaned forward, his black eyebrows knitted in anticipation. 'Go on then, Gilmour. Let's hear it.'

She began by telling him what Mags had said about the children's home and kids being used. Then she told him about Gemma turning up on her doorstep, and watched his angry frown as he heard how she and TJ had her back to the home.

'Who the fuck's TJ?'

'A friend. Just a friend.' She looked away from McGuire's piercing eyes. 'He's fine though, don't worry. I can trust him.'

McGuire said nothing, but continued to look straight into her eyes. She assured him again it was fine. She confessed that she'd visited the children's home at the weekend. He covered his face with his hands when she told him she'd gone into Woodbank and spoken to Gemma and her friend.

'I don't think I want to hear this. Christ almighty, Rosie, what are you playing at?'

'There was nothing else for it, Mick.' She looked pleadingly at him. 'They started talking about it and I just asked a couple of questions.'

McGuire shook his head. 'No you didn't, Rosie. You broke the fucking law.'

But Rosie persisted.

'Listen, Mick. Just wait till you hear what the kid told me.'

She then began to relate the story exactly as Trina had told it to her.

When she was finished, he took a deep breath and let out a sigh.

'Jesus wept!' he said. 'This goes all the way to the very top. Jesus!' He shook his head. 'Those kids. That's fucking awful. Could they be making this up?'

'No.'

'Jesus.'

'I know,' Rosie said. 'The poor little bastards are already victims by the time they get to that home. Then this happens. It's unbelievable.'

'So,' McGuire asked, 'do you have a plan? Or are you just going to trample all over the child protection laws until you end up in the High Court? We have to handle this very carefully. You know, Rosie, despite how serious this is, we've no real defence for what you did. You can't just walk into a children's home and start quizzing kids. It's a jailing case.'

'I know, but let's cross that bridge when we come to it. Let's get the story first and worry about the details later.'

McGuire shook his head. 'You know perfectly well that you are not allowed to question or interview a kid without an adult being present. Even worse, that these kids were in care. It's a jailing case.'

Rosie told him they had to be careful of their next move. She had no idea how many people were involved. Maybe more cops. Mags did say there were other things the cops were involved in. What if they were part of this sexual abuse ring as well?

'That's wishful thinking on your part, Gilmour.' McGuire was shuffling papers on his desk.

'Yes, maybe, but what if it's all linked? Can you imagine the impact of that? We have to work out a way we can watch this children's home. We have to get an in, so if they do take the kids away we can follow them or something.'

McGuire buzzed Marion and told her to put his meeting back for fifteen minutes. They discussed various possibilities of how they could monitor any outings Trina and the kids made from the home. Rosie said she would visit Gemma again as a relative or friend. Since there seemed to be scant security that might not be too difficult. McGuire said he would pretend he didn't hear her say she would visit the home. Rosie hoped she could pick up some information from the kids as to when they would be going, though they both assumed the children wouldn't be told until the last minute.

They considered working on the caretaker, Paddy, who seemed to be central to the whole affair. Rosie suggested they could monster him by putting the frighteners on him, tell him they knew everything, and threaten to expose him and turn him in, unless he gave them the details. That was risky, though, as he might spill the beans to whoever was handling him, then the whole scam would stop.

'At the end of the day, Rosie,' McGuire said, 'I'm not

bothered if it isn't linked. It doesn't matter. At the very least we will crucify the cops on two levels, because while they were out shagging prostitutes, kids along the road were being molested by people in high places. That's if we can get any proof that it's happening to the kids at all.'

He was pacing the floor now, imagining the front page. 'I mean if we take it all as two separate stories, we'll have a couple of belters that'll rock the establishment on its heels.' He put one hand out. 'First we expose the cops and the hookers. Then, while everyone is wiping the blood off the walls, we take it even further and expose the sex abuse ring. Who needs to link them? There will be bodies leaping out of tall buildings from here to Downing Street. It would be good to get the two stories, but either one of them individually is brilliant.'

He grinned. 'Mind you, it might ruin my chances of a knighthood.'

How typical of McGuire! In one breath he was full of the fight for justice, and in the next he was considering how it would impact on his career.

'And apart from your knighthood,' Rosie said, 'we might even be able to stop the abuse of kids by monsters at the very heart of our establishment.'

'Of course, Gilmour,' McGuire said indignantly. 'Absolutely.' He looked serious. 'And don't think for a minute I'm not driven by that. I know you think I'm a cynical bastard and I only care about myself. But honestly, I want these fuckers exposed for the sake of the kids – and for these poor hookers who stand out there freezing their tits off every night!' He looked her in the eye. 'Believe me, Gilmour. I want that badly. Now get out there and make it happen.'

It was just what she needed. She turned and left.

In the coffee shop later in the afternoon, TJ sat silently, watching Rosie as she told him everything that had happened. Neither of them had mentioned the other night at his flat, but she knew that even though they hadn't called each other since, it was going to have to be dealt with sooner or later. It was there, the elephant in the room.

When she'd finished her story about Trina and the danger she believed Gemma was in, she sat back and took a deep breath.

'Jesus, Rosie,' TJ said. 'This could get really dodgy. You're going to have to be very careful. I know it's not your style, but you are going to have to take a step back and think about this.'

Rosie looked at him, incredulous. She was too hyped up for common-sense talk.

'What? Do you mean just chuck it because it might get a bit tough? Give me a break, TJ. You don't know me at all!' She felt her face burn.

TJ watched her in silence for a moment.

'Oh but I do know you, Rosie. Maybe even better than you do yourself.'

'What's that supposed to mean?' She was irritated. She had wanted TJ to back her, to agree with her that she must go at this investigation all guns blazing, but he seemed to want her to pull back. She wondered if it was anything to do with the other night. Just because they got drunk and went to bed together. He thought he knew her. Now he wanted a say in how she should operate. That was not on the agenda.

'Doesn't matter,' TJ said. 'Never mind.'

But Rosie was riled. She wanted to talk now. She put down her cup and leaned forward.

'It does matter, TJ. I told you all of this because I trust you and I value your help and support.'

'And that's it?' TJ lit a cigarette. 'My support and help.'

Rosie sighed.

'Look, TJ,' she ventured. 'About the other night. I mean, don't get me wrong. It was fantastic and I really loved being with you. You're very important to me . . .'

Her voice trailed off as TJ put his hand up as though to silence her.

'Please, Rosie.' He looked hurt. 'Don't. I get the message.' He shook his head. His dark eyes burned. 'I get the message. There's only one thing that's truly important to you, and that's all this shit. Unless you're up to your knees in it, you're not happy.'

'Hold on a minute.' She reached out to touch his arm, but he pulled away.

'You see the thing is, Rosie . . .' TJ moved to get out of his chair. 'You see, as long as you're lost in all of this stuff, you don't have to sit down and look at your own life because there's no time. And it's better if there's no time because then you don't have to face things.' He stood up.

'Oh, TJ, sit down, for God's sake. Face what?'

She remembered crying in the bed beside him, how she had let her guard down and exposed herself. Now it was coming back to haunt her. She knew what he meant – and she knew that he was absolutely right. But this story was more important right now than anything in her own life, and she had to make him understand. She didn't want to lose him. She would sit down and talk to him about everything.

'Listen,' she said, taking a deep breath. 'Look, TJ. I'm sorry. Let's just start again. From where we left off the other night.'

TJ lifted his sax case and got out of the booth.

'You're not ready, Rosie,' he said. 'You're not ready.' He slung the sax case over his shoulder. 'When you're ready, call me.' He turned and walked away.

CHAPTER NINETEEN

It was an Oscar-winning performance from Chief Superintendent Gavin Fox. It had to be. All the movers and shakers from the entire police force, as well as some lawyers from the top drawer were at Jack Prentice's funeral, so it was crucial that he didn't put a foot wrong. This was about giving Jack a proper send-off, fit for a cop from the old school. Foxy even amazed himself at how well he delivered the speech, charting the life and heroics of one of the city's finest ever policemen. He had written the speech over the last couple of nights, and found himself a bit choked when he was going over it again just an hour before the funeral.

He had stood at the entrance to the crematorium in the crisp frost, shaking hands with the mourners as they filed past him. Everyone was there: the uniformed contingent from the various police stations across the city, as well as detectives they had worked alongside as they rose through the ranks, plus others, older now and retired, who always turned up to see one of their own away. Foxy felt proud that he was a leader in this company. Sure, there were a few who thought they had the inside story on Foxy, some of the younger ones who were on the fast-track promotion ladder. They were the ones who'd got there because they were university graduates, not because they knew anything about life on the streets. The force was changing, and the older guard like Foxy knew that. But he was confident that nobody out there had the balls to take him on. He got results, and that's what mattered to the men at the top. He was untouchable.

The service had begun with the rousing hymn, 'Will Your Anchor Hold?', the Boys' Brigade anthem that most of the men now sat before him had belted out as young boys. Once the Bible readings were over, Foxy squared his shoulders and strode up to the lectern to deliver his tribute.

He knew the press, sitting at the back, were listening to his every word, looking for a line that would allow them to make a story out of Jack's suicide. But Foxy was too clever for that. Tomorrow's newspapers would tell the story of how DCI Jack Prentice, a tragic and exemplary policeman, was struck down with depression after years of coping tirelessly with the stress of fighting crime on our streets. He told how he had gone through the ranks with Jack Prentice, and how he and Bill Mackie had sometimes been criticised for what people saw as the unorthodox way they handled the small-time gangsters who made life misery for decent people. That got a small chuckle. Policemen and civic dignitaries in the congregation nodded wisely as he spoke.

Chief Superintendent Fox told them he believed passionately that it was officers like Jack Prentice who made a difference to the lives of ordinary people, because men like Jack Prentice cared. One or two people in the press seats nudged each other and rolled their eyes. Most of the older hacks knew the stories of the notorious 'three amigos', as Fox, Mackie and Prentice were called. Gangsters had always queued up to tell reporters how they were framed by these three. But when you had a record as long as your arm, nobody gave a toss about the fight for freedom of some crook who belonged behind bars anyway.

Foxy spoke of Jack's struggle with depression.

'And you know,' he said, his voice faltering just a little. 'You know, deep down I feel a certain responsibility that Jack is gone.'

Bill Mackie shifted in his seat and examined the backs of his hands.

Fox's eyes scanned the congregation as he spoke. 'Depression is such a crippling, debilitating illness. Yet the problem, as we all realise now, is that Jack, by and large, managed to hide it from those closest to him. I saw him just the other day and I had no idea he was anywhere this close to breaking point.' He gripped the lectern and sighed. 'I wish I could have done more.' The press would love that, he thought. The soul-baring humility of it all.

He took a deep breath and touched the corner of his eye. A small tear. In the congregation, there were one or two sniffs. Jack's widow sat with her head bowed. His daughter Alison looked straight at Foxy, her face stern.

Alison stood outside shivering in the cold. Her face was pale and her eyes had dark shadows underneath them, but she had never shed a tear. The mourners shook hands with her, and some hugged the weeping Myra. When her mother had called her mobile after they found her dad's body in the car, Alison had collapsed from the shock and had to be taken back to her flat in Edinburgh by one of her student friends.

Two days later she returned after being at home with her mother and saw, among the mail scattered on the floor behind the door of her flat, a brown envelope, addressed in what she recognised as her father's handwriting the moment she saw it. She sat down and opened it with trembling fingers.

The letter was eight pages long and she was almost terrified to read it. But from the third paragraph she could see that it was a confession. Her head swam as she read the words, thinking at first that her father must have lost his mind to write a letter like this. Words like prostitute and cocaine leapt out of the pages. She felt sick. Surely not her father . . . A photograph fell out of the sheaf of papers – a photograph of a man she didn't know, his arm around two tarty, half-naked women. Her Uncle Gavin was in the background, not face on, but she could see it was him. She recognised the surroundings as his boat where, as a kid, she had spent many happy sailing trips with her dad.

She kept reading, and the more she read, the more she understood that he was telling of another, secret life. He wrote of corruption, confessing that Gavin Fox, Bill Mackie and himself had been on the payroll of gangster Jake Cox for many years. There were convicted men in prison, he said, who they had framed for crimes they didn't commit. He named several of them. But the most gut-wrenching of all was the confession that a girl called Tracy Eadie had died on the boat six months ago, and they had got rid of her body by throwing her over the side.

Alison put her hand to her mouth in horrified disbelief. She had seen the story in the newspaper at the time, when the fourteen-year-old girl went missing, and again last week when she was washed up on the beach. Her father did this? Her uncles Gavin and Bill? Another name leapt out. Mags Gillick, a prostitute found several days in Glasgow with her throat cut. Her father knew about this too . . .

Alison had to stop reading. She felt sick. She went to the kitchen and drank a glass of water, her hands shaking. She came back in and sat down, staring at the letter for a time, and then forced herself to read on. When she got to the end, she stared at his signature, 'Dad'. 'Please forgive me,' he had written. 'I am praying now for your forgiveness and for the forgiveness of God. I love you. Please never forget that I love you. Dad.' She had had so many birthday cards and notes from him all her life, with that same 'Dad', the way he always wrote it, with the big elaborate 'D'. It was from him, there was no doubt.

Alison hadn't slept a full hour since she read the letter, but she knew she had to keep up some kind of bold, supportive front for her mother. For the whole of the next day, she stayed in her flat, walking around in a stupor. Twice, she almost put the letters and photograph in the fire, but stopped herself.

Now, as she stood freezing outside at the funeral, she shook hands with Bill Mackie, who put his arms around her and hugged her. She stood limply and looked into his eyes, red-rimmed from crying. Foxy came forward and hugged her, then looked into her face.

'Your dad was so proud of you, Alison,' he said. 'You were everything to him.'

Alison stared blankly back at him and eased herself out of his grasp. He moved away, patting her shoulder. She watched as he went down the steps, shaking hands with people on his way to his waiting car.

CHAPTER TWENTY

In the cafe, Gemma and Trina blew bubbles with their straws in the dregs of their iced fizzy drinks and giggled at the gurgling noise. They had wolfed down burgers and chips, and cola drinks with a dollop of ice cream, and were now lounging back in the booth.

'I'm stuffed,' Trina said. 'That's the best dinner for ages.'

'See?' Gemma looked proud. 'I said she was brilliant. I've been here with Rosie and my mum . . .' Her voice trailed off and she looked sad.

Rosie had been surprised how easy it was to get the two of them out of the home for a couple of hours. She went on a Saturday afternoon hoping that, like on the Sunday of her first visit, there would be less security. The same fat woman was at the reception and when Rosie told her this time she was Gemma's aunt, she didn't ask any questions. Now, sipping her coffee, Rosie wanted to probe the girls gently to see if there had been any more visits to the house in the country. She'd be in deep shit if anyone found out what she was doing, and she hadn't told McGuire when she was going. He'd said he didn't want to know.

As it turned out, she didn't have to worry about how to pose her questions, because Trina started to talk.

'We were away on a run last night,' she said, matter-of-factly. 'Gemma was there too, and Paddy says she might get to go every week.'

Rosie tried to look only vaguely interested.

'Who's Paddy?'

'The janny, I told you before,' Trina said. 'It's Paddy who decides who gets to go and he takes us there in the van and brings us back. Sometimes he gets us chips on the way home. But he didn't last night.'

Rosie looked from one to the other. Gemma seemed happy that she was now a part of something Trina was doing.

'So where did you go?'

'The big house again,' Trina said flatly.

'It's brilliant,' Gemma said. 'It's got trees everywhere and hundreds of windows. And a fire in the big room.'

Rosie nodded. 'Sounds great. So where is it?'

Gemma and Trina looked at each other. Trina looked like she was trying to remember.

'Don't know really.' She screwed up her eyes. 'It's near

some place called pebbles or something. The road was dark, but I saw that name because it's like a stone. Is that a real place? Pebbles?'

'Peebles,' Rosie said, feeling her heart skip. 'Peebles. Was that it? It's a wee place right out in the country. Did you go along dark country roads?'

'Aye,' Gemma said. 'I was a bit scared, 'cos one of the boys, Brian McCann, started telling creepy stories on the way back.'

Rosie needed more. She looked around the cafe and leaned towards the girls.

'So what did you do in the big house?'

Trina looked at her, as though she was surprised she didn't know.

'Games. We play games with the big people.'

Gemma giggled. 'It was funny. Some of it. But I didn't like when they took our pictures.'

'Pictures?'

Trina gave Gemma a disapproving look, and Gemma raised her eyebrows in surprise.

'It's okay, Trina,' she said. 'Rosie's my pal.'

'Awright . . . Well, the man took pictures of us,' Trina said. 'We were in our vests and pants. He just took pictures of us jumping around in front of the fire, and then he said we had to take everything off. But I wouldn't take mine off. Rhona Hutchison did though. I think that's why Paddy didn't get us chips on the way home.'

'And were there many men there?' Rosie asked.

'Six,' Trina said. 'No, maybe five . . . Dunno. But they all gave us money. I've still got mine. Look.' She pulled out three pound coins from her pocket. Gemma also produced three. They held them in their small hands.

Rosie felt sick and a cold sweat broke out on her back.

'So, tell me about the games.'

'The man sat Rhona on his knee,' Trina said. 'With no pants on. He was laughing and bobbing her up and down but Rhona wasn't laughing and then she said to stop.'

'And did he?'

'Aye.' Trina screwed up her face. 'But I didn't like him much. He had big hairy hands and a pink fat face. His face was all red.'

'And do you know whose house you were in?' Rosie knew they would soon lose interest in this conversation.

Gemma and Trina looked at each other, then shook their heads.

'Hmm, nope,' Trina said. Then after a few seconds she said, 'Oh, yes, Paddy says it was the judge's house. He says we could get put in jail dead easy if we didn't do what the men said. It was judge somebody or other. Can't remember. Lord somebody. Lord Snooty.' She sat back and tickled Gemma. They both giggled.

'What if you saw a photograph of him? Would you recognise him?' Rosie could only imagine how the newspaper's lawyers would react to a photograph being identified by two kids in care.

'Aye,' Trina said. 'Aye.'

'Maybe,' Gemma said. 'Paddy says if we behave we'll get to go again. He says we're the best ones.'

Enough questions.

'Remember now,' Rosie said, looking at both of them. 'Remember you've not to tell Paddy or anyone that we were talking about this. He wouldn't be very happy.'

'I know,' Trina snorted. 'He's a fat bastard.'

Gemma burst out laughing.

'He is!' Trina giggled.

'You shouldn't be swearing like that.' But Rosie was barely able to control her own laughter.

Rosie drove them back to the home, telling them again not to mention to anyone they had been talking about the big house. She would come and visit them in the middle of the week, and by then they might know if they were going on a visit on the Friday.

'Why? Do you want to come, Rosie?' Trina said. 'There isn't any women, it's all men. But maybe they would let you come.'

'No,' Rosie said quickly. 'No. Definitely. I don't want to come. I just wondered, that's all.'

Both girls gave her a hug as they got out of the car, and Gemma said, 'Remember, Rosie, you said we could come and stay with you one night? You *said* it.'

'Of course. Soon. I promise.'

CHAPTER TWENTY-ONE

Alison was suffocating with the anger raging inside her. She had come back to Edinburgh the day after the funeral because she couldn't stand being around her mother, knowing what she now knew. Listening to her mother glorify her father to anyone who would listen made her sick. The truth was Myra had made his life a misery. She had watched her mother pick away at him down the years, and she hated her for it. And anyway, Alison had always felt Myra resented her. It was plain that her dad had more time for his daughter than his wife. When she was growing up, her mum would send her to her grandmother's on a Saturday night so that she and her dad could be alone, but Jack had always protested. It was often the only night he got to tuck Alison into bed because of the odd hours he worked. And Alison didn't like being sent away overnight when she would have preferred to sit on the sofa, leaning beside her dad as they watched a film together. Then mass on Sunday, hand in hand with her dad, while her mother cooked lunch.

When Alison left the house after the funeral, she had embraced her mother before getting into the taxi for the train station. But there was a coldness between them. Alison knew her parents' marriage had been a sham, their whole lives a lie. In the letter Jack said he'd only stayed with Myra while Alison was growing up; that once her studies were finished he'd planned to leave.

But events had overtaken Jack, and his daughter didn't recognise the man he painted in the letters. It was disgusting. He spoke about the women that used to come onto Uncle Gavin's boat, although he did not specifically say he had sex with them. But when he tried to blame Myra by saying she'd never shown him any proper love, Alison knew that he must have used the prostitutes. It was cowardly crap. She was angry and confused. She hated the way her mother had treated her dad, but nothing could justify the double life he had been living.

And it wasn't just that, but the widescale corruption he'd been pursuing along with Foxy and Bill. He seemed to think that by offloading his sins in a suicide note, Alison would somehow exonerate him. He was wrong. She would not. But she was determined to do the one thing he'd asked of her – to make sure that Foxy could not go on like this. He was out of control and it had to stop. That was why he was taking his own life. The coward's way out, he'd called it. It didn't matter if his name was ruined, he just wanted it all to stop. One girl had died and another girl had been murdered, and he didn't know where it would all end. Put a stop to it, he pleaded. And she vowed to herself that she would.

Now Alison sat in front of the gas fire with the letter again in her hand. She had read it so many times that she knew it almost by heart. For two days she had sat in the Edinburgh flat, sleeping in snatches on the sofa and eating hardly a thing. She wished she had someone to talk to; all she could think about was how to stop Foxy. How to make him pay for what had happened to her father. She wanted to blame him and Bill because she needed to believe that her father was not a bad man. Finally, on the third morning, as she sat with the duvet wrapped around her, she made up her mind. She would go and confront Foxy in his office. She could ruin him if she really wanted to. She had evidence.

In his office, Foxy skimmed through the day's newspapers, scanning for anything on the death of Jack Prentice. There had been the usual speculation for the first couple of days in that rag of a paper, the *Post*. They commented that Jack had lost the plot in recent months, and they had the nerve to say that he died as police were under pressure with two prostitutes dead in the past week. What the fuck did that mean? Either they were just fishing and chancing their arm, or they knew something.

Foxy had got Bill to give the *Post*'s crime reporter, Reynolds, a ring and ask him what he was playing at. He was supposed to be on their side. Reynolds told them he'd written the story fairly straight, but he hinted that the editor had some kind of bee in his bonnet about it. Foxy remembered it was the same situation when the hooker Tracy was washed up. That bitch Rosie Gilmour had written some speculative story that the prostitute was connected to people in high places. What was that supposed to mean? It meant nothing to anyone except Jack, Bill and himself, but it niggled away at him. She had to be watched, that Gilmour . . .

He'd made a call to the Big Man to keep tabs on the journalist, but he stressed that, this time, he didn't want a finger laid on her. Just watch her. So far, all they had come back with was that she was pissed with some guy at a salsa bar and went back to his flat for the night. Big deal. But she had also been seen up at Woodbank, and later in a cafe with two kids. Foxy couldn't understand why Gilmour was interested in the wee kids – unless she was trying to dig up some more stuff on that Tracy bitch. He wished he'd never set eyes on the whore.

He would ask Reynolds to do a bit of digging, just in case. See what Rosie Gilmour was up to.

So far, though, everything was reasonably calm. Foxy was genuinely gutted about Jack, yet part of him was glad because, with him out of the way, there was no chance of anyone's bottle crashing. Bill wasn't the type. He could tell a lie that would get you hanged, and he wouldn't buckle under pressure.

They'd both got plastered the night of the funeral, and ended up laughing and crying about the old days. It was fine now, though. It would all die down.

He answered the buzz on his phone. It was his secretary.

'There's a girl here to see you,' she said. 'It's Alison Prentice. She doesn't have an appointment.'

Foxy was puzzled, but he supposed Alison needed to be close to her dad's best pals. He could understand that. He would make time for her. He immediately put on his most fatherly tone.

'It's okay, Patsy,' Foxy said jovially. 'I've always got time for Alison. Show her in please.'

The door opened, and Patsy ushered Alison in. The girl's face was pasty and she looked tired. Foxy got up from behind his desk and strode across to greet her with a hug.

'Alison, darling. How are you, sweetheart?' He noticed she didn't hug him back.

'Jesus, pet. You look terrible. Not sleeping? Don't worry, that'll come. I know it's tough for you. Tough on all of us.'

Alison said nothing, but sat on the sofa next to his desk. Foxy came and sat on a chair opposite her, pulling it in a little closer. He buzzed Patsy and asked her to send in some tea and biscuits. The kid just needed a bit of sympathy.

'So, Alison. How's your mum?'

'Bearing up.' Alison's voice was a monotone.

'Time,' Foxy said. 'It'll take time.'

He was relieved when Patsy came through the door with the tray. He poured the tea and handed Alison a cup.

They sat in silence. She looked like she was about to explode. He didn't know how he would cope with her if she burst into floods of tears.

'I miss him too,' Foxy said. 'Jack was a great man. You know, we were mates right from police college. God, we had some laughs down the years, but he was a solid mate. Great man, Alison. I know you must be suffering.'

'I didn't know him at all.' Alison's words hung in the air.

He put down the cup and looked at her. What was she on about?

'I didn't know him at all,' she said again. 'I didn't know any of you. Not you, not Uncle Bill. I didn't know any of you.'

She fixed him with a stare.

'What do you mean, darling? Course you knew us. We were like family.'

Another silence. She took a deep breath.

'I know everything now, Uncle Gavin.'

Her eyes were cold. Maybe she was on drugs . . . ?

'In fact it makes me sick even to call you uncle. I know what you are. What Dad was. What Uncle Bill is. I know it all.'

Foxy felt his face go white. She must be on something. 'What?' He shifted in his seat. 'What are you talking about?'

Her voice was calm.

'I know everything.' She looked him in the eye. 'I know about the boat, and the drugs. And the girl you, Dad and Bill threw over the side of your boat. I know about the prostitute who got her throat cut. Yes, I know about the years of corruption with you, Dad and Bill. The backhanders from Jake Cox. I know the whole disgusting lot.'

Foxy felt as though someone had just shot him in the chest. He opened his mouth to protest, but Alison kept talking.

'Dad sent me a letter.' She was triumphant, her eyes blazing. 'Eight pages, and a picture. I still can't believe it.' Her voice quivered and tears came to her eyes.

'Alison . . .' He got up and went towards her.

'Don't touch me!' She stood up and put her hands up.

'Don't ever touch me. You're an evil man. An evil, corrupt man and you ruined my father. He's dead because of people like you. You destroyed him.'

'Alison.' Foxy could feel the sweat breaking out. He motioned for her to simmer down. 'Please, pet. You don't know what you are saying.'

'Yes I do.' Her voice was shrill. Her lip trembled. 'And you had better listen to me. You'd better get your resignation sorted out and get out of this job in the next few days, or I'm going to tell the world about you and your stinking, evil set-up.'

Foxy's knees were shaking. Christ almighty!

'Enough, Alison,' he said, regaining control, his voice firm. He had to be careful. She obviously did have some serious information about them, and she must have got it from somewhere . . . That daft bastard Jack and his Catholic guilt, right to the end. He couldn't even bump himself off without dropping everyone else in it. Fuck him. Keep calm.

'Alison. Listen, pet. I'm going to open the door now and let you go home before you say anything else that will get you into trouble. What you are saying just isn't true, Alison. And if your dad said these things then it was all part of his illness. You must understand that. Alison . . .' He just about managed to stop his voice from croaking.

'We'll see,' she said. 'We'll see.'

'Come on now, Alison.' Foxy folded his arms across his chest and looked defiant. This little bitch could make serious trouble. 'Now don't be silly. Who's going to believe a suicide note from a man who was clearly off his head? Look – just get the letter to me and we'll forget about everything. You need a wee bit of help, pet. You need some sleep. Maybe you should talk to somebody.'

Alison walked to the door. She turned towards him, her face flushed.

'If I don't read that you and Bill have resigned in the next three days, then I'm going to the papers.' Her voice was deadpan.

He tried to force a smile, but it was more of a grimace. 'They'll laugh you off the park.'

'We'll see.' She stared at him. 'We'll see.' She opened the door and walked out.

Foxy went back to his desk and phoned Bill Mackie. 'Get up here,' he said. 'Smartish.'

Then he rang the Big Man's mobile.

CHAPTER TWENTY-TWO

Rosie stretched her legs out in the front seat of Matt Harper's car and sighed. 'Christ I hate stake-outs.' She turned to Matt, whose eyes were focused straight ahead on the grey minibus in the yard of the children's home.

'The problem with you reporters,' Matt said without looking at her, 'you've just no patience. You want to swing in like the SAS when it all kicks off, grab the glory and then disappear to the pub. We snappers, on the other hand, are like the panther. Poised in the long grass. Patient. Deadly.' His eyes narrowed.

'Gie's peace,' Rosie snorted. She liked Harper, even if he was regarded as a bit loopy by all the other journalists and photographers. He might be eccentric, but he was the best there was, especially on a snatch job like this, where you only got one fleeting opportunity to bag a picture of your victim. Harper would lie in wait for hours, days if necessary, but he always came back with his picture. He was also discreet. That was why McGuire told the picture editor to give Harper the job with Rosie. She wasn't even comfortable with telling the picture editor the story she was working on, but he had to know.

McGuire had told the picture editor straight, while the three of them were in his office, that he would sack him on the spot if he found him blabbing about this investigation to anyone.

'You see, I could sit here all night if it was necessary.' Matt caressed the camera on his lap. 'Nobody is coming out of that place to go anywhere unless I've got a shot of them. So just settle down, darlin', and tell me some stories. What about your sex life? Are you getting your leg over?'

'Piss off, Harper. And do you think I would tell you if I was?' She shook her head and looked out of the window.

'Well,' Matt sighed. 'I just thought it would break the monotony, you know, hearing a wee bit about what you do when you're not pissing the polis and everyone else off. What do you do for relaxation?' He flicked his tongue across his top lip and grinned.

'I'm in a sewing bee,' Rosie said without looking at him. 'Every Thursday. Most uplifting.'

Harper chuckled.

She thought about TJ, wondered how he was. He'd looked hurt the other day at the cafe, and she'd never seen that side of him before. She would get in touch with him as soon as she could. She thought about the night in his flat and how she had loved being with him – the intimacy and tenderness had felt so natural, so right. But she quickly put the thought out of her mind. What was the matter with her? She didn't have the time or the inclination to throw herself into the rollercoaster of a big love affair again. No more of that, thank you very much. She would call TJ as soon as she had time, but where she was and what she was doing right now was more important than anything.

'Uh-oh,' Matt said, sitting forward. 'Something's moving, Rosie. Look.'

Rosie saw kids coming out of the back entrance to the children's home. She counted five of them, scanning their faces. She saw Gemma first, then Trina behind her, and two boys with one other girl. Matt was already snapping furiously through the windscreen, twisting with the zoom lens.

'Get the guy,' Rosie said, as a balding, fat little man, who looked about fifty, opened the door of the minibus, and ushered the kids inside. 'That'll be the janny. Paddy. He's the bastard who organises it all.'

'Don't worry. I hosed him as soon as he came out of the building.' Matt started the engine of the car.

'Okay,' Rosie said, feeling the familiar rush of adrenalin. 'All we have to do now is follow them, but at a discreet distance. Really discreet. I'm depending on you, Matt.'

'You're talking to the man who gives masterclasses in discretion. Bear that in mind if you ever need someone to keep your feet warm at the bottom of the bed.' Matt handed her the camera as he watched the minibus reverse then drive out of the gates of the home. 'Unless something untoward happens we'll tail them right to their destination.'

'Great. Problem's going to be, though, when we get into the country. There'll be less traffic and he might notice if the same car is behind him for a while.'

'We'll just have to take our chances.' Matt pulled out behind the van after allowing a car to go in front of him. 'Give me that bottle of Coke over.' His face was set with concentration. He swigged from the bottle, then said, 'Here we go, Rosie. I just love this shit.' He glanced at her and winked. 'Game on.'

Rosie could feel excitement in her stomach and prayed they wouldn't be spotted. She'd spent the last two days making sure that the man who'd be driving the girls was indeed Paddy the janny. Trina and Gemma had pointed him out when she visited them the other day, and they'd told her the outing was on for Friday. Paddy had been working in the yard as she said goodbye to them.

Rosie and McGuire had decided that the best way

forward with the investigation was to try and track the next trip to the big house. She had already established whose house it was. When she told McGuire, he had punched the air with excitement.

She couldn't believe it when she went trawling the files to find out which judge lived in or around Peebles, and came up with Lord Dawson, one of the most senior and respected High Court judges in the country. But, sure enough, there he was in a huge country pile, complete with grounds and forest much as the girls had described it. She swigged from Matt's Coke bottle. So far, so good. The minibus was heading out of the city onto the motorway in the right direction. Matt stayed two cars behind.

'Looking good, Rosie. Looking good, pal.'

'Here's hoping. What I wouldn't give to nail this one down,' Rosie said.

Matt stepped on the accelerator as the van sped along the motorway, but remained two cars behind.

It was still light by the time they came off the motorway and headed down the road towards Lanark and Peebles. They had already taken a run out to the location of Lord Dawson's house yesterday to do a recce, and Matt had found a tiny road that seemed to rise up above the estate, where he could get a clear view of cars coming and going into the long driveway of the big house. The plan was to follow the van for as long as they could, then overtake and head for the high ground so that they could watch, and photograph it as it arrived. They both knew there was no way they could keep behind the van when it got closer to the house, because they would probably be the only two vehicles on the road.

As the car turned towards Peebles, Matt put his foot down, overtook and sped on. Rosie kept her head down in case any of the kids looked out and spotted her.

Matt cursed as his car wove in and out of the potholes on the twisting road. 'I'd better be getting covered for damage,' he said, as they bumped along.

Rosie was beginning to feel queasy. She didn't know if it was the road or her nerves.

'Shit. I feel like throwing up.' She rolled down the window.

'Well, make sure you upchuck into your handbag, sweetheart. I don't want any more damage to my motor.'

'Thanks for your support.' She leaned towards the window to gulp the fresh air.

Finally they reached the top of the hill. Matt reversed the car and turned it so they were facing Lord Dawson's house. They could see five big cars in the driveway. Rosie had binoculars and could make out Jags and Mercs. Matt aimed his camera and said he could see the number plates. He read them out to her along with the makes of the cars as he photographed them, and Rosie jotted them down.

She would try to get them checked out. Lights were on in several of the downstairs rooms in the house, and in one or two upstairs. Matt got out of the car and attached his massive lens to the edge of his camera. They waited and watched.

'Here it is,' Matt said. 'You fucking beauty!' His camera whirred furiously as the minibus drove up the gravel drive and parked outside the front of the house.

'Jesus!' Rosie said. 'I would never believe it if I wasn't seeing it with my own eyes. Keep snapping, Matt.'

The janny jumped out of the driver's seat and quickly went to open the door. The kids piled out, and Rosie could see them with her binoculars. Some were laughing and smiling, but Gemma looked pale and subdued. Trina's arm was around her as if she was trying to comfort her. Rosie wondered if the journey had made her feel sick. In the doorway of the house, a large, thin man in a black suit appeared and opened the doors. He motioned for the children and Paddy to follow him. Matt kept taking pictures until the last of them disappeared behind the large front door.

'Did you get the guy?' Rosie asked. 'He might be the butler or something.'

'Yep. Everyone.' Matt was already looking at his images on his digital camera.

He came back into the car and they sat in silence,

staring down at the house. Rosie's heart sank, thinking of what was going on inside that place. Matt shook his head.

'Fuck it,' he said, eventually. 'I'm going to go down and have a look in the window.'

'What?' Rosie turned to him. 'You're bloody joking!'

'No. Look, Rosie, I know what I'm doing. The last thing these bastards will be thinking of is someone shuffling around the bushes taking photographs. It just won't enter their heads.' He started to get out of the car. 'Trust me. You don't have to come. Just let me do it. We don't have enough. One snap. That's all I need. One frame of something in that room that will bury every fucking one of them. Come on, Rosie, it's your call.'

She looked at him, then back at the house. McGuire had told her at all costs to keep her distance, and not to do anything daft that might blow the whole investigation. But Matt was right. They didn't have enough to string everyone up.

'Okay, go for it. But if you've got any doubt at all as you get closer then come back. Don't do anything that will bugger it up.' She turned away and looked out of the window. 'Shit, I don't believe I'm doing this. I must be as mad as you.'

'Don't worry, Rosie.' Matt flashed a smile. 'Trust me. I'm a snapper.'

Rosie watched as he started to walk down the road with his camera tucked into a small rucksack on his back.

She sat back and waited.

It took about ten minutes for Matt to get down the road and find a suitable place to enter the grounds without being noticed. No one was around, but there was always the chance a dog might come tearing out of nowhere. He sneaked up to the back of the house where a light was on, and peered through the window. The tall thin guy who'd answered the door was sitting alone in an armchair by an unlit fire in the huge kitchen, reading a newspaper and smoking a cigarette. Matt ducked back down and crept alongside some bushes, popping his head up now and again to steal glances into each room. All were empty and dark. Soon he was close to the front of the house, and outside a window where he could hear voices. He stuck his head up and looked into the room. He ducked down quickly with his back to the wall. He could hear his heart beat. He'd seen three or four children, dressed only in their underpants, with their arms folded across their pale skinny chests as if they were embarrassed. Men sat on the large sofas around a blazing fire, smiling and drinking. From the corner of his eye, he saw a camera flash go off inside the room. He twisted round, and lifted his own camera then pressed it against the window. Now he could see quite clearly. A silver-haired man was taking pictures of the children sitting on top of each other, and horsing around in front of the fire. The children weren't smiling or laughing. They just looked bewildered. Matt zoomed in on their faces. One of the little girls had tears in her eyes. His camera roamed across the room, taking pictures of every face. One of the men took a little girl on his knee and caressed her thighs. Then he took her by the hand and left the room.

Matt kept taking pictures. He had plenty, but he kept going. After a few more minutes the silver-haired man who had been photographing the kids went out of the door, leaving it open. Matt could see Paddy sitting on a long-backed chair in the hall, and took a quick snap of him. The silver-haired man made a gesture to Paddy, who got up, went into the room and seemed to tell the children to get dressed. When he returned to the hall, the man handed him a wad of notes. Then he went back into the room and gave some coins to each of the children.

After he'd taken his last picture, Matt crouched down and made his way out of the bushes and into the back gardens. He climbed the fence, and reached the road, where he sprinted up the hill towards the car.

When he reached Rosie he was puffing and panting, his face red. She jumped out of the car.

'Holy shit, Rosie.' He was bent over, hands on knees, getting his breath back. 'Holy shit.'

'Was there stuff happening?' Rosie asked, anxiously.

'And how.' Matt shook his head. 'Rosie – we've got enough pictures here to bury whoever these fuckers are.'

He told Rosie how the kids were cavorting half naked in front of the fire, and that one of the men took a little girl away.

'Bastards. Did you get all that on film?

'Oh yeah. Everything.'

'What about the kids? How did they look? Were they scared? Crying or anything?'

Matt turned and looked back at the house. 'Don't know ... Not crying, just kind of confused looking. Fucking awful.' He got into the car and they drove back down the twisting road.

CHAPTER TWENTY-THREE

Gavin Fox had never felt so rattled as since this whole bastard of an episode had begun that morning on his boat. Even then, as Bill and Jack had slung the dead girl's body over the side, he'd never considered that all this would come unstuck. But now that weird-bitch daughter of Jack's was threatening to blow it all sky high. She always was a snooty little bugger, her head constantly in books, always the one to disagree or to ask questions if they were having dinner at Jack's. Little smartass wasn't going to bring *him* down . . . His buzzer went, and Patsy announced that Bill had arrived. Foxy said to show him in.

'How's it going, boss?' Bill was chipper. 'You sounded a bit edgy. What's up?'

'What's up?' Foxy got up from behind his desk. He blew hard and shook his head. 'Tell you what's fucking up, Bill. Sit down.'

Bill sat on a chair and Foxy stood over him.

'Fucking Alison Prentice has been in here.' He rubbed his hand across his chin. He noticed he was trembling and hoped Bill hadn't seen it.

'Jack only left a fucking suicide note,' he said. 'No, Bill. Correct that. Not just a suicide note. A fucking signed confession sticking all three of us in. Complete with a photo, according to her. The ratbag bastard. He's given Alison enough material to put us away for ten years.' He threw out his arms. 'I mean when the fuck did Jack take pictures? That must have been ages ago. I can't even remember.'

Bill's face had turned chalk white. He stood up and walked around the room without speaking. Then, 'Oh fuck, Foxy,' was all he could say. 'Oh fuck.'

They stood in silence, Bill watching Foxy taking long, deep breaths.

'Well,' Bill's voice had a quiver to it. 'Either we chuck it – resign, as fuckng Alison demands – or we stay here and tough it out. And I'm not fucking resigning. We have to get to her somehow. Get that stuff back. She's not clever enough to have done anything with it.'

Foxy nodded agreement. He bit his lip.

'That's what I wanted to hear, Bill. It's already done. I talked to the Big Man, told him he has to be careful. I don't want another stiff on my hands. And I told him to keep watching that Gilmour woman. Just in case.'

'Good,' Bill said. 'Good. Reynolds says she's been very shifty this past week. Holed up somewhere in the West End, not in her own flat. He followed her.' He gave that address as well as Rosie's home address to Foxy, who wrote it down.

Alison had walked around the city for two hours after she left Fox's office, until she felt calm enough to go home. She didn't want to go back to Edinburgh and be on her own, but she had to be sure she wouldn't crack in front of her mother. It wasn't that she really cared if her mother felt betrayed by her dad, but she didn't trust her. She knew that, rather than risk a scandal that would ruin her husband's reputation, her mother would do everything she could to keep a lid on the situation, but she herself was determined to see it through.

She left the following afternoon. On the train to Edinburgh, she sat drinking a cup of sweet tea and looking out of the window at the countryside whizzing past. For the first time since her father died, she didn't feel like crying. There was no choking sadness in her every time she was alone. Suddenly she felt strong. She knew she could carry this through. Uncle Gavin had been a lot more upset than he pretended. He had tried to fob her off and treat her like the kid she once was, but she knew that underneath the bluster he was terrified. His lip had even trembled at one point. She'd never seen him upset before, and she knew that the show he'd put on at her dad's funeral was just that – a show.

Alison tried to work out how she should handle this. She knew Uncle Gavin would not resign. He thought himself too powerful to buckle under the threats of someone like her, but she had to give him a couple of days to see if he did. If nothing happened she would go to the papers, but she didn't know any reporters. Her father had always said they were scum, constantly looking at ways to undermine the police and not to be taken seriously. But since moving to Edinburgh and studying at university, Alison had developed her own views. Her friends were intelligent and they questioned everything. Growing up as an only child, she had felt isolated at home. Her parents were very strict Catholics. Even though her dad doted on her she knew his word was law, and would never answer him back or question his judgement. How wrong she had been about him! All those years of deceit. Now it was driving her forward.

She got off the train and started to walk towards her home a few streets away from Haymarket Station, but stopped in her favourite cafe and drank a cappuccino. Sitting at the window, she watched people making their way home from work and wondered what burdens they carried. Everyone had something – but she doubted many of them would have what she had right now. She finished her coffee and headed up the side streets to her flat in the West End. Through habit, she took the keys to her flat out of her handbag and put them into her jacket pocket. The streets were empty and it was beginning to get dark. Alison quickened her step. Then she heard footsteps behind her, quickening to her pace and was afraid to look around. She told herself she was panicking for no reason, and slowed down. Suddenly she felt a hard push against her back and she was grabbed from behind, swung around, and had her head pushed against the side of a building. She was dizzy, confused, trying to work out what was happening.

'Gimme your bag, bitch.' She smelled drink off the guy's breath and could taste tobacco on his hand as he covered her mouth.

'Wait,' Alison said. 'Don't hurt me. I have money. Here. In the purse. There's thirty pounds. Take it. Please don't hurt me.' She started crying.

'Shut it, bitch.' The guy, who wore dark glasses, ripped the bag from her shoulder and pushed her head against the wall again, so hard she heard it clunk against the brick. He punched her stomach and ran off, leaving Alison doubled up and sinking to her knees as she gasped for breath. She touched the back of her head, and felt a bump but it didn't seem to be bleeding. She got slowly back to her feet and looked around. No one was about. Cars had driven past and must have seen what had happened. Why did nobody stop to help her? Sobbing, she staggered along the road and up the hill towards her flat. When she tried to open the main door of the tenement building, her hands were trembling so hard she took three attempts to get the key in the lock.

When she reached her first-floor flat, she saw the lock had been forced and the door was already open. Terrified, Alison stepped inside, but she could see at once the place had been ransacked. She glanced into her bedroom: all the drawers were pulled out and the contents scattered on the floor. She dared not go into the living room in case they were still there. She stood in the hall, sobbing, before slumping down the wall to the floor. After a while, she got up and stepped cautiously into the living room. There, too, every drawer was emptied, everything turned upside down. The sofa cushions were thrown everywhere and all the ornaments had been brushed off the mantelpiece and onto the floor. A picture of her with her father, taken last year, lay smashed on the wooden floor.

Alison staggered to a chair and sat down, weeping. It could only have been Uncle Gavin. He must have sent someone to look for her dad's confession and the picture. Now she knew for sure the kind of people they were. They would stop at nothing to maintain the sham they'd built up over the years. She rushed into her bedroom where she had hidden the letter under the floorboards below her bed. She pulled the bed out quickly and grappled with the loose floorboard, pushing her hand into the gap. Relief flooded through her when she felt the envelope. She took it out and held onto it. She had to do something now. She considered phoning the police and reporting a break-in, but decided against it. Word would filter back to Glasgow. She wondered if she should go to the police in Edinburgh with the confession, but she couldn't trust them either. She looked around the room at the books and newspapers thrown everywhere. Uncle Gavin and Uncle Bill had so much to lose. But her father had already lost everything.

Her eyes finally rested on a copy of the *Post* she had bought a couple of weeks ago on the way home from university. She saw the name Rosie Gilmour on the front page. She picked up the telephone from the floor and put the receiver back on the hook. Then she lifted it off again, dialled directory enquiries, and asked for the number of the *Post* in Glasgow.

CHAPTER TWENTY-FOUR

Rosie was beginning to feel seriously frightened for the first time in this whole investigation. Lying in bed, she couldn't help listening for every noise. Footsteps in the stairwell, cars pulling up outside. Jesus. She was getting paranoid. She tried to sleep, but her mind kept going over and over the phone call from Alison Prentice. She could never have predicted that, not in a million years. Alison had called her that evening as she was about to leave the office. She said she had a very important story to tell about her father and police corruption. Gavin Fox was the main player, she'd said, and it had all happened on his boat. And she had evidence – a written confession from her dad and a photograph. When she said that, Rosie knew it couldn't be a crank call. She agreed to meet her in Edinburgh, but after Alison told her of being attacked in the street, Rosie decided it would be wise to take some help. Before she went to bed, she called her friend Adrian, the Bosnian refugee.

The following morning, she drove to the top of Hope Street and pulled over when she saw Adrian standing on the corner. His expression didn't change when he caught sight of her. No smile or wave. He just came over to the car and got into the passenger seat, stretching out his hand and clasping hers.

'Hallo, Rosie.' His voice was deep and rich. 'My friend.' Finally a smile cracked his granite face. 'How are you? I have not see you in some months.'

Rosie smiled. 'I'm good, Adrian, I'm good.' She looked at his pale face, black shadows under his dark eyes. He always looked as though he never slept. 'For me it's been busy. A lot of work. What about you?' She handed him a coffee she had bought from the takeaway.

'Thanks.' He shrugged his shoulders. 'Sometimes some hotel work, sometimes in the biscuit factory.' He shook his head. 'I hate the biscuit factory. They are treating us like slaves. But I like the hotel, the tips are good.'

They drank their coffee without talking. You could do that with Adrian. He was comfortable in his silence, almost unnervingly comfortable sometimes. He'd once told her that people talk too much, and that there is more to hear if you are quiet. Rosie hadn't worked that one out yet.

She recalled how they'd met – two years ago – and how he'd said he would never forget her kindness. She'd been sitting at the window of a coffee and sandwich shop in the centre of town, waiting for a taxi back to the *Post*. The place was filling up with office workers out buying lunch to eat at their desks. She was vaguely aware of the big Eastern European guy loitering by the sandwich bar. He was gaunt and pale, probably in his early thirties. In his shabby clothes, he looked no different from the dozens of Bosnian refugees you saw these days in the streets and housing schemes of Glasgow. They had flocked here to escape the conflict in their own war-torn land, only to end up in high-rise flats in drug-infested Sighthill. Definitely a cruel irony there.

Rosie had watched as the guy slipped two baguettes under his jumper, but then she noticed that one of the girls behind the counter had also seen him do it and was whispering to her boss. When he made to walk out of the door, the manager came after him. The big man completely froze as he was approached and asked what he was doing with the baguettes up his jumper.

'Excuse me,' Rosie heard herself saying. 'He's with me.' She looked at him and he looked back at her, confused. She glared at him and took the baguettes out of his hand, saying, 'What are you doing?'

She turned to the manager. 'Sorry,' she whispered,

discreetly. 'He gets confused, you know what it's like. He works for me. I told him to pick up the sandwiches and bring them to me in the car so he mustn't have noticed me here. Must have got lost in translation.' She gave the manager a slightly frustrated look. He had no reason to doubt her, and apologised. She told the big man to come and sit beside her. There were tears in his eyes.

'Why you do that? I not understand.' His face was white.

Rosie looked at him. 'You remind me of someone I used to know. A long time ago . . .' She smiled. 'Hey. But why did you do it? Steal the bread?'

'I am hungry. Sorry. I will pay you back.'

She told him to forget it. She paid for the sandwiches and watched as he ate both of them. Over two mugs of tea he told her, in fractured English, his story. A Bosnian Muslim, he had been a farmer north of Sarajevo who, alongside his villagers, had fought against the Serbian soldiers who rampaged through the region. How he got here, and the horrors he had witnessed in his village before he escaped, was heartbreaking. He had lost both parents and a brother in a massacre.

Rosie knew what he was talking about. The memories of her time in Bosnia, of the brutality and atrocities, still haunted her. She got him a job as a porter at one of the big hotels and, over time, he proved to be a valuable contact. Occasionally they would share a coffee or lunch, and Adrian said she would be his friend forever. He told her he was very strong, and if she ever needed anyone to protect her, she should call him. She had only asked him once before, when she went to doorstep a loan shark. His sheer size had proved enough of a threat, and he hadn't had to lift a finger.

CHAPTER TWENTY-FIVE

Rosie had asked Alison Prentice to meet her in a cafe at the Corstorphine side of the city to save her driving through the madness of Princes Street. It was also better that they meet away from Alison's flat in case she was being watched.

She drove along the motorway blinking back tiredness, hypnotised by the windscreen wipers and the driving sleet. She explained carefully to Adrian the basics of the story about the police corruption. He didn't seem surprised. It was the same, he said, in his country. He couldn't understand the point of writing a story in the newspaper, he was sure nothing would change, and he nodded impassively when she told him about Alison being attacked.

'When you go to meet her in the cafe,' he said, 'drive past first and show me where you are, then I get off along the road. I will watch. I will see if someone is following. You. Or the girl.' He stared straight ahead.

Adrian wasn't a lot of laughs, but Rosie was glad he was with her. She was dog tired. She hadn't slept a wink last night after seeing Matt's pictures of the kids at the big house. She, Matt and the picture editor had sat in McGuire's office with him, going over the snaps. They hardly spoke as Matt explained what he'd been doing and what else he noticed in the room. Rosie and McGuire shook their heads in disbelief when they realised the man with the silver hair, taking pictures of the children, was Lord Dawson. McGuire quoted some of the high profile court cases Dawson had been involved in. McGuire looked shattered, Rosie noticed, as though he didn't know whether to celebrate or despair at the property in his hands. He knew it was almost too hot to handle.

'Will we ever get this in the paper, Mick?' Rosie asked.

McGuire looked at the photographs spread out on his desk, then at her.

'We will get a story in the paper,' he said, emphatically. 'How much we'll be able to say is another matter. But these pictures tell a story, Rosie, and I'll do everything I can to make sure we print them, whatever happens.'

'There'll be all sorts of pressure from upstairs,' the picture editor said. 'Political pressure, I'd say. Wait till you see, Mick.'

'I know,' McGuire said. 'I'm not in any doubt about that. But before this goes anywhere, before we even take it to the lawyers, I want everything nailed down as tight as we can. I want it watertight.' He looked at Rosie. When the others left the office, she and McGuire stood over the photographs.

'This is fucking dynamite, Rosie.'

'I know. I just keep seeing Trina's face, especially when she's taken out of the room by that man. God knows what happened to her, Mick. I'm going to find out who he is. I'm going to find out what the bastard did to that poor wee girl.'

McGuire touched her arm. 'What you're going to do, Gilmour, is not get all emotionally hung up.' Seeing she was about to protest, he went on. 'You will nail this down. In a totally cold, clinical way, as only you can. You can save your bleeding heart for the day after publication. Right now, there's a lot to be done.'

He had asked how things were going on the cop story and almost choked when she told him about Alison Prentice's call.

'Be safe, Rosie,' he said, as she left the office.

Now, walking towards the small cafe where they'd arranged to meet, Rosie steeled herself. She had dropped Adrian off a couple of blocks down the street, then parked close to the cafe.

There were only three people in the cafe – two elderly, well-heeled Edinburgh ladies with hats on, and an unhappy-looking girl in the far corner. The girl's face was grey and her eyes looked red and swollen from crying, and Rosie guessed this was Alison. She made eye contact and headed for the table.

'Rosie?' Alison whispered, moving as though to stand up.

'Yeah.' Rosie slid onto the bench, taking off her coat. 'How're you doing?' She reached across and touched the back of Alison's cold hand. 'Don't worry.' She hoped she sounded reassuring. 'Everything's going to be fine.'

Alison's eyes filled with tears, but she seemed to shake herself out of it. She rubbed her face and sat forward. The waitress came and Rosie ordered herself coffee and another for Alison.

'On the phone' – Rosie didn't see the point of wasting too much time – 'you were saying that you had something to tell. Something about your father and others. Other police officers . . . ?'

Alison closed her eyes and sniffed. 'I'm so scared, Rosie.'

'I know. I know you're scared. Just take your own time.'

They sat in silence for a moment. The waitress came over with the coffees and looked at both of them. Rosie gave her a cold stare and she shrugged and walked off. Rosie wondered if this was a good place to talk, or even if Alison was up to it. She would give her another few moments then suggest they go for a walk.

'He left a note,' Alison said suddenly. 'My father. He left a letter. He posted it to me before he died. It . . . It tells everything. Everything. And there's a picture . . .' Rosie could hear her heart beat. She squeezed Alison's arm encouragingly.

'Go on.'

Alison composed herself, and told her everything that was in the letter. Rosie kept her eyes looking straight into Alison's as she spoke about Fox. She called him her Uncle Gavin, whom she had grown up respecting. She told how he was behind everything and described how she had confronted him a couple of days ago. She believed that was why she'd been attacked.

'Where's the letter and the picture now?' Rosie prayed she hadn't destroyed them.

'They ransacked my flat, but they didn't find them. I've got them in my bag.' Alison placed the brown leather bag on the table, and Rosie breathed a sigh of relief.

'Don't take them out here,' she said, as Alison moved to open the bag. 'We'll drink our coffee then go to my car.'

She asked Alison if she thought anyone saw her leaving her flat. She said she'd left by a back entrance and had been doing that for the past two days.

Rosie knew that Fox would not rest until he had destroyed any evidence that could damage him. She would call McGuire, they'd have to make an arrangement to get Alison away somewhere. When they'd finished their coffees, Rosie got up.

In the car, Alison sat in silence as Rosie read the letter. She had leafed through it briefly, noticing it was signed 'Dad' and not Jack Prentice's name, but she would get more samples of his handwriting to authenticate it. She spotted the main names throughout the letter, Gavin Fox, and Bill Mackie. Jake Cox. Now she read it again, slowly. It was unbelievable. When she had finished, she sat back and let out a sigh of disbelief. Alison was crying.

'I'm so sorry, Alison.' She turned to her. 'This must have been awful for you. But you *will* get through this.' Jesus, she was sounding like the parish priest. But what else could you say to a girl who worshipped her father, then found out he was a complete bastard?

Then Alison rummaged in her bag, and handed Rosie a picture. She immediately recognised Jake Cox, the Big Man, with his arm around a woman. It looked like Gavin Fox in the background, but it was a side-on view. They seemed to be on a boat. Rosie rolled down the window and took a deep breath. The cold sleet felt good on her face.

'Can I have this picture and the letter, Alison?' she said. 'I take it that's what you want? I can expose this.' She was terrified that Alison would say no, but she knew in her heart she had to give her the opportunity. And she knew she had to give her the chance to pull back. 'Are you absolutely sure you want all this to come out?' she said. 'All this about your father?' McGuire would have had a heart attack if he'd heard her.

Alison nodded. 'Yes. I want the truth to come out. It's not just about my father, or the shame on me and my mother. It's about people being killed. Murdered. That young girl on the boat, Rosie? I read that story at the time and thought how sad it was. My dad was there. He did that. Not killed her, but he threw her into the sea.'

She broke down. 'I mean, well, he might even have had sex with that young girl. It's awful. She was only fourteen. I was physically sick when I read that.'

She sobbed.

Rosie put the snap inside the letter, folded it over and put it into a zip compartment in her handbag. Despite herself she felt a pang of guilt. McGuire was right. She never really had that killer instinct. *Save the bleeding heart for the day after publication.* His words rang in her ears.

'Alison,' she said. 'What do you want to do? If I'm going to investigate this story and do it in the next week, or however long it takes, I don't think you'll want to be around. I can get you away somewhere. Abroad if you like. Or if you want to go somewhere with a friend . . . Have you got a close friend? One you can trust?'

'Yes.'

'What about going up north or something? I can send someone to look after you. You wouldn't be in any danger.'

'I'd like that.' Alison blew her nose. 'Just get away for a bit. Until it all comes out in the paper.'

'What about your mother?'

'I'll tell her I'm going for a break.'

'Yes, but what will happen to her when all this comes out? She'll be shattered.'

Alison looked away. She took a deep breath, then she stopped crying.

'I don't really care. As you can see from the letter, she made my dad's life a misery. He was probably all fucked up because of her, and he probably took all those back-handers to keep her and her greed going. She wanted so much, always had to have the best of everything. I want the truth to come out more than I want to protect her.'

Rosie told her to go back to her flat and contact the friend who would go away with her. They might be away for a couple of weeks, so she should be prepared.

Alison seemed relieved. 'Thank you,' she said, as she opened the door of the car to leave.

Rosie didn't really know what to say. She squeezed her hand reassuringly and said, 'Okay, Alison. I'll call you in a couple of hours. Take care.'

She watched in her rear-view mirror as Alison walked

up the street into the grey afternoon until she disappeared from view, then she drove along the road until she saw Adrian standing in a shop doorway. He got into the car and they drove off. He pulled down the sun visor and looked in the mirror.

'They are following us, Rosie. Two men. A black BMW.'

CHAPTER TWENTY-SIX

There was no way Rosie's Vauxhall could outrun a BMW. Even if she drove with her foot to the floor, ripping up the inside lane on the M8 to try to lose it, she knew the BMW would catch her.

Adrian kept checking the mirror. 'Still there . . . four or five cars back . . .'

'Shit.' Rosie's heart was pumping. She gripped the steering wheel, her knuckles white as she zipped into the fast lane, almost taking the nose off a car in the middle lane, whose driver honked his horn indignantly. 'Yeah, yeah, asshole,' Rosie snapped. 'You want to be where I'm sitting.' She saw the driver giving her the finger.

'Coming now,' Adrian said. 'On inside lane.' He turned to Rosie. 'Do you think they will shoot us when they pass?' he asked, as though it would be a minor inconvenience.

'What?' Rosie was stunned. '*Shoot* us? Jesus, Adrian.'

Adrian shrugged. 'I am thinking, maybe, if they want something you've got they will shoot us. I think, maybe, you should drive off the highway.'

Rosie dropped a gear, cut back into the middle lane, then across to the inside. She saw a sign for Bathgate. Her tyres screeched as she took the slip road too fast and she struggled to keep control of the car.

'Shit,' Adrian said. 'They're behind us.'

Then suddenly the BMW was on her bumper. It tried to overtake her on the narrow country road and she swerved to block it. 'Christ almighty,' Rosie muttered. 'I don't believe this.' A long stretch of road ahead and the BMW was right beside her. She glanced quickly and saw a bald, heavy man in the passenger seat. It was a mistake to take her eye off the road. The car started weaving and she was heading fast into a field.

'Oh, fuck, Adrian!'

'Take your foot off the gas.'

She did. They ploughed into the field. She waited for the car to roll over, the airbag to pop out, and her whole life to flash in front of her. But it didn't. The field was soggy and the car stopped. The BMW was nowhere to be seen, but running towards them were the bald, fat guy and a big, burly man in a woolly hat.

'Quick.' Adrian opened the door. 'We must run.'

They got out of the car and ran. Rosie had no idea where

to, she just kept running. She couldn't breathe. She held tightly onto her bag. Up ahead she saw a large building.

'In there.' Adrian held her arm. 'Hurry, Rosie.'

The building was derelict, with smashed windows; rusting machinery sat in the yard. Adrian pushed open the front door and they went inside. It was dark, but not pitch black. Another half hour and it would be. They picked their way through the warren of rooms with overturned desks and chairs scattered around.

'In here.' Adrian motioned Rosie into what looked like a long cupboard. They stood there, trying to get their breath back.

'Ssssh, they're coming.' He put his finger up to his lips and stepped out of the cupboard. Rosie looked at him. 'Wait there,' he whispered, then disappeared behind a pillar. Rosie could hear his footsteps walking away. Sweat broke out all over her body and she felt sick. Please, God, don't let me be sick . . . She heard footsteps in the distance. She breathed softly and waited. It seemed like a good time to pray. Where was the Holy Ghost when you needed him? Where was Adrian? I promise I'll change, God. I'll never do anything bad. Don't let me die.

'Rosie.' It was Adrian's voice. She breathed a sigh of relief. She peered into the semi-darkness. Her heart jumped. Adrian was being held by the fat guy who was behind him, holding a knife at his throat. Adrian's face was grey.

'Your fucking pal just stabbed my mate.' The bald guy took a step towards her, pushing Adrian, the blade nearly through his skin. 'He'll pay for that.' He stretched out one hand.

'Gimme the stuff, bitch.'

Rosie didn't answer.

'Hurry the fuck up.'

'What stuff?' she managed to say.

'Aw for fuck's sake. Hurry up, or I'll cut his throat and you'll be next.' He grinned. 'I just do this for fun, hen. It's no for the money.'

Rosie reached into her bag and tried to fish the envelope out. Her hands were shaking as she held it out towards him. He was reaching out a hand to grab it, when he gave a loud gasp.

'Bastard.' The fat guy slumped over clutching himself between his legs. He looked shocked. He let go of Adrian, who turned swiftly and grabbed the knife from his hand. Rosie watched in shock as he plunged the knife into the man's stomach.

'Let's go.' Adrian wiped the knife on the man's jacket as he lay bleeding on the ground. He was gurgling. Then he stopped. Rosie seemed unable to move. Adrian tugged her arm.

'Come on, Rosie. We must go.'

'Have you killed him?' She stepped over the body.

'Does it matter?' Adrian said, flatly. She followed him out of the building and ran back to her car.

'I will drive,' Adrian said. 'If I can get the car out of this field.'

Rosie got into the passenger seat in a daze. She didn't feel sick any more. Adrian put the car into reverse and was soon out of the field and onto the road, the tyres screeching as he sped away. Rosie wondered if he had a driving licence, if he was insured.

At that moment, it didn't seem to matter.

CHAPTER TWENTY-SEVEN

In the internet cafe off Buchanan Street, Rosie drank a second cup of tea while she sat staring at the blank screen. She was somewhere between hysteria and collapsing from exhaustion, and she wasn't sure what would come first. On the way back to Glasgow, Adrian had driven like a maniac and she had to keep telling him to slow down. The last thing they needed was to get pulled over by the cops. But Adrian told her it was important they got far away from that place as fast as possible because the other guy had got away. He might have called for help and there could be others on the way.

'Do you think the fat guy is dead?' The image of him lying gurgling was even more vivid now.

'I don't think so.' Adrian pursed his lips. 'Maybe.' He glanced at Rosie as they overtook another car on the M8.

'Maybe. But I didn't pull the knife up to his chest. Then I would be sure.'

'I have killed men before. Three.' He counted on his fingers. 'No. Four.'

'Great,' Rosie said. 'That's all right then.' She shook her head, incredulous. 'Jesus wept, Adrian, forgive me. But it's not something I see a lot of in my work.'

Adrian smiled, for only the second time today. 'No. Rosie. Please. You must understand me, please. I do not kill for sake of it. Never. The men I killed were bad people who came to our village and murdered people. Me and other men in the village had to fight back.' His eyes were black. 'The soldiers were butchers, just like that man. He was going to kill me anyway, even if you gave him the things he wanted. And maybe he would kill you also.' He shrugged. 'If he is dead, that's fine.'

There was no answer to that, Rosie decided. They drove the rest of the journey in silence. She was relieved when they reached that rise of the M8 after Townhead and you could see the West End spread out before you. Home at last. When they got to Charing Cross, Adrian stopped the car and turned to her.

'I think now I have paid you back, Rosie. For being kind to me that day. And saving me from things.'

There was no answer to that either. They both got out of the car and Rosie came around to the driver's side where he stood, buttoning up his jacket against the wind.

'I must go now. Tomorrow I am at work in the biscuit factory from six. Long day.' He reached out both hands and took Rosie's, holding tight. 'If you need me, you know how to find me, my friend. Take care.'

'Thank you, Adrian.' Rosie wanted to say more. She wanted to probe, to try to understand how someone could experience the horror of what had just happened, then seem to completely forget about it. She watched Adrian stride along the street, wondering if he would turn to wave. He didn't. He was used to moving on.

In the cafe, Rosie reached into her handbag and took out Alison's letter and photograph. She had decided to scan them onto a disk which she could hold onto, just in case they disappeared when they got to McGuire's office. Matt had already given her a disk of the pictures he took at Lord Dawson's house. It wasn't that she didn't trust McGuire. In all the time she had known him, she'd respected his integrity and the way he acted on his instinct. But, deep down, she worried that when McGuire's back was really against the wall and political pressure was raining down on him, he just might fold.

They now had two explosive stories on the go. Lord Dawson and the paedophile ring, and the bent cops at the top of the tree. You could wait all your life for a sniff at stories like these and never get near them. But Rosie knew they were too hot for safety. If push came to shove, she wanted to have the option of resigning and taking them elsewhere, but she hoped it wouldn't come to that. She called McGuire and told him that everything had gone well and that the letter and picture were in the bag. He was waiting for the car that was taking him to a dinner with the Secretary of State for Scotland, and he didn't want her to give the material to anyone but him. He would see her first thing in the morning. Rosie was relieved. She was completely drained. You're a star, he told her, as he hung up. If only he knew . . .

She finished her tea and sat back, waiting for the disk to complete. She felt achingly alone and exhausted. She'd been running on empty for the past few days, yet when she lay in bed at night, sleep wouldn't come. She kept thinking about Gemma and Trina, remembering their innocent faces that afternoon in the cafe when she promised she would take them to her home one night. They needed so little to make them happy. She knew she wouldn't sleep tonight either, after everything that had happened. There was only one person in the world she wanted to talk to.

'What took you so long?' The sound of TJ's mild sarcasm made Rosie feel warm. 'What's wrong?' TJ's voice was suddenly concerned.

'TJ.' Rosie choked back tears. 'Can I come over? I need to see you.'

'Of course you can, Rosie. Where are you? Do you want me to come and get you?'

She took a deep breath. 'I'll be there in ten minutes.'

The disk popped out. Rosie put it into her handbag and walked out of the cafe into the night. She looked over her shoulder as she got into her car. Her hands were shaking and she gripped the steering wheel hard to stop them.

CHAPTER TWENTY-EIGHT

When TJ opened the door, they stood looking at each other for a moment. Then he put his arms around Rosie and held her tight. She buried her head in his shoulder, and the tears came. He didn't speak, just held her there in the hallway, caressing the back of her head.

'I'm shattered, TJ.' She eased herself away. 'I'm sorry. I've got nowhere else to go but here. I'm just . . . I just feel lost.' Tears rolled down her cheeks. TJ stood with his hands on her shoulders, then he wiped her face with the palms of his hands and kissed her on the lips. She was ashamed of cracking like this in front of him.

'Come on, Rosie. Sssh . . . It's okay now. You don't need anywhere else to go. Come on.'

He put his arm around her shoulders, and she allowed him to lead her down the hall and into the living room. He sat her down on the sofa in front of the flickering fire.

'Tell you what I'm going to do with you, Rosie.' He turned her face towards him. 'I'm going to pour you a large drink and run you a hot bath. I'll scrub your back for you.'

He went to the table and poured from an open bottle of red wine. He handed Rosie a glass, then disappeared. She took a long slow drink. She could hear water running. She sniffed back her tears, but the heaviness still pressed on her chest. TJ appeared in the living room and drank half of his wine in one gulp. He refilled both their glasses.

'Bath's ready. On you go, you look done in.' He smiled. 'Don't worry. I'm not going to molest you.'

Rosie caressed his face gently, then she took off her jacket, and went past him into the bathroom. In the candle-light, it smelled of incense. She stood in the steam watching little rivers of condensation run down the blue and white tiles. She stripped off and sank into the bubbles, moaning softly as the water warmed the raw chill of her body. She lay watching the flickering candles, and closed her eyes. The door opened and TJ came in with her glass of wine.

'You'll need this.' He handed her the glass as she sat up.

She saw him looking at her body and she smiled up at him. He knelt down by the side of the bath, took the sponge and began to wash her. He rubbed the sponge gently across her shoulders and back, then her breasts, caressing them with the sponge, then with his hands, making her nipples immediately hard. He touched them softly with the tips of his fingers and Rosie felt a twinge of desire. TJ looked into her eyes and pushed back her hair. He leaned forward and kissed her.

'I can see you now, Rosie. More clearly than ever.' He got up and sat on a chair beside the bath so he was facing her.

'Talk to me. Tell me what made you who you are. Tell me why you cry in your sleep, Rosie.' He drank from his glass and looked at her.

She lay back in the bath and closed her eyes. Now she would talk – for the first time in her life. She was tired of fighting from behind the wall. She took a deep breath and began.

'It's always the phone ringing.' She swallowed. 'Always the phone, TJ. That's what wakes me up. And when I finally open my eyes I know I've been crying. Because – because I know where I've been.'

TJ studied her face. 'Tell me.'

She began at the place where her childhood had ended.

She had walked slowly home from school that day, slower than usual. That's what had always preyed on her mind afterwards. Perhaps if she had run home from school like the rest of the kids, she could have been there on time and then maybe it wouldn't have happened. But Rosie was never in a hurry to go home because she knew what she would find. Her mother would either be asleep on the chair or couch, the mug by her side and an ashtray filled with fag ends, or else she would be fussing around the house trying to look sober, drinking from the mug as she bumped into furniture or dropped pans while she attempted to cook. Rosie wished her mother wouldn't bother with the pretence of pouring the cheap wine or strong lager she drank into the mug, trying to pass it off as tea. She might as well have swigged it from the bottle, instead of trying to hide it. Rosie knew that her mother was drunk from the moment she opened her eyes in the morning until she collapsed on the bed at night. Usually, that was after the men visited, and were taken into the bedroom while Rosie was sent to the shop for sweets.

Sometimes she sneaked back into the house and listened outside the bedroom door where she could hear the groaning noises. Through the keyhole once, she saw a man with his trousers at his ankles lying on top of her mother and moving up and down, huffing and puffing. At first she thought he was trying to murder her and she considered bursting through the door and hitting him with the poker. But then she heard her mother moaning, and she didn't sound as though she was being hurt or in danger.

After that night, she didn't look through the keyhole any more.

Her mother never spoke about the men to Rosie. She thought maybe her mum was just lonely, because her father had been away for so long. Rosie waited and waited for him to come home, and the memory she had of him faded with each passing year. All she had to remember him by was a cracked black and white photo of the man she last saw when she was four years old. That seemed to be the time when her mother started to drink. And the more she drank the more she cried, and the less she cared about the state of the house. Rosie would come home from school and start to peel potatoes for the dinner. She cleaned the house and went to the shops while her mother slept off the booze. That was why she didn't rush home from school, because while she wasn't in the house, she could pretend she lived a different life. The kind of life that the other kids lived, with dads who had jobs and mums who had dinner on the table when they got home from school.

These kids used to tell Rosie how they sat at night and told stories around the fire and sometimes played card games with their dads. Rosie used to tell them her dad was in the Merchant Navy, and was coming back next year with presents and exotic things from every country he had ever visited. She wondered if they believed her. And she wondered if the stories they told her about their own lives were real, or if they were all living like her.

There was nobody she could talk to about her mother. If she did, they would send the social welfare in and take her away to one of those big damp children's homes where the nuns would bash you up every day. Rosie had heard stories about them and she was terrified of being sent there. Her mother wasn't much, but she was all she had. And anyway, she wasn't a bad person. She loved Rosie and would sing to her sometimes, and they would sit some nights, just the two of them, and her mum would tell her of places they would visit some day when they had enough money. Nights like that, Rosie would fall asleep in her mother's arms on the couch and dream of the countries they would see together. She only told her pals at school of her plans once though, because they all sniggered after Ann-Marie Grattan said it would be hard for her ma to go anywhere because she could hardly stand up, she was that drunk. Deep down she knew they would probably never go anywhere, but there was no harm in dreaming.

She felt the tears coming on again. TJ came and knelt beside her.

'It's okay, Rosie. Just let it go.' He stroked her hair.

She went on. The day it all happened, Rosie had walked home from school in her usual slow way, stopping to look in some of the shop windows and sitting for a while on a wooden seat at the bus stop. She liked watching people and wondered what their lives were like.

She walked up the steps of the tenement to the top flat where they lived. She could hear music coming through the door. She hoped her mother wasn't drunk, just happy, so they could sit together after dinner and talk. She pushed the door open, and was about to shout hallo to her mum that she was home, when she looked up and saw her. It was her feet. In mid-air. She was swinging from the ceiling. For a second Rosie felt the room sway, and she fell against the wall. There was a rope around her mother's neck and her face was blue. It had this shocked expression. And bulging eyes. Then the phone rang. It rang and rang. But she couldn't look away from her mother hanging there, wearing the fur slippers Rosie had bought her for Christmas from the nearly-new stall at the church jumble sale. She loved the slippers.

Rosie was crying now.

'The next thing I remember,' she said through sobs, 'is Mary McGarvie from next door and her husband Danny coming in through the open door and shouting Jesus, Mary and Joseph. Then there were other neighbours. And the police. The McGarvies took me to their house.'

She swallowed, composing herself.

'And then . . . and then someone in a blue uniform came into the McGarvies and took me away. They told me my mother was dead now. I was an orphan.' Rosie's lip trembled. 'I used to hear people in the close whisper the word orphan, and I was ashamed because I was one now, with nobody else in the whole world.'

It was the first time since she was nine years old that Rosie had spoken about that day. For nearly twenty-eight years she had woken up at least twice a month with that memory of her mother's suicide, and the phone always ringing in her dream.

'You know, TJ,' Rosie said, 'there were times in my life when I was mad at my mother for giving up and leaving me like that, all alone. But I suppose I grew to understand how sad her life must have been. How terrible it must be to have no hope. Maybe that's why I never give up on anything.'

Rosie told him she'd never got to the funeral because she was in the children's home, and to this day she had no idea where her mum was buried.

'So there you have it. Or most of it. So you see, TJ, if you thought I was off my head, then you're absolutely right. Now you know why, or partly why.' She looked at him. 'I can't find peace anywhere in my life. That's why I got annoyed the other day in the cafe when you said that I fill my life with work so I don't have to look at myself. You touched a raw nerve.'

'Sorry,' TJ said, coming over beside her with a big bath

towel. 'I'm sorry, Rosie. I didn't know things had been this bad for you. I knew there was stuff somewhere, it's in your eyes. But I had no idea. I'm sorry. Come on.' He held open the bath towel and Rosie got out of the water. He wrapped the towel around her and dried her body, gently rubbing her back and hair, then her legs, kneeling down, drying her feet. Rosie stood, allowing him to dry her as if she were a child.

'Come on. Let's go in and relax in front of the fire.' TJ gave her his bath robe and tied it around her waist.

Rosie smiled and, putting her arms around him, kissed him on the lips.

CHAPTER TWENTY-NINE

The bar was heaving for one of the biggest farewell parties the *Post* had seen in a long time. Dan Divers, the legendary features writer, had taken a deal and was off to write his memoirs on some little Greek island with his latest girlfriend. An hour earlier, Dan had taken the long walk across the editorial floor for the last time, to the traditional banging-out ceremony reserved for only the most respected newspaper figures. There were misty eyes amid the thunderous applause as he turned and bowed, before walking through the revolving doors.

Now he was holding court at Blacks, the notorious journo watering hole within spitting distance of the office. It was there that journalistic legends were built up or torn down; it just depended on who was wielding the knife at the time. Everyone who was anyone was there for Divers' send-off. Journalists, photographers, management, telesales and, of course, the printers, plus the usual collection of lawyers and detectives that you found at any newspaper party.

Divers was one of the last great characters who could tell stories of a golden era when journalists partied as hard as they worked. Blacks was where they took refuge in hard drinking and black humour. Down the years, many had paid the price, and newspapers were littered with alcoholic casualties. But Divers lived to tell the tale. Here he was in sparkling form, a Guinness in his hand and a growing line of whiskies on the bar. He would deal with all of them before the night was through.

In mid-sentence, he stopped and winked when he saw Rosie squeezing through the crowd.

'Ah the beautiful Rosie,' he said with a theatrical flurry. 'The delightful Rose among so many hairy-arsed thorns. Come here, sweetheart, till I kiss you full on the bare lips.' He planted a wet kiss as promised, almost hugging the life out of her.

'You know something?' He turned to the half dozen people around him. 'I love this woman so much there's nothing I wouldn't do for her. If only she'd have me.' He kissed Rosie again and everyone laughed.

'I don't know why she wouldn't have you, Div,' somebody shouted. 'Sure everyone else has.'

'This woman . . .' Divers was already half drunk, but

Rosie knew he would still be the last man standing by the end of the night. 'This woman is the best journalist I've ever known. Bar none. And you know what? I taught her everything she knows.'

Rosie laughed. He ordered her a gin and tonic and they clinked glasses.

'All the very best, Div.' Rosie kissed his cheek. 'I'll miss you more than you'll ever know. Nobody did more for me than you.'

Divers had a special place in her heart. When she had started out at the *Post*, it was Divers who took her under his wing as she punched above her weight to survive as a young female reporter among so many macho personalities. It was Divers who was there when her heart was broken. And it was he who had pushed her career by using his considerable clout among the editors to suggest she be allowed to prove herself. Now and again, they would have a boozy lunch together and Rosie would sit spellbound listening to Divers' stories.

Now he leaned towards his protégée and whispered in her ear.

'It's time to get out, Rosie. I can see it in your eyes, darling. You're burning out and none of these fuckers is worth it. Nothing is.'

Rosie looked at him and didn't answer.

'I know you're on a big one just now.' He studied her

face. 'I know it's a secret, and I don't even want to know what it is, but who's going to give a shite about it two days later? Time to go and lead your own life.'

Rosie sighed. She didn't want to have this conversation. Not tonight. She gave him a look that brushed it away.

'Just don't leave it too late,' Divers whispered. Then he put his arm around her and pulled her close. 'And something else, Rosie, sweetheart. This story you're on? Watch that bastard Reynolds. He's sneaking about like the polecat he is, trying to find out what you're doing, so I'd guess it must be something that will upset his Freemason pals at the polis. Luckily, he can't find his arse in the dark, but just watch your back, darlin'.'

Rosie said nothing. Much as she loved Divers, she was glad when someone else threw their arms around him and dragged him away from her.

She looked around the bar. The younger reporters were grouped in the corner, and looked as though they were already coked up. They nipped in and out of the toilet, coming out like they could conquer the world. Cocaine was everywhere these days, from the editorial floors to the boardroom, and no self-respecting dinner party was complete without the host bringing out the Peruvian marching powder with the after-dinner mints. It wasn't Rosie's bag at all. She had tried it, once with a trusted journalist friend then, just to make sure, she tried it again.

She decided that anything that made you feel that good had to end in tears, and should be avoided like the plague.

The hacks waved her over. She waved back, but she had no intention of joining them. Annie Dawson was among them, giggling and happy. Too happy, Rosie thought. She hoped Annie hadn't slipped into the coke habit and made a mental note to watch for telltale signs.

She turned and joined a group of feature writers and advertising girls who were already three sheets to the wind. Jimmy Kavanagh, the oily show business reporter, was running true to form, talking about sex. It was all he ever did. But he talked about his conquests so much that people stopped believing him, and he was becoming a figure of fun.

'I'm telling you,' he said to the group. 'These pills I got from this guy. Not Viagra, but something like it. They're unbelievable. I'm at it four times a day. I'm shagged out.'

'Just think how knackered you'd be if there was somebody with you,' Rosie said to loud guffaws.

'Aye, very funny, Gilmour,' Kavanagh said. 'Hey. What would you say to a wee shag?' He slid his arm around her waist.

'Hallo, wee shag.'

He turned to one of the advertising girls. 'You just ask your pal about me. They all know me, the girls upstairs.' He winked. 'Some better than others.'

The advertising girl sniggered and said, 'I did. Betty Reilly talks about your manhood all the time.'

The girl knocked her drink back and slammed the glass on the bar. 'She said it was like a penis. Only smaller.' The group erupted in giggles.

'Aw fuck off. You deadbeats are just jealous.' He walked off and joined another group.

Rosie was on her third drink and feeling good. The pub was filling up with the night-shift subs and backbench editors, now that the newspaper had been put to bed. McGuire put in an appearance. He always did at these parties, but never stayed too long. He handed over a wad of notes to the barmaid to give everyone a drink. On the way past Rosie he touched her shoulder and said to join him for a quick drink.

She reminded herself to have only one more gin. She couldn't cope with a hangover on top of everything else. She felt someone's arms go around her from behind.

'Hi, Rosie.' It was Matt Harper. He was already half drunk. 'Why don't you take me home and ride me till the environmental health comes and drags you off.'

'It's finding the time, Matt,' Rosie laughed, kissing him on the cheek. 'I'm just so busy.' She ran her hand through his curly hair and whispered. 'Hey, Matt. Thanks for the disk with the pictures. It'll be some stuff if we can get it to work. I'm up to my eyes with that, and another story as well.'

'I can't get it out of my mind,' Matt said. 'Those wee kids. If we can get these pictures in the paper it will be the most important job I've ever done.' Rosie hoped he wasn't drunk enough to start running off at the mouth. Reynolds was hovering in the background, along with two guys who looked like coppers out noseying around.

'Listen, Matt. The most important thing just now is to keep your head. All of this might take some time so we've got to be patient. Keeping everything really tight is the most important thing. If any of this gets out before the time is right we can just forget it. Okay?'

'You're the boss, darling.' Matt gave her the thumbs up and moved on as a young telesales girl put her arms around him.

Rosie moved to cross the room to speak to the editor, when Reynolds grabbed hold of her arm.

'Rosie, I want you to meet a couple of guys.'

She went towards the two short-haired guys. They were wearing double-breasted suits, the uniform of every copper who was trying his best not to look like a copper.

Reynolds introduced her to both men. One was a DS, and the other a DI. They made small talk and chatted about an upcoming court case that both were involved in. Then they were making jokes about how important it was to tell the truth, the whole truth and nothing but the truth in the witness box.

'I've never met a copper yet who could lie straight in his bed.' Rosie couldn't resist the dig.

The cops laughed, but the DI didn't look happy.

'Of course. You're the reporter who never gives us guys a minute's peace.'

'Me? Not at all. As far as I'm concerned, all cops are honest and true upstanding figures. Where would we be without them?' She looked the DI straight in the face. He glared at her.

'I've got to have a word with the editor,' Rosie said, turning away. 'Excuse me, gents. Nice meeting you.' She smiled at the DI. 'Enjoy yourselves, guys. The disco's due to start. Reynolds here was the Hucklebuck champion in 1967.' She could feel Reynolds's eyes on her back as she walked away.

McGuire was drinking a pint with one of his assistant editors when Rosie made her way across. He excused himself and took her to one side. He bought her a drink and another for himself.

'So how's it going? How're we doing on the cops story?'

'Well, you've seen the picture and the suicide note. I'm ready when you are, Mick.'

Rosie hadn't told him about the men who chased her, or the stabbing. She would keep that one for her memoirs. She looked at McGuire. 'It's pretty much up to you now, Mick, I can start writing it up any time you want. There's a lot of stuff. We could run it over two, maybe three, days. The rest of the papers will be into it as well. Especially Prentice's confession about the guys who got framed – the fit-ups.'

McGuire beamed. 'I haven't even run it past the lawyers yet. I'm not going to until I see the copy. Then, of course, you've got to go knocking on Gavin Fox's door. I'd love to be a fly on the wall for that caper.'

'What about the paedo ring? Lord Dawson and the rest?' She watched as McGuire's mood seemed to change.

'That will be the hardest one. Honestly, Rosie.'

'But we've got him actually taking pictures of kids from a children's home.' Rosie sensed he was beginning to buckle already.

'I know, I know, but we have to be very careful with this one. Ultra careful. This is a High Court judge, and one or two more of the guys in that room may also be top people.'

'So fucking what?'

'Just calm it, Gilmour.' His voice was soft. 'We're not there on that story yet. Okay? We've got the pictures, but we need more. I don't want to be the editor who has to go to Lord Dawson with this unless it's absolutely one hundred per cent.'

'Maybe you don't want to go to him with this at all.' Rosie knew she was pushing it. 'Tell you what. I'll be happy to knock at his door, any time at all.'

McGuire raised his eyebrows. 'I know, Gilmour. Look – let's just get this cop story in the bag and we'll take things one at a time.'

'We have to get the paedo stuff in the paper, Mick. We can't betray these kids.'

'I know. But just remember one thing, Rosie. We'll get fucking hammered when they find out how you got this information. How you were acting unlawfully by interviewing minors. You could be the one in the pokey. And me.'

'You just say you didn't know anything about it,' Rosie said.

He laughed. 'Oh don't worry, sweetheart. I'll be the one standing in the witness box saying, I know of no Rosie Gilmour, nor what she does.'

McGuire slapped her on the back and went to the bar to order more drinks. Rosie watched him. Still, deep down, she wondered what would really happen if the chips were down.

CHAPTER THIRTY

For nearly three hours Rosie and Matt had watched caretaker Paddy Quigley go from pub to pub. They'd sat outside the children's home since early that evening, waiting for him to finish his shift so they could see where he went. Earlier in the afternoon Rosie and McGuire had put their heads together and decided their best option to get to the paedophile story was to intimidate the caretaker by telling him they knew enough to incriminate him, and that he would be the one who'd be facing jail for what he'd done. Chances were he would crumble and spill the beans to protect his own skin. It was a risky strategy – if a guy was prepared to take children from a home and offer them to paedophiles, he wasn't big on integrity. McGuire and Rosie knew that this could blow the whole story out of the water and they could be left with nothing. Rosie told Mick she would go with her gut instinct and make a decision once she'd figured what kind of guy the janitor was.

Quigley had been in the first bar for a while before Matt went in for a drink in order to eyeball him. The man was at the bar alone, drinking a pint with straight whisky chasers. He had three in twenty minutes. When he came out of the second bar, he was unsteady on his feet. He stopped outside and lit a cigarette, then spat on the pavement and made his way to a small bar on the corner of the street. It was one of the roughest bars in the East End of Glasgow.

Rosie remembered the bar from her childhood, as the place where her mother sometimes went on a Saturday afternoon for the sing-along. Sometimes Rosie would stand outside with a bag of chips, waiting for her to come out, watching the door in the hope that the next person to leave would be her mother. Even if she was staggering, it wouldn't matter, just as long as she came home. The smell of stale beer, tobacco and dampness that hit her every time the door swung open, had stayed with Rosie all her life. She could smell it even now, sitting in the car with the windows closed.

'That's a shithole of a pub,' she said.

'I wouldn't have thought it was a place the likes of yourself would hang out,' Matt replied.

'No.' Rosie looked out of out of the side window. 'But

I remember it from years ago. I lived around here a long time ago, Matt. A lifetime ago . . .' Her voice trailed off.

'Yeah? I was a West End boy. Top floor of a tenement. It was quite nice though, even if we didn't have any money. There was always somebody polishing the banister and bleaching the close. It was as if they were trying to bleach and polish some respectability into their lives to make up for the shame of being skint. Never quite understood it.'

'Know what you mean.' Rosie never had Matt down as being profound before.

'Mind you' – he chuckled – 'the closes were great for a bit of a shag against the wall. Some of the knee tremblers I had in there! Jesus!'

That was more like the Matt she knew, thought Rosie, and just then spotted Quigley coming out of the pub. 'Look here he comes.'

Quigley staggered along the pavement towards the broken neon light flickering on and off outside Mario's fish and chip shop, and went in. They drove closer to the shop so they could see him standing inside.

'What happens now?' Matt said. 'Fancy a puddin' supper?'

'No. I'm watching my waistline. Just let's see where he goes.'

'We're going to have to hit him soon, or he'll be going home.'

Rosie felt a twinge of nerves.

Quigley came out of the shop, opening his chip bag as he went into the street. He looked up and down, stuffing chips and lumps of fish into his mouth. Then he walked towards a bench close to the bus stop. He sat down and continued wolfing down his fish supper.

'Paddy's eating out tonight,' Matt said. 'These jannies really know how to live.'

'Well . . .' Rosie buttoned her coat. 'I hope he doesn't mind a bit of company, because I'm about to join him.' She told Matt to snatch pictures while she approached Quigley, but to stay at the car.

'Don't come until I give you a wave. I want to be first to let him know that his world's about to come tumbling down.'

She got out of the car and went towards Quigley. He looked up momentarily, then went back to his food. Rosie stopped at the bench and stood in front of him for a moment, then sat down beside him.

'Howsit goin', doll?' Quigley said, giving her a sideways glance. 'Awright?'

'Aye, fine.'

'This is no a bus stop, by the way, doll.' Quigley spoke with a mouthful of food. 'I mean the bus doesnae stop here. Not even at the bus stop. Fuck knows why. So if it's a bus you're waiting for, you're in the wrong place. Awright, doll?'

Rosie looked him in the eye for a few seconds.

'I'm not waiting for a bus.'

'Oh.' Quigley looked her up and down. 'You on the game? If you are, you must be new, 'cos it's only a fiver for a hand-job down here in the cheap seats. And the birds that hang about here can hardly stand up, they're that smacked out their tits.'

Rosie said nothing.

'Sorry, doll. Sorry, darlin'. I mean, I'm just sayin' what it's like. Know what I mean?'

'I'm here to see you, Mr Quigley.'

Quigley's face froze.

'How do you know my name?' He seemed to sober up. 'Who are you. Polis? Or what?'

'No, not police. I just want to talk to you, Paddy. You and me are going to have a wee talk.'

Quigley glanced around him. He put his chips down on the bench. His face looked grey.

'Talk about what?' he snorted. 'Who the fuck are you?'

Rosie kept looking at him in silence. He stood up.

'Sit down, Paddy,' she said. 'Don't make this hard for yourself. You're in enough trouble, believe me, pal, and that's why I'm here. To give you a chance to get out.'

'Fuck are you talking about? What? What the fuck is

this all about? Look, doll. I don't know what kind of psycho you are, but I'm going home. Now get yourself tae fuck.' Rosie caught him by his sleeve and tugged him back.

'Sit down, Paddy.' Her voice was calm. 'I want to talk to you about your Friday night bus runs to the big house in Peebles.'

Quigley rocked back on his heels. Rosie thought he was going to faint.

'Look, I know all about it, Paddy. You. The kids from the home. The judge's house. Every single bit of your stinking little scam I know.' She waved to Matt. 'And I'll tell you something else, Paddy. See that guy behind you?' Matt was coming towards them. 'He's got it all on film. Everything, the lot. Including you, pal.'

Quigley turned around so fast he staggered and almost fell. He came face to face with Matt, towering above him, smiling. He spun around again and looked at Rosie.

'So sit down, Paddy,' she said. 'Before you fall down.'

Paddy slumped onto the bench. Matt lifted his bag of chips, ate one, then put them on the ground and sat beside him. Quigley fumbled furiously in his pocket and brought out his cigarettes. He shoved one between his lips, but his hands were trembling so much he couldn't light it.

'Wait and I'll get that for you, wee man.' Matt took

Quigley's lighter off him and clicked it under the fag quivering in his lips. He puffed hard, then took the cigarette out and held it in his trembling hands.

'Look. What the fuck's going on?' His voice was shaking.

'Paddy.' Rosie swivelled her body so she was facing him. 'We are your worst nightmare. We're about to expose you for what you are, so let's be clear here. We have been watching you and we know what you're up to. But you're only a bit player in this, Paddy. You're nobody. It's not you we're after, so if you help us we'll make sure you get left out of it.'

There were beads of sweat on Quigley's upper lip. He stared at them.

'Are you with the papers?'

'You should be on *Mastermind*, Paddy,' Rosie said. 'We're working on the story about the kids going to the judge's house and the stuff that goes on in there. You know, the pictures of the kids, etc. We're going to blow it all sky high.'

Quigley stared at the ground. Eventually he spoke.

'And me? What happens to me?'

'Nothing. If you help us. Tell us everything that's going on. Every detail. If you do, we'll not use the fact that it's you who organises the Friday nights and drives the kids to the big house.'

Quigley looked from one to the other.

'That's right, mate,' Matt said. 'We've got it all on film, from the moment you leave the children's home.' Matt produced a digital camera from inside his jacket and showed Quigley a picture of himself outside the big house, holding the door of the minibus open as kids climbed inside.

Quigley buried his head in his hands. For a moment there was no sound. Not even his breathing. Rosie looked at Matt. Quigley's shoulders started to shake.

'Oh fuck! Oh fuck! I'm fucked! I'll end up at the bottom of the Clyde! It's not me who organises it. I just drive the bus.'

'You help us, Paddy,' Rosie said, 'and nobody will know your involvement.'

Quigley drew on his cigarette. Tears ran down his face.

'Don't give me that shit. How're you going to do that? Who are you going to say takes them to the house? Fuck's sake! If you're going to tell the whole story, how the fuck can you leave me out? Do you think I'm buttoned up the back?'

Rosie was quiet. She knew it would be impossible to tell the story without exposing Quigley's part in it. The fact that it was the caretaker of the home who drove these kids to the judge's house was one of the crucial parts of the story. But she had to convince him they would find a way out for him, even if at this stage she had no idea whether she could or not.

'Tell you what,' she said. 'If you can help us all the way down the line, then before we're ready to go with the story we'll make sure you know in advance, so you can get off your mark. Disappear.'

He sat puffing his fag, breathing fast. He wiped away tears, shaking his head. He looked pathetic.

'I was only doing it for the money, ' he said. 'I'm up to my neck with the moneylenders. These fuckers are into me for thousands. It's my laddie. He's a smackhead. He owes so much to the drug dealers they were going to kill him. If I don't keep up the payments they'll do me in.' He turned to Rosie, his face streaked with tears. 'Don't you think I'm fucking disgusted at what I do? These sickos make me want to kill them every time I go there. You say you could destroy me? That you're my worst nightmare? My whole life is a nightmare, but I had to do it. My laddie was going to die.'

Rosie looked at Quigley. Poor bastard.

'Will you help us?' She mustn't let this story get to her.

He said nothing, just kept sobbing quietly. Rosie looked at Matt, who shrugged.

Eventually, Quigley took a deep breath. 'Aye,' he said, his head in his hands.

'Okay.' Rosie moved closer to him. 'How much do you get paid each time you take the kids to the judge's house?'

'Two hundred pounds.'

'Every week?'

'Aye.'

'I don't know the name of the judge,' Rosie lied, and put her hand on Quigley's arm. 'I want you to tell me the name – and the names of the others in the house.'

'It's a lord. Lord Dawson,' Quigley said. 'You know him. He's famous. There's a few others there, but I don't know their names. One's a judge, but I only know that two others are sheriffs and one is a lawyer.'

'Who asked you to get involved in this?' Rosie's heart was beating fast.

Quigley sniffed again and flicked his cigarette end away.

'My boss. Duncan Davidson. He's the manager of the home.'

Rosie and Matt exchanged glances. She hadn't expected this.

'The manager of the home organises for the children to be passed around paedophiles? Is that what you're saying?'

He nodded. 'That's right.'

'Jesus,' Rosie said. 'I was told it was the manager, but I didn't believe it.' Another lie.

'Who told you about this?' Quigley asked.

Rosie told him there was no way she could tell him that. 'Listen, Paddy. 'We're well down the line with this investigation, but we do need your help. As I said, it's not you we're after. Would you be prepared to wear a hidden tape recorder when you talk to your boss while he's arranging a meeting at the big house?' She didn't know what she would say if he refused, but she knew he'd run out of choices a long time ago.

Quigley stared into the middle distance. Then he turned to Rosie. 'Okay,' he said. 'Okay. I'll do it.'

Bingo! Done up like a kipper. Nothing could stop them them now. And even if he walked away there and then, Rosie had their entire conversation on tape. At least that was something. She asked Quigley for a phone number and gave him her mobile. They would meet tomorrow and she would give him the wire and tape.

'Okay, Paddy.' She stood up. 'We're going now. It's up to you what you do. You can walk away and tell your boss everything, but it won't stop the story. It'll just put it off. And remember, you're up to your neck in it but I can give you an out. I hope you understand that? I hope you're going to help us. Then you can disappear.'

Quigley nodded.

'I'll help.' Tears came to his eyes again. 'As long as I can get out of here with my laddie.'

Rosie shook his hand, greasy from the fish, then turned and walked away, Matt following her. She had no idea if there was any way to save Quigley's skin. Part of her felt a twinge of sorrow for him, for the shitty deals that life sometimes threw at people. But right now, that was not her problem.

CHAPTER THIRTY-ONE

Gavin Fox filled up Bob Reynolds's whisky glass, and poured a little into his own and Bill Mackie's. He winked when Bill caught his eye, as Reynolds protested that he didn't need any more whisky. Foxy felt smug. The hour-long session with Reynolds had gone even better than he had anticipated. He sat back in his leather chair and stretched out his long legs, admiring the shine on his shoes.

'I fully understand, Bob,' Foxy said. 'I can see why you feel pushed out.'

Reynolds swigged from his glass. His face was flushed and his speech slurred a little, but he still seemed coherent enough. He was talkative, and Foxy was glad of that. In truth, he hated Reynolds as much as he despised all the journalists he'd ever met. Parasites, he called them in private, even though he'd often been seen lunching or dining with the hierarchy of the newspapers during his career. He knew they thought he was slippery, but once they'd spent a couple of hours having their egos bolstered by him, most of them were putty in his hands.

Reynolds was easy meat. He was so keen to be first on all the major crime exclusives, he would have sold his granny. Foxy and Bill had thrown him some big stories over the past fifteen years, and Reynolds always made sure the cops came out smelling of roses, even if it meant massaging the truth. Reynolds had already called Bill earlier in the week to mark his card that Rosie Gilmour was working on something about Jack Prentice's suicide. Fox's only agenda was to find out what Gilmour was doing and what evidence she had. That business with the two heavies Big Jake had sent to Edinburgh after her meeting with Alison had been well fucked up. One of them nearly got stabbed to death by Gilmour's big minder, and Jake was not happy. That reporter was too fucking smart for her own good. Foxy would make sure she'd be sorry. If he didn't, he knew Jake would . . .

'The way I see it, Bob,' Foxy said, 'is you're just being frozen out altogether, pal. Maybe they're looking to get rid of you and this is a ploy. Keep you in the dark about stories. That's what it seems like to me.'

'I know, Foxy,' Reynolds said. 'It's been like that for the

past two years. Any time there's a big investigation going on it's always that bitch Gilmour that's running the show, and I end up playing some bit part. You know something? I was doing this job when she was wearing gym knickers. It makes me sick.' He shook his head.

'Know how you feel, Bob,' Foxy said. 'But she's reading something into all this that just isn't there. I mean, what the hell is she looking at Jack Prentice's death for? What's that got to do with anything? We all loved Jack, but we knew he was going round the twist for months.'

'I know, I know.' Reynolds drained his glass.

Foxy put on his gravest expression. He explained to Reynolds that they had information that Gilmour was planning to run a story about corruption inside the police force. A story that would name himself, Bill and Jack as rotten. Apparently, it was based on a letter written by Jack Prentice before he died. The fact was, it was all a set-up by a rogue cop with an axe to grind against Foxy. He had already been quietly dealt with and moved to a rural police station in the back of beyond, but it was important that this crap didn't come out – for the good of the force. But the story, Foxy emphasised, was absolute rubbish. There were allegations about prostitutes and drugs, and the Big Man. And even some nonsense linking them to the wee hooker that washed up on the shore. All shite.

If Gilmour and the *Post* came out with that story, he said, they'd be fielding off lawsuits from everywhere, especially from him. Bob would be doing his editor a favour if he warned Gilmour off. The editor would be grateful in the long run. Reynolds seemed delighted to get this much information. He promised he'd sort it for them. He'd lean on Gilmour, tell her the story was a set-up. That would probably be enough for her to have doubts about it. Her ego was too big to be brought down by something that wasn't watertight.

Foxy stood up.

'Right, Bob. So let's see how it goes. That's all we can do. But the story is just a farce, Bob. A total farce. Mind you, we would get the last laugh if the *Post* printed it because one thing's for sure: that wee bitch Gilmour would be out of our hair for good.'

They all guffawed.

'Might be worth just letting her go with it,' Bill said, as Foxy shook Reynolds by the hand and slapped him on the back.

'Don't you worry, Bob, you're still the kiddo up here. You'll always be welcome here. The only man we can trust, eh, Bill?'

'Absolutely,' Bill said.

Foxy walked Reynolds to the door with his arm around his shoulder.

'Right, Foxy. I'll be in touch. You can count on me.' He walked out of the door, and Foxy closed it behind him.

He looked at Bill. 'Prick,' he said.

Across the city, in a smoke-filled basement room, four men sat around the poker table. There was twenty grand in the pot, and Big Jake Cox was almost gleeful as he reached across the table and dragged the hundred-pound bundles towards him. His straight flush had put them all out of the game and it couldn't have felt any better – especially sticking it right up that wanker Tam Ryan, who once took thirty grand off him during a three-day poker game at York races. The silence hung in the air, thick with tension. All four men glanced from one to the other, then all eyes rested on Tam. A slight redness rose in his neck. Then Tam's belly shook a bit as he seemed to simper to himself.

He looked at Jake. 'Fuck me, Jake. You're some fuckin' man. Some fuckin' man.'

Jake chortled. 'You fuckin' better believe I am.' He knocked back the remains of his Jack Daniels and Coke in one.

When the players left, Jake told his minder to wait outside while he made a phone call. He keyed a number into his mobile.

'Bob,' Jake said, when he heard the voice. 'Jake Cox.'

He waited for DI Bob Fletcher to answer. Eventually, he heard a curt hallo.

'Bob? Listen, big man, I'm gonnae make your day.'

Silence.

Jake spoke. 'Call it a wee payback for that cunt Hamilton you never managed to bag for that murder. I know you were never in any doubt what happened, big man. But it had to be done. Big Foxy fixed it for me.'

Silence.

'So, it's like this, Bob. I've got something for you. A wee package. I hear you're now in Internal Affairs, so this will give you a hard-on. You can bury Foxy and Mackie. No need to worry about that dead prick Prentice. Listen: that wee bird that washed up? I've got stuff to give you on it. But I want guarantees, big man. Guarantees.'

Silence. Big Jake looked at his watch. It was ten-thirty.

'If you're as smart as you think you are you'll meet me now,' he said.

'Where?' Fletcher said.

They sat in the corner of the deserted pub next to Jake's club, and the barman brought drinks to their table. Fletcher sipped a straight whisky, and Jake enjoyed watching him, savouring the fact that Fletcher had come running.

'You know it was Foxy who made that knife disappear

in the Dick Hamilton murder case, don't you, Bob?'

Fletcher didn't answer. It had been his first big murder investigation, ten years ago, and he'd been convinced he had Hamilton nailed down for stabbing the young woman who'd fallen to her death from the balcony of the high flats in Petershill.

It had appeared at first to be suicide, but the stab wounds in her chest told a different story. Hamilton, one of Cox's scumbag enforcers, had been seen by a witness running from the building, and a fingertip search of the area by police found the bloodstained knife the following morning. Most of the blood had been wiped off, but there were traces of Hamilton's prints all over it. Gavin Fox was Fletcher's DCI at the time, in charge of the case. He had instructed Fletcher to bring Hamilton in, and charge him with murder, but, by the end of the week, the knife had disappeared from the police station. There had been an inquiry into how a bagged and tagged possible murder weapon that would be used as a production in the trial, could simply disappear. But nobody ever found out.

'He gave it to me,' Jake said. 'Hamilton is an arsehole. No bottle. I couldn't afford to have him standing in the witness box singing like a fucking canary. He knew too much. Of course he was well out of line for killing that wee bird, but I dealt with him myself.'

Hamilton had gone missing after he was released from custody when the Crown Office decided not to prosecute. It was eighteen months later that Spanish police discovered the remains of a dismembered body in a suitcase in the Sierra de Mijas hills, above the sleepy white village of the same name near Malaga on the Costa del Sol. The remains turned out to be Hamilton's.

'That's in the past.' Fletcher looked at his watch. 'What have you got for me, Jake?'

Jake looked hard at him. 'I need a guarantee from you right now, before I tell you anything, that I will be nowhere near this. I'll be in Spain by the time it all kicks off, but I need a guarantee.'

'You've got it. Tell me.'

Jake told him about the trips on Fox's boat, and how he had twice brought hookers for Fox, Prentice and Mackie. He had taken pictures when they were all drunk or coked up – a bit of insurance, he told Fletcher, because if he ever needed to get out, it was always his intention to shop Foxy to save his own skin.

Fletcher listened to the story; his face showed nothing.

'Where's the stuff?'

'You'll get it. Wait for my call.' Jake beckoned the barman and told him to phone his driver.

'You need dropping off somewhere?' Jake grinned at Fletcher.

The DI stood up. 'From you? Aye. Like a fucking hole in the head.' He looked down at Jake who was finishing his drink. 'Phone me.' He turned and left.

CHAPTER THIRTY-TWO

It was almost midnight by the time Rosie typed the final sentence into her laptop. She stabbed the full stop key, sat back in her chair, put her hands behind her head and took a deep breath. She called up on her screen the three articles she had written over the past twenty-four hours, holed up in the flat. There was enough material here to run the scandal of Gavin Fox and his cop cronies over three full days. The revelations in Prentice's suicide note – that they fitted up men who were serving time for crimes they didn't commit – could make a day's coverage in itself. These convictions could now be deemed unsafe, and there would be appeals flying all over the courts. All she had to do now was to let McGuire see the copy before it was shown to the lawyers.

Rosie turned away from her screen and stared out of the window, rubbing her eyes. She took a long gulp of tea from her mug. She was knackered, but there was still a long way to go. The lawyers would baulk at the revelations, but with the photograph of Big Jake on Fox's boat, and Fox in the background, plus the letter from Jack Prentice, the story was copper-bottomed and safe. She couldn't wait to see the look on Fox's face when she door-stepped him with the allegations. McGuire had decided that they would not take the story to the press office in the usual way; that the showdown would be done at Fox's home, with a photographer there on the doorstep to snap him as his bottle crashed. Rosie relished the thought of it. She put a disk into the laptop and burned the three stories onto it, then another disk for a back-up copy in case anything happened to the first. Just because you were paranoid, the hacks used to joke, didn't mean they weren't out to get you. She had already made two extra disks of the photograph and Prentice's letter. They were safely tucked away so that McGuire wasn't the only one who had the material.

She lifted her mobile, intending to call TJ for a chat, when it rang. Reynolds's name came up on the screen. She was immediately on her guard.

'Rosie. Howsit going, darling?' She could hear the sound of traffic. If Reynolds was out and about at this hour he had to be drunk.

'Bob?' Rosie was chirpy. 'Jesus, you're late on the road tonight. Don't tell me they've got you working.'

'No, no, darling.' His voice was slurred. 'I've just been out with a few contacts. You know . . . pressing the flesh.'

'Good.'

'So what's happening, Rosie? You've been missing for a few days. What're you up to? Some secret squirrel mystery?'

Alarm bells went off in Rosie's head. Someone had been talking. Reynolds never phoned her at this time of night. Slimeball was fishing. 'Okay.' Reynolds sounded irritated when she didn't answer. 'Look, doll. No sweat. Anyway, I know what you're doing, and I'll tell you something, Rosie. I'd be right on your side if it was true. But it's not, darling. It's not.'

Either Reynolds was just chancing his arm, or he really knew something.

'Look, Bob,' she said. 'It's midnight and I'm ready to go to bed. What do you mean, you know what I'm working on? Well? So tell me then, smart arse.'

'Foxy,' Reynolds whispered. Rosie could hear him breathing.

Shit.

'Foxy?' She tried to sound surprised.

'Oh come on now, Rosie. You know. Gavin Fox, the chief super. It's me you're talking to, Rosie. Don't come the wide-eyed bird with me.'

'Reynolds. Words like fuck and off are coming into my head.' She tried to keep calm.

'Come on, Rosie. I'm your mate.'

'Bob, listen. I don't know what you're talking about. You're obviously half-pissed so I'm not going to waste my time. I'm going to hang up now.'

She waited.

'You've been set up,' Reynolds blurted out. 'The whole thing's a set-up. That letter from Prentice. It was all a set-up, I know who did it.'

Silence. How did he know about the letter? How could he have known? It couldn't be a set-up. The picture said it all.

'Everything was a set-up, Rosie.' Reynolds said as though he was reading her mind.

Rosie felt light-headed. She took a deep breath.

'Reynolds. What the hell are you on about? Listen, I've no time to talk to you.'

'Rosie,' he persisted, 'listen, darling. I admire and respect you all the way, but you're wrong on this one. You're sticking your neck out and it'll ruin you. Rest assured, you're making a big mistake.'

She snapped. 'Reynolds! That sounds like a fucking threat!'

'No, Rosie, not a threat. I'm telling you. I'm doing you a good turn. You've been set up.' The phone clicked.

Rosie stood looking at her phone. Her first instinct was to call McGuire, but she stopped herself. She sat down on the sofa and tried to put Reynold's call into perspective. He had obviously been got at by Fox, and the ploy was to create doubt in her mind. Could the whole thing really be a fake? Even the picture? Perhaps they had been set up by some prostitutes to extort cash from the cops. Or perhaps the hookers had been sent there by some gangster so that he would always have something on Foxy. Jesus. Maybe Prentice's suicide note to his daughter wasn't even written by him, but she immediately dismissed that. Alison would have recognised his handwriting, unless someone else had gone to elaborate lengths to make it look like Prentice's.

She wondered how Fox found out that it was she who was doing the investigation . . . Perhaps Mags had blabbed to another hooker before she was killed – prostitutes were notorious for being unable to keep secrets, and many of them were used by police for information. The only other person who knew the details was McGuire, and he was desperate for the story to come out. And TJ, of course, knew, but he was one hundred per cent reliable.

She went over to her desk and opened her laptop again. She called up the stories and put them in the trash and emptied it. Then she took a copy of each of the CDs, including the pictures and the letter, and went into the bathroom with a screwdriver. She levered off the bath panel and hid the CDs behind it, then replaced it so it looked like it had never been disturbed. She wanted to talk to TJ, but decided it was too late. Tomorrow she had to see McGuire with the story and get everything ready for the lawyers. She was tired but she knew now she wouldn't sleep. She poured herself a large glass of red wine and ran a bath.

She was in a fairground at night, clutching the strong hand of a tall man with tousled black hair. Her mother took her other hand, and smiled at Rosie the way she did when she was happy, her eyes wide and shining. She was dressed in the lime-green print dress with the roses splashed along the bottom. The pattern seemed to dance as her mother sashayed along, proud with her family. Rosie was always afraid in fairgrounds, especially at night, with the din of the rides and the flashing lights. But she was safe in the grip of her father's strong hand. She was eating candy floss, and her mother leaned over and wiped the side of her cheek with a handkerchief. Everyone seemed to be laughing.

They went into the hall of mirrors and suddenly they were all shapes and sizes. Rosie's father looked squashed like a midget. Her mother guffawed when she caught her image all lanky in another mirror. Everywhere they walked in the hall, their faces were a different shape. Rosie could hear the sound of her father giggling, and shouting to her mother to come and look at him. But Rosie felt afraid in the eerie corridors. Suddenly, she looked around and she couldn't see them any more. She ran along the narrow, dark hall and came to a small corridor. When she turned into it, she could see her father and mother's image in a mirror at the end. They were smiling at her. Rosie was shouting, 'Where are you, Mum? Dad?' But they just kept on smiling. No matter where she looked she only saw herself in the mirror. Dozens of different images of her, there was nobody else. Then she heard a phone ringing and ringing, and she was back in the house looking up at her mother's body hanging from the rope. The phone rang and rang, but she couldn't answer it.

Rosie was drenched in sweat when she awoke to the sound of her own phone ringing. She reached out to her bedside table and lifted the receiver, still not sure if she was dreaming.

'Rosie,' the voice said. 'It's Matt.'

She looked at the clock on the table. It was eight o'clock. She had been sleeping for nearly seven hours.

'Matt?' Rosie was surprised to hear him. 'What's up?'

'Rosie. I've just been listening to the news on the radio. It says two wee girls have gone missing from that children's home. From Woodbank.'

'Jesus!' Rosie sat up. 'Christ, Matt. Did they say any names?'

'No, no names. Just that they've been missing since last night.'

'Okay. Thanks, Matt. I'm just getting organised. I'll see you in the office.'

On the drive from the flat, Rosie had the radio on waiting for the news bulletin, but she didn't need to hear the names. She knew it would be Trina and Gemma. When she came into the office, she called up the news wires on her screens. The names Gemma Gillick and Trina Houston flashed on the story of the massive police search. Rosie sat back in her chair, trying not to catch Reynolds's eye. She buzzed through to McGuire's secretary and asked to see him urgently.

'Rosie,' McGuire breezed, as she went into his office. 'The very woman. Did you get your copy done yesterday? I'm itching to get my hands on it.'

'I did.' She handed over the CD and sat on the sofa.

'A CD? Why not send it to my private email in the usual way?'

'Too dodgy, Mick. The tighter we keep this the better.' She was about to tell him about the phone call from Reynolds last night, but thought it best to let him know that the girls were missing.

'Listen, Mick,' Rosie said, swallowing. 'There's a problem.'

He looked up from his computer, where he had been trying to insert the disk.

'I hate it when you say it like that, Rosie.' His eyes narrowed.

'Those two wee girls on the paedophile story? They've gone missing from the children's home.'

'Fuck me!' McGuire sank back in his chair. 'Jesus, Rosie. There was a line on the radio this morning as I was driving in, and it did cross my mind. Do you know any more?'

'Don't know exactly, just a couple of lines on the wires, but there's a big search for them. Shit, Mick. What if something's happened to them?'

He ran his hand across his chin, anxious. 'Did you give your name at the desk when you went to see them? Tell me you didn't give your own name, Rosie?'

She told him the false name she'd given.

'Thank Christ,' he said. 'The law would've hung you out to dry for that.'

Rosie was irritated. Two girls were missing and all he was worried about was how it affected him and his paper.

'Don't worry.' Her face burned. 'If I'm in the shit, Mick, I'll make sure that I tell them you didn't know anything about it. Which is true, anyway.'

McGuire softened. 'Look, Rosie, I'm sorry. Listen, of course I wouldn't let you hang out to dry. I was just trying to look a few steps ahead, that's all.'

Rosie looked away from him. 'Yeah, sure, Mick.'

'Well.' He stood up and began to pace. 'The thing is,

we're in possession of information that could have something to do with the girls' disappearance.'

'I know. But my main worry at the moment, Mick, is what has happened to these kids. I mean, what if they've been abducted or something? Or worse?'

McGuire looked intently at her. 'We can't tell the cops anything,' he said. 'Not just yet. Let's give it twenty-four hours.'

'But what if something happens to them?'

McGuire bit the inside of his cheek. 'Shit, Rosie. I don't know. I just don't know.'

'We have to let the cops know. We have to.'

'Listen,' McGuire said, 'if we tell them anything, we have to tell them everything. Simple as that. And that blows our whole story. I mean, we're not even there yet on the Lord Dawson stuff. Are we?'

Rosie told him about the meeting with Quigley and that he had agreed to wear a wire for evidence. McGuire was surprised, but delighted. She told him that Quigley had agreed to help in return for an escape route before the story was published. McGuire rolled his eyes upwards when she told him that part.

'Shit.' He put both hands on his head as though he was going to tear his hair out. 'We're on the verge of breaking the biggest story this paper has ever seen, and it could all fall apart. Fuck. We're fucked, Rosie.'

'I know.'

'Okay.' McGuire went back to his desk and sat down. 'We have to tell the cops, nothing else for it. The bastards will string us up. We're in for a very bumpy ride, Miss Gilmour.' He grimaced. 'But don't worry, I won't run out on you – unless, of course, I'm going to lose my job.'

'That's what I like to hear.'

Rosie tried to smile, but her heart sank to her boots. As soon as she made the call to the cops everything would be over. Gavin Fox and co. would be down upon her like a ton of bricks because she spoke to children in care. She would be discredited to the point that the story about his web of corruption would be so weakened, it would never be believed. She looked at McGuire. He shrugged sympathetically, but there was nothing more to say.

Rosie's phone rang in her pocket. She fished it out.

'Rosie?' It was Matt. 'I see they've got the wee girls. They're all right.'

'Jesus, Matt. You're kidding! Are you sure? What happened? Where?'

'It's just been on the radio news. They were on a bus to Stirling, and the driver spotted them. Apparently they were going to see one of their mothers in the jail. No other details of where they were from the time they went missing. Silly wee bastards. I need to go now.' He hung up, and Rosie blinked back tears of relief.

'They've found them, Mick. The girls. They're fine. They were going to Cornton Vale. Trina's mum's inside for shoplifting and assault. Jesus! Can you believe it?'

'Oh thank Christ,' McGuire said. 'I could kiss you, Rosie. I could fucking kiss you.'

They both laughed.

'Let's not get carried away.'

'I hope you appreciated how I was going to stand by you,' McGuire said. 'Even prepared to ditch my two big stories for you.'

'Actually,' Rosie said. 'I was only testing your loyalty. To see how far you could be pushed.'

McGuire laughed again and went back to inserting the disk into his computer.

'Right, fantastic. We're back in the driving seat. Now fuck off while I read this crap you've taken a whole day to write.' He waved her away and turned his eyes towards his computer screen.

CHAPTER THIRTY-THREE

'I'll need to get a move on,' Quigley said. 'I usually get a phone call from the boss about four to come and see him, so he can let me know if it's on for the big house.'

'Won't be long now,' Rosie said, fiddling with the tape recorder and microphone. They had been sitting in her car in the East End for nearly half an hour as she tried to fix the wire onto him. She was useless with gadgetry, and though she had used these tiny hidden microphones before, she had always had someone to fit them for her. But with this job there was nobody she could trust enough to help her. She fixed the recorder inside the breast pocket of his jacket, and the tiny microphone was attached behind his lapel. Quigley's hands were shaking, as she showed him how to switch the device on and off when he was ready to record.

'What if he finds it?' Quigley asked.

'Don't worry, there's no chance of that. I mean, why would he suddenly think his janitor is wired up with a tape recorder? Don't worry, Paddy.'

Once it was fitted, Paddy made three trial runs with Rosie talking into the tape, and then seemed more confident. He looked at his watch, then stared out of the window.

'You think I'm a scumbag for what I do, don't you?'

Rosie looked at him. Years of drinking had left his face blotchy and bloated. His eyes were bloodshot and he stank of last night's booze. She wondered at what stage his life had flipped to the miserable existence it was now, or whether it had just been a slow decline.

'What I think or don't think doesn't matter, Paddy,' Rosie said. 'I try to understand. But to be honest, it's hard. I can't say I accept or condone what you do, because I don't. But I'm not in your shoes.' Deep down, though, she didn't want to be breathing the same air as the kind of pond life that was prepared to hand over kids to perverts.

'I'm not a bad man, Rosie. I was just an ordinary guy like the rest of them, working away. It was the drugs. Everything round here is drugs. You always think it won't come to your doorstep, but it does. And when it does, it tears your family apart. You do things that you hate yourself for. You lose who you are, who you once were, just trying to survive it.'

Rosie nodded, but she didn't feel like helping him justify

what he had been doing. She just wanted to get the job done and get him out of her life. She knew that, realistically, she couldn't help people like Quigley. It was all a means to an end. You walked in and out of people's lives. You did the job, zipped it up, then you went home and tried to live your life. But for too long now the script hadn't been working that way for Rosie. It was getting harder and harder for her to distinguish between what was her job and what was her life. In fact, sometimes the job was better than her life. At least it was somewhere for her to go. Maybe she needed a break. She didn't want to hear any more about Paddy's pathetic life. Just tell the story, she said to herself, and move on to next business.

'Don't worry, Paddy. Let's just get this done. You know, the people who you hate for doing this, they'll get their day, Paddy. Believe me. They'll get their day.'

'And me?' he asked. 'What about me?'

'We'll sort you out when the time is right.' She looked straight at him. 'You'll be fine, you have my word on that. Now, call me tonight if there's anything to report, and don't worry. I'll come and see you if there's anything on the tape, and after that you're out of the frame. Okay?'

'I trust you, Rosie,' Quigley said, grabbing her hand. 'I trust you.'

She pulled her hand away and looked beyond him as he got out of the car.

As he made his way down the road towards the children's home, she drove off with his words ringing in her ears.

CHAPTER THIRTY-FOUR

It was the first time Rosie had ever heard TJ open up about his life.

They'd eaten at a restaurant close to St George's Cross. Rosie had asked TJ to come and check her flat with her, since she hadn't been there for nearly a week. Paranoia had set in after what Alison had told her about the break-in at her place in Edinburgh, and after her conversation with Reynolds, Rosie was worried that she was being watched. When they met up at the restaurant, she gave TJ the lowdown on the investigation over the last few days. He shook his head when she told him they had Quigley wired up to tape his boss. Almost a bottle of wine down, Rosie was feeling more relaxed than she had been for weeks. She wasn't prepared to listen to TJ's predictions that none of the stories would see the light of day.

'Come on.' Rosie took one of his cigarettes. 'Let's talk

about something else. Tell me about Havana, TJ. You're always a bit mysterious about that. Come on.'

TJ lit her cigarette, saying, 'It's a long story. You don't want to hear all that.' He looked beyond her out into the street.

'I'm not going anywhere,' Rosie said.

To her surprise, he took a sip or two of his wine, lit himself a cigarette and began talking. He said he had never meant to fall in love. For most of his life he had managed to navigate his way around relationships with women all over the world, pursuing his own agenda of having fun with no ties. As a musician that was easy. Why settle into one relationship when he could have a different woman every night in a different town? More often than not, he did.

'When I went to Havana, everything changed.' TJ ran his fingers through his hair.

'You fell in love?' Rosie said. 'You met someone?'

'You sure you want me to tell you?' Their eyes met.

'If you're okay with it, TJ.'

He had gone to Havana, to Cuba, with his best friend, who he'd been living with in New York for the past couple of years. His friend played trumpet, and with TJ's sax, they had no trouble getting work in the bars in Havana. The city was awesome, with tourists from all over the world, and the beautiful Havana girls.

'We were just a couple of crazy musicians living the wildest life you could imagine. It was brilliant. We loved our music, the Cubans loved us. It was so good to be a part of something that was like stepping back fifty years. Everything was different in Havana. It gets inside you.' He sighed.

'Then it all changed the night a beautiful creature called Martina walked into this smoky little bar where we were playing. His dark eyes were fixed on Rosie. 'Love at first sight, Rosie. It's for eejits, right? A fairy story – or so I thought. But that's what happened. I fell like a ton of bricks.'

Martina was fifteen years younger than he and initially had shown no interest in him. But TJ pursued her, and within weeks she was sharing his apartment in the heart of the city. He guessed that part of it may have been to get away from the ramshackle home she shared with her mother and two brothers, but he didn't care. He could have looked at her all day and she was devoted to him. When he awoke in the mornings, she was watching him, like a puppy. She said she liked to look at him sleeping, wait for him to wake up to share her day. Nothing had ever felt like that before.

Rosie split the last of the wine between each of their glasses.

'Then I lost her,' TJ said. 'One ordinary day. In the blink of an eye.' He was silent.

Rosie waited. She thought he was going to cry. 'What

happened, TJ?' She stretched her hand across and touched his fingers.

'Stupid accident,' he said. 'Nothing exotic. It happened right outside my house. She got hit by a car on her way back from the market after buying some food. As soon as I heard the bang and the screams, I just knew. I ran downstairs and into the street, and she was just lying there. Her face was white, her eyes open, and there wasn't even a lot of blood. The driver was screaming and weeping that it wasn't his fault, that she stepped out in front of him. But Martina was still alive . . .'

Rosie brushed the back of her hand on his cheek.

'I knelt down and held her in my arms until the ambulance came. It took ages. I could see blood trickling from her ear . . . She was whispering my name. She slipped away in my arms.' He closed his eyes and pinched the bridge of his nose with his thumb and forefinger.

'I'm sorry, Rosie. I've never told anyone that before. It happened four years ago.'

They sat in silence, not looking at each other. Eventually, Rosie spoke.

'What happened after that?'

TJ sipped his wine and lit another cigarette. He passed it to Rosie, and sighed. 'What could I do? I had nothing. Nowhere to go. It was the first time in my life that I really wanted something to stay the same, and it didn't.'

'Did you stay in Havana?' Rosie took a draw from the cigarette and handed it back to him.

He nodded. 'Yes. I stayed, because I didn't want to leave. It was as though by leaving I would have left too much behind. It was the strangest feeling. So I stayed for a while, nearly a year, but I knew it couldn't go on. Then I just got up one day, packed my bags, and went to the travel shop and booked a flight to New York. I knew if I went back there, I could get something of my old self back. But you know, Rosie? I never did. So whoever I am now, that's not who I used to be. I play that sax outside O'Brien's every night, and it's like if I keep playing then the pain will go away. Sometimes it works.'

'Well,' Rosie said. 'Whoever you are now, I like you.' She reached across the table and squeezed his hand. 'And now? I mean, how are you now? Is it any easier, TJ?'

She wanted to ask him if he could love like that again, but she was afraid. Her feelings for him had grown strong in these past few weeks. In her arrogance, she had never even considered that he may have loved someone else. Now she sensed that, whatever she was to him, she could never mean as much as Martina had.

He looked into her eyes. 'I don't know, Rosie. Yes, of course it's easier, and I suppose it's something that will get better in time. My life has moved on, but part of me is still with her. A wee bit of me died that day too, so that's why it's hard for me to have relationships.'

She wanted to ask if it had been a mistake for them to go to bed, but supposing his answer was yes?

TJ seemed to be reading her mind.

'Rosie.' He took her hand in his. 'Please don't think that with you it didn't mean anything. Of course it did – of course it does. I do have a lot of feelings for you. Strong feelings. But part of me will always be somewhere else. I felt it was only fair to tell you that, because . . . because I do think I love you, Rosie. Do you understand that?'

Fear and relief flooded through Rosie. Fear because, if you love, you have to make changes to your life. You lose control.

'TJ,' she said. 'I know. Well, I kind of know what you mean. Don't worry. I do have a lot of feelings for you too. I think I've loved you longer than I've even admitted to myself.' She sighed. 'But if I'm honest, the thought scares me because I'm no good at relationships. You may have noticed.' She smiled.

'I noticed,' he said, and smiled back. 'Trouble with you, Rosie, is that you move around so fast. Sometime, you have to think about waiting for your soul to catch up with you. Maybe then you'll see things different.'

Rosie looked at him. Nobody had ever read her so well.

'Yeah. Maybe you're right. But I just don't know what will happen to us, TJ. I do love you, as my friend and as my lover, and I want to be with you – I think. I just don't know if it's right. I'm scared, TJ. It's easier for me if I just keep working, and sticking to relationships that never go anywhere. That way, nobody gets to hurt me.'

TJ sat back and drank his wine, then said, 'Rosie, nobody gets to go through life without falling in love and getting hurt. That's what it's all about. You do it, and you grow from it. You have to understand that.'

'I know,' she said. 'I know.'

They sat in silence until the waiter came over and put the bill on the table. They hadn't noticed that all the other diners had left and the waiters were shuffling around at the bar waiting for them to finish.

'Okay,' TJ said, lifting the bill. 'Enough soul-searching. Let me buy you dinner.'

'Fine.' Rosie finished her wine. 'I'll cook breakfast.'

He smiled, and put his arm around her as they walked out the door and into the cold night air.

As soon as Rosie switched on the light in the living room she knew. Someone had been in the flat. She stood looking around the room for telltale signs.

'What's the matter?' TJ came towards her and ruffled her hair.

'Someone's been in here, TJ. I just know it.'

'But the place looks fine.' He glanced around. 'As far as I can remember being here, though I was pissed at the time.' He leaned over and kissed her neck, slipping his arms around her waist.

'Sssh, TJ.' Rosie eased herself away. 'Honest. Something's up.' She walked over to the computer and pushed the button. It was switched off. She never switched it off. Even when she left last week to stay at the rented flat. She opened one of the drawers in her desk and could see that it had been rifled.

'Look, TJ. My CDs. They're all scattered. Look.' She pointed to the drawer where the CDs were kept. She opened another drawer and papers she had kept for years, nothing important, just private scribblings, had also been moved.

'Look. That stuff's been in there for about two years. I hardly ever go into that drawer but I know where everything is. It's been tampered with, TJ.'

'Are you sure?'

She was absolutely sure. Someone had been looking for the material Alison had given her – as if she would be daft enough to keep in her desk drawer. 'At least whoever it is doesn't seem to know that I've not been living here. My other place is safe. At least I hope so.'

'What do you want to do?' TJ said. 'It's not as if we can call the cops.'

'I know. I don't think there's much we can do, but it gives me the creeps knowing that someone's been here, rifling through my things.' She looked at TJ and went into her bedroom. Nothing looked as though it had been disturbed. She opened her wardrobe. A box at the bottom where she kept old papers had its lid off and the contents jumbled up.

'Look,' she called to TJ. 'They've been in here too. Bastards!'

He came into the bedroom and put his arms around her.

'Listen, Rosie, do you think we should stay here? Maybe we should just get the hell out. Go back to my place.'

Rosie nodded agreement, but as they went back into the living room, there was a loud knock at the door. They looked at each other. Rosie's stomach turned over. 'Shit!' she said.

TJ put his fingers to his lips. 'Sssh.'

The door was knocked again, louder, as though a fist was slamming against it. Rosie walked towards the door and looked through the spyhole. She saw officers in uniform, standing behind two plain-clothes men.

'Cops,' she turned and mouthed to TJ.

'Who's there?' she called out. 'Who is it?'

'Police. Open up, please.'

'Jesus! What do they want?' she whispered to TJ.

'Open up, please, Miss Gilmour?'

Rosie took off the chain and opened the door. A man in a black raincoat stuck his foot in the door. He showed her his warrant card with the name Detective Inspector McIver.

'Rosemary Gilmour,' he said. 'We have a search warrant for your home. We have received information that you are in possession of a quantity of drugs.'

His plain-clothes colleague stepped inside.

She was being set up. She hadn't been through every drawer in the house, but she could guarantee that when they did, they would find the cocaine that had been planted by whoever had broken into her house. She stood aside to let them in. The two uniformed officers came in after them. One was a WPC with a face like flint. She gave Rosie a sour look. All four walked past her down the hall.

'Wait a minute,' Rosie said. 'What the hell's going on here? What do you mean, drugs? I don't do bloody drugs! Anybody knows that.'

'Can I see the warrant?' TJ asked. He gave Rosie a look that told her to simmer down.

'Who are you?' the inspector snapped.

'I'm her friend,' TJ snapped back. 'Just let me see the warrant please?'

McIver looked at his colleague and handed over the piece of paper. Rosie tried to read it along with TJ, but it was just a blur. She couldn't concentrate.

'Okay?' the inspector said. 'It's all in order. Now if the two of you remain here, we will get on with our job.' He turned to his partner. 'Alex, you take the kitchen.'

Rosie stood fuming as DI McIver began opening the drawers of her computer desk and rifling through them, scattering the contents onto the floor. He pulled the bottom two drawers out and emptied them out. At the bookshelf, he pushed books aside carelessly, knocking some to the floor. A glass ornament Rosie had picked up on a trip to Rome fell on the floor and smashed.

'Watch what you're fucking doing!' Rosie was across the room. TJ pulled her back. She fought hard to keep back tears of rage.

The inspector walked around the living room, then into the hall and pushed open the door of her bedroom, Rosie and TJ following. He pulled out the drawers of her bedside cabinets and rifled through a chest of drawers. Rosie stood watching, biting her lip. He stuffed his hand to the back of a drawer, and kept it there for a moment. Then he turned to look at them. He pulled out a small clear plastic bag. All she'd ever kept in that drawer were swimsuits. The inspector had a smug expression on his face as he turned and looked at Rosie, holding up the bag of white powder.

Suddenly her legs went weak. It was over. The whole investigation. Of course, it had crossed her mind that they might pull a stunt like this, but she never really believed they would. The inspector shouted for his colleague to come through.

Rosie turned to TJ. 'I knew something had happened as soon as I walked in the door. It's been planted. Shit, TJ.'

He held her close and whispered into her hair.

'Look, Rosie. Sssh. Don't say a single word. Nothing at all.'

McIver put his 'find' into an evidence bag, tagged it, and handed it to the other cop. Then he turned to Rosie and read her her rights.

She gritted her teeth. Bastards! She would die on the floor before she would burst into tears in front of these arseholes.

'Come on. Let's go, Miss Gilmour. You're in custody until the court in the morning.' The WPC moved toward her. Rosie stepped back.

'I have to make a phone call to my editor,' Rosie said.

The inspector looked at his colleague and shrugged.

Rosie went into the living room, TJ behind her, and pulled her mobile out of her bag. Her hands were shaking so much she could hardly get McGuire's name up on the consul. She pleaded under her breath for him to answer.

'Gilmour?' McGuire sounded as though he was in a bar. 'I'm out for dinner. What's up?'

'Mick,' Rosie said, her voice shaking. 'I'm at my own flat. The cops have come in here and found cocaine in my drawer.'

'What?' Mick said. 'Cocaine? Fuck me!'

'Christ, Mick! It's not mine! I came back tonight and I knew someone had been here because stuff had been disturbed. Suddenly the cops came and found this shit in my drawer.' She was trying not to break down. 'I swear to God, Mick, it's not mine. It's been planted. I've been set up.'

Silence at the other end of the phone. He doesn't believe me, she thought. Then he spoke.

'Right,' McGuire said. 'Okay, Rosie. Don't panic. Where are they taking you to?'

She turned and asked the inspector which station, and he told her it would be Central. She told McGuire.

'Right. Don't you worry, Rosie, the fuckers will not get away with this. You better believe they won't. Listen to me, don't say a word. Just go down there with them and keep your mouth shut. I'll get the lawyer straight down to you. Don't worry, darling.'

Rosie couldn't speak for a moment. She took a deep breath.

'Okay, Mick. Thanks. I won't. Thanks.'

'Chin up, Gilmour.' The line went dead.

CHAPTER THIRTY-FIVE

Rosie sat on the edge of the bed in the police cell, chilled to the bone. The mixture of nerves and the booze wearing off made her feel nauseous. She had been left here for nearly an hour since she had been formally charged at the bar. They did the full humiliation job, fingerprints and mugshot. Just imagine if you were actually guilty, Rosie thought. She knew this was a scam organised by Fox to wreck her credibility, and he would get away with it because cocaine was actually found in her home. That would be enough evidence to take to the Procurator Fiscal. Whether he pursued it to court was another matter, but the damage was done. The newspapers would already have been tipped off.

She could visualise the headlines in tomorrow's papers: 'TOP JOURNO ON COKE RAP'. The *Post*'s enemies in the tabloid world would have a field day. Rosie was not everyone's favourite journalist – she had pulled the rug from beneath the feet of enough rivals to have made some enemies. But people who really knew her would never believe she was involved in drugs. She had written exposés before about drug dealers and was hated by them. She was certain she would be cleared of any drug charges, but none of that changed the dilemma of the moment. If there was doubt about her credibility, it would be impossible for the *Post* to publish revelations about police corruption. She took comfort from the fact that they had a full testament from Jack Prentice, as well as a photograph. If it had been a set-up, as Reynolds had warned, Foxy wouldn't have bothered to plant the coke in her flat, he would have let her make a fool of herself. She began to feel better. Planting the coke was an admission of guilt.

She looked at her watch. Suddenly she remembered Quigley. He could be phoning her any time to let her know about the tape. She was glad that TJ had her mobile. The cops had told him there was no point in coming to the police station until the morning. He had kissed Rosie on the lips as she left the flat with the cops. She was beginning to feel edgy. She had to get out of here to talk to Quigley. She knew he wouldn't speak to anyone else, and the state his nerves were in, he was likely to do a runner. She looked at her watch again. Come on, McGuire, come *on* . . . Time was running out. She put her head in her hands.

'You must have upset somebody pretty high up, Gilmour?' It was the smiling face of Tommy Hanlon, the young hotshot lawyer for the *Post*.

Rosie looked up. 'You bet,' she said.

Hanlon came in and shook her hand.

'Christ almighty, Rosie.' He kissed her on the cheek. 'What the fuck's going on?'

Very quickly, she told him what had happened, from when she left the restaurant with TJ until the police arrived at her flat. He told her McGuire had given him information that the *Post* was about to expose Gavin Fox.

'Don't worry,' Hanlon said, 'it's being kept really tight. Christ, I hope you get to turn over that bastard Fox, Rosie. I really do. But this is a big setback, legally. You do know that, don't you.'

Rosie nodded. She loved Hanlon. His sunny disposition never changed, whether he had just walked out of court having got someone off a murder charge, or a hoodlum had been sent down for fifteen years. It was all a game. Whoever has the quickest brain and the best line in bullshit wins hands down every time, he would say. And there was nobody better than Hanlon. He was one of the highest-paid criminal lawyers in the business, but there were no airs and graces about him. His charm made him as much at ease with punters in a pub as he was with top lawyers or politicians.

He and Rosie were old friends, although sometimes at loggerheads. He had 'legalled' some of Rosie's most controversial stories and he knew she would fight tooth and nail to get every last detail in the paper. Often he would have to stand his ground and cut out the juiciest parts in order to save the newspaper from a lawsuit.

'C'mon,' he said. 'I'll make sure they send you down a good curry and a bottle of decent wine.'

'Piss off,' Rosie said, trying to smile. 'Can you get me out of here tonight?'

'Course I can, but they want to talk to you first. That big inspector, McIver, Christ, he's a mean bastard. I've come across him before. You should think yourself lucky you've got no broken ribs. Most of my clients fall down the stairs every time he's in charge of them.'

'What happens now?' Just having Hanlon here lifted her spirits.

'We're going for an interview,' he said. 'They'll try to interrogate you, but you say absolutely nothing, okay? Just take your cue from me, Rosie.'

'Okay. Then what?'

'Well . . .' Hanlon straightened his tie and smoothed his hair. 'With a bit of luck, they'll let you go, and they'll send a report to the Fiscal. But if it all goes pear-shaped, they'll keep you here all night and you'll be up with the custodies in the morning. That's what they'll want to do. Let's hope that doesn't happen.'

'Aw please, Tommy,' Rosie said. 'Please don't let that happen. The papers will have their fill of it as it is.'

'I know,' he said. 'They're outside. That wee fat bastard from the *Sun*, and the *Mail* is here as well. Cops must have tipped them off. Obviously all part of the plan. But don't worry, Rosie, that'll all look great in the final story. No sweat. Just trust me. I'm a lawyer,' he grinned.

The cell door opened and the DI appeared, along with a woman detective. Rosie was surprised when she smiled at her. The inspector nodded grudgingly in Hanlon's direction. He told them to follow him, that they were going to have a little chat. Hanlon winked at Rosie as she stood up and walked out of the cell behind McIver, and glanced at her before they went into the interview room, putting a finger to his lips.

She and Hanlon sat at one side of a table and the inspector and the woman sat opposite. Rosie looked at the depressingly grim green walls. She took a deep breath. She still felt sick.

'Right, Miss Gilmour.' The inspector shuffled papers on the table. 'You know what you have been charged with. Now we want just to have a chat about the substance found in your flat. Understand?'

Rosie said nothing. She could feel the woman detective staring at her. Hold your nerve, she kept telling herself.

'Where did you get it, Miss Gilmour? The cocaine. Where did you get it?'

Still Rosie said nothing. McIver leaned forward.

'It would be in your interests to give us some information,' he said. 'You wouldn't be the first hack to do the odd line of coke, and you'll not be the last. You guys can do what the hell you like. Me? I'm only interested in where you're getting the stuff. That's all. You can do yourself a lot of good, just by throwing me one name.'

Rosie bit her lip. She wanted to throw him a name, all right – three names, actually – Gavin Fox, Bill Mackie and Jack Prentice. She wondered if he knew everything that was going on, or if he really was just acting on the information about the drugs. She suspected he knew. Her face burned with rage.

Hanlon detected her tension. 'Inspector McIver,' he said. 'My client has nothing to say. She will not be making any comment whatsoever. Not on any of the matters you ask her about. So I trust this interview is over. I would like to take my client home now and wait for the due process of the law to take its course.'

The inspector took a deep breath and let it out slowly. He held the pen in his hand so tight that his knuckles were white. The woman detective looked at Rosie, then at Hanlon, then at the desk. Rosie wondered if she believed any of this. She had a look about her that distrusted the process going on here. Perhaps she had fallen foul of Foxy herself . . . He did have a reputation for using ambitious young policewomen for his own ends, then dumping them.

'It may not be possible to release Miss Gilmour tonight. We're taking advice at the moment. She may have to be in court tomorrow.' He looked as though he hoped so.

'Well,' Hanlon said. 'We shall just have to wait and see. But on my advice my client will not be making any statement.'

They sat in silence. Rosie could hear the minute hand ticking on the wall clock. The door handle turned and the door opened a little. A young WPC stuck her head round and beckoned to the inspector. He went out. Rosie and Hanlon looked at each other.

'Tough time,' the woman detective said to Rosie once he had left. 'I've read a lot of your articles. I like what you do.'

'Thanks,' Rosie said, surprised. 'I appreciate that. Not many cops like what I do.'

The detective raised her eyebrows. 'Only the bad ones don't,' she said.

The door opened and McIver came in with his face like fizz.

'You can go,' he said to Rosie. 'A report is being prepared

for the Procurator Fiscal. You're lucky, Miss Gilmour. You must have friends in high places.'

'No.' Rosie stood up. 'Only in low places. It's enemies I have in high places.' She walked past him and out of the door, Hanlon holding her arm.

'Don't push it, Gilmour,' he said, ushering her down the corridor.

As they walked towards the door, they could see press photgraphers and reporters outside. Rosie knew most of them and realised there was nothing they could do. It could have been her standing there.

'Don't smile,' Hanlon said.

Rosie looked at him. 'Like I've got something to smile about?'

She kept her face straight and her head down as they headed towards Hanlon's Jaguar. Cameras flashed as she crossed the car park.

'What's going on, Rosie?' Tim Clarke from the *Sun* shouted. 'Are you on a drugs charge? Coke?'

Rosie said nothing and got into Hanlon's car.

'I'd love to get out and punch that bastard's lights out,' she said.

'You know, Gilmour,' Hanlon said, 'you should get McGuire to make you the diplomatic correspondent. Your talents are wasted in the gutter.'

CHAPTER THIRTY-SIX

Rosie was praying that Quigley would turn up. He'd sounded so edgy on the phone that she'd had to drop everything to go and meet him immediately. She had been sitting in McGuire's office with Hanlon, going over the events of the night before, when the call came through on her mobile.

On the way to the East End, Rosie reflected on how bullish McGuire had been over the fact of her arrest. He was certain it was a set-up and it further strengthened his resolve to get the story in the paper. He told her that he had actually been in the company of the divisional commander of Glasgow Central police station when Rosie's call came that she had been arrested. McGuire said he had hinted to the commander that he believed his reporter was being set up because of an investigation into a top policeman, and it was the commander who mentioned the name Gavin Fox. He said he'd heard on the grapevine that Fox was about to come a cropper, and he wasn't sorry. They had been enemies for a long time. He had wished McGuire well with his investigation, and told him he'd be in touch in the next few days, then he made the phone call to his division to get Rosie released. Rosie had told McGuire it was lucky he was in the right place at the right time. He replied that you make your own luck. He had read Rosie's copy and was planning three days of revelations. He was as buoyed up as she had seen him in a long time, and she was even more keen now to get the story out.

She had woken up this morning to headlines in the newspapers that she was facing drugs charges. The broadsheets were fairly matter of fact about it, but the *Post*'s two rival tabloids had a field day. Her picture was on the front page, leaving the police station with Hanlon. TJ had tried to make light of the picture when he'd brought the newspapers into her bedroom earlier, but Rosie was fuming. She had gone back to her secret flat after she was released by the police, and phoned TJ to come and join her. She fell into his arms when he arrived. They drank a bottle of wine and TJ took her to bed. It had been a very long day and she had barely slept, but she was fired on adrenalin.

Rosie was relieved when she saw the shabby figure of Quigley coming towards her car. He was breathing hard as he opened the door and sat down beside her.

'I've got it.' His hands were shaking. Rosie could smell alcohol on his breath.

'Have you listened to it?' she asked, as he handed her the tape recorder and microphone.

'No. I was scared in case I pressed the wrong button and scrubbed it. I just spoke to him in his office an hour ago and as soon as I got what you wanted I left and phoned you. I went for a quick drink first because I was shitting myself.'

Rosie prayed that the tape had worked. She put in the earpiece and rewound the tape. It was perfect. Quigley even had the sense to say 'Mr Davidson', when he was talking to his boss so that the man was identified. The conversation was clear as a bell, and Davidson had hung himself out to dry. He told Quigley there was a meeting planned for Lord Dawson's house later that night, and to organise some of the kids. Jesus, Rosie thought. He even named the judge. He said to make sure there were no problems, and not to pick any kids that were whingers. And even more damning, he also said that he would be talking to him next week about another location. Some of the men at the big house wanted to have something at another place. It was to do with filming, but he would be told nearer the time. It might mean more money, Davidson had said.

Rosie was ecstatic. She felt like doing a lap of honour round the car. The tape was pretty damning evidence to have as part of the investigation. It might not guarantee the story would make it into the newspaper, but the lawyers would certainly feel a little more comfortable. She knew they weren't ready to publish just yet though. She still had work to do. McGuire might want them to photograph the kids one more time, leaving the children's home again to show they went to the judge's house not just once but at least twice. With the taped evidence, and Quigley's own evidence when they first met, she knew they were nearly there.

The big problem would be when they put it to the judge, and any of the others they identified, that the newspaper was about to expose them. Then pressure would be brought to bear from the very top level. That was when Rosie might lose control of the whole story . . .

She enquired how Gemma and Trina had been since they'd gone missing, pretending to Quigley that she was only interested because it had been a news story. Quigley smiled.

'You know, the wee buggers had everyone in a flap,' he said. 'Nobody could believe it. It was obviously that Trina's idea to slip out and go to Stirling. It's her ma that's in the jail. I mean, that wee girl Gemma would have never thought of anything like that. She's a great wee kid. Her ma was a prostitute, you know, and she got done over.'

'I know.' Rosie decided to say no more than that. 'But how are the girls?'

'They're all right. They think they're celebrities because their pictures were in the evening paper and on the telly, but they're keeping a real watch on them now.'

Rosie wanted to say that it seemed a bit late to keep a watch on them, but it was best to leave it alone, quit while she was ahead.

'So what happens now?' Quigley asked. 'I mean, you said I would get away before it went in the paper.'

Rosie looked at him, then out of the window.

'I know. But we're not there yet, Paddy. I'll let you know before it all kicks off. You have to trust me on that.'

'Okay,' he said. 'I better go.'

He shook her hand and left the car, walking fast across the road and into the nearest pub. Rosie sighed, then played the tape again. She started up the engine and turned the car around, heading back to the office. McGuire would be delighted, but she knew he would also be worried. The cages they were about to rattle contained more dangerous and powerful animals than the head of the CID.

CHAPTER THIRTY-SEVEN

Rosie was awakened by the aroma of fresh coffee, and she stretched luxuriously in TJ's bed. She blinked against the sun streaming through the window. She sat up and looked at her watch. It was already nine and she had to be at McGuire's office by ten for a session with Hanlon and the boss of the law firm that the newspaper retained at huge expense. The lawyers would explain what would happen in the coming weeks if the cocaine charges were pursued by the Procurator Fiscal. Then they would go through the Gavin Fox investigation line by line.

The lawyers had had Rosie's copy since yesterday, and Hanlon had already been on the phone asking her specific questions. She was pleased that he seemed positive. It was looking good, he said, but the lawyers were being typically cautious, asking if there was more back-up that would nail Fox and his cohorts to the wall. They were told that everything they had was there. It was now their call and, ultimately, McGuire's.

Over dinner the previous evening, Rosie thought she had detected a reticence in TJ. He had seemed quieter, preoccupied. She'd wondered if he was about to tell her it was all over, but by the time they finished dinner he was back to normal. When they went to bed they made love for longer than ever before, and fell asleep exhausted in each other's arms.

'Morning, darling.' Rosie came into the lounge where TJ was sitting on the sofa, drinking coffee. She was wearing his blue bathrobe and rubbing her hair with a towel.

'You look good enough to eat.' He stroked her leg and she ruffled his hair as she walked past him to the kitchen.

'Any time.' She fetched a mug of coffee and sat beside him.

They drank in silence. Something wasn't right. Rosie glanced at TJ. He looked pensive. She got up and went into the bedroom to get dressed.

'I'd best be going soon,' she said, as she came back in, fully dressed. 'I've got to meet McGuire at ten. Could be a long day.'

TJ looked up at her and nodded his head.

'Sit down, Rosie. I want to talk to you.'

So she had been right last night. Something *was* wrong.

She sat down. She felt her mouth go dry and took a sip of her coffee.

'Rosie.' TJ sat forward and turned his body so he was facing her. He ran his hand through his hair. Rosie looked at the grey flecks, like silver in the sunshine. She loved them.

'Rosie.' He looked nervous. She'd never seen him like that. 'Listen. There's no easy way to say this, sweetheart, but I'm going away.'

Her stomach fell. He was leaving her? She hadn't even seen it coming.

'Away?' It was all she could say.

He took a deep breath. 'Yes,' he said. 'I want to go away from here, Rosie. This whole place. I don't mean you. Of course not. The problem is, I want to be with you. I really do. But not like this.'

Rosie was confused. She swallowed hard. She didn't know what to say.

'These past few weeks . . .' TJ said. 'No, not just these weeks, I mean months, for a long time – even before we got involved like this – I've had real feelings for you. Feelings I didn't think I would ever have again. And then, when we're together, like last night, I feel that I really want that, to be with you. But not here. I just don't think you've got any room for me here.' He kept looking at her.

She didn't want to lose him. She had better say something quick.

'Course I've got room for you, TJ,' she said, but her eyes flicked a glance at her watch. She saw him noticing and cursed herself.

'See what I mean?' TJ threw his hands in the air. 'You're looking at your watch. You're already somewhere else.'

'Sorry.' Rosie was sheepish. 'I'm not, TJ, I'm listening. It's just a reflex action with me.' She smiled, trying to make light of it. 'Come on . . . Of course I've got room for you, I love being with you – I want to be with you.' She touched his hand. 'More than you know.'

'But Rosie,' he said, 'how can you ever get away from all this stuff? This job? It's eating you up. I don't think you can ever be anything to anyone unless you pull back from that.'

Rosie sighed. She had to make him understand.

'Look, TJ.' Her voice was pleading. 'I can't just give up work. I can't. What am I going to live on? And anyhow, I like it, it drives me.'

She knew he was right. For too long the job had devoured her life and she had allowed herself to be devoured. There had been no need for anyone else. But now it was different.

'Yes,' TJ replied. 'I know it's important, but what about your life? What about doing some other kind of journalism? A freelance, or a travel writer. Anything. You could work anywhere in the world. You could write books. Just get away from this shit that's pulling you down. You have to develop as a human being. You're not just a journalist, that's just your job. It's not who you are.'

She resisted the urge to look at her watch again. She knew it must be getting close to ten, but she daren't mention it.

'Please, TJ, don't go into all that soul stuff again. Believe me, I know you're right. The other night when you told me about the way I run away from myself, I felt so close to you because nobody had ever seen me so clearly before. You were right, but I just don't know if I'm ready to wait for my soul to catch up. How am I going to know, TJ? Tell me that. You're sure of things, sure of yourself. I'm not. How am I going to know when I'm ready to stop all this?'

TJ took her face in his hands and looked into her eyes.

'You're not going to know, Rosie. You're not going to be sure. That's the whole point. You have to be prepared to take a chance. Are you prepared to take it?' He let go of her face, but kept his eyes on her.

Rosie said nothing. She didn't know if she could take a chance, but there and then she wanted it more than anything.

'You'll be late for work,' he said. 'You'd better go, Rosie.'

She leaned over and kissed him on the lips. He kissed her briefly, then turned away.

'Don't be like that,' she said, trying to lighten the mood. 'Come on, TJ. Let me get this stuff out of the way first. Give me some time. Please . . . ?'

He nodded, but said, 'I'm going away, Rosie. Maybe Cuba, maybe New York. I want you to come with me. Think about it.'

Rosie stood up. Jesus. Right now, the idea seemed impossible.

'I'll call you tonight,' she said, turning back to him at the door.

'Sure,' TJ said, not looking at her.

She closed the door quietly behind her.

CHAPTER THIRTY-EIGHT

The Big Man was not happy. He had been ranting for half an hour and his face was flushed. Foxy had called Jake Cox on his private mobile and told him they had to talk. Jake said he was too busy to see him, but Foxy insisted that it wouldn't wait and Jake had to postpone his poker game for nearly two hours.

Now Foxy sat on the red leather sofa in Jake's tacky office on the top floor of the nightclub he owned. He hated having to lower himself by coming here, but Jake had said there was no option. Foxy knew the Big Man loved to feel he had power over you. Useless bastard! He stayed sitting behind his desk so that he was talking at Foxy as though the cop was one of his minions who had messed up a drug deal. Foxy watched Jake's mind turning over all the possibilities of what might happen.

'This is not good, Foxy,' Jake said, toying with the cigar

in his fingers. 'I mean, if this shit gets in the papers, hell will break loose. Cops investigating cops . . . We've seen that before, but this one won't be brushed away. They'll bring some fucker up from the Met or something.'

'I know, Jake.' He squirmed in his seat. Bastard was talking down to him.

'You see the thing is,' Jake said, 'I don't want to fall out with you, Foxy. You're my mate. Solid. But to tell you the truth, I blame you for letting this go so far.'

Foxy was startled. He sat forward. 'What? Christ, Jake, how can it be my fault?'

Jake blew smoke across his desk. 'Well,' he said. 'You shouldn't have given me so much grief for getting that wee whore done over, then I wouldn't have told my boys to lighten up when they were dealing with that fucker Prentice's nutcase daughter.'

Foxy sighed. He had worried that Jake might pull something like this, but before he could reply, Jake carried on.

'I mean, my boys actually saw that lassie with the reporter. They actually saw her in the car after they were in the cafe, and they saw her handing over something to the reporter. What's her name? That Gilmour bird. They should have fucking gone in there straight away and beat the shit out of the two of them. At least we would have the fucking material in front of us, instead of it sitting in the fucking office of the editor of the fucking *Post*. But no. My boys hung back. Then when they caught up with the bitch, she had some big fucking Lurch guy protecting her. Stabbed one of my boys, you know.' He snorted. 'He'll fucking suffer for that – when we find him.'

Foxy tried to reason with him. 'I know, Jake. That was bad, but we don't know that Alison didn't take a copy of the stuff. She might have had a copy somewhere else, so moving in and doing people over doesn't mean we wouldn't still be in the shit.'

Jake opened his drawer. He took out a small plastic bag with cocaine in it and emptied some of it carefully onto his desk. Foxy watched as he chopped two lines with his credit card. He snorted one line then sat back, sniffing and wiping his nose.

'Foxy,' he said. 'We're not in the shit, pal. You're in the shit.'

Foxy suddenly felt weak. He was glad he was sitting down.

'No, Jake.' He was flustered. 'What I mean is, that the letter Jack wrote talks about stuff we've done down the years. It mentions your name all through – money changing hands – it's quite damning stuff.'

'Fuck it.' Jake snorted the other line of coke, then grinned. 'It's not as if people think I'm the parish priest. What the hell do I care if they say I'm a gangster? They've been saying it all my life. I don't give a shite.'

Foxy insisted. 'Yes, but if an investigation starts they'll be all over you like a rash. Tax. VAT. Everything.'

Jake shook his head. 'I know. But they'll have to fucking find me first. *And* all my money. Hey, Foxy. You don't think I've been daft enough to keep it in the Post Office, do you?' He chuckled. 'I'm one of the untouchables, pal. Un-fucking-touchable.'

Foxy sighed. He was getting nowhere. Coked up like this, there was no reasoning with Jake, he was just a psycho from the streets, only interested in protecting himself. Foxy had never been naive enough to think it would ever be any other way, if push came to shove, but neither had he imagined that everything in his life would fall apart the way it had at the moment. He could never have imagined that Jack Prentice would have a crisis of conscience and stick them all in before he topped himself. How do you make plans for that kind of crap? He had hoped Jake would be a bit more helpful. He should have known better.

'So,' Jake said, looking at his watch. 'What do you want me to do, Foxy? I can rough the reporter up if you want. Christ, I can shoot her if you want. Fuck, I might even shoot her anyway, but it doesn't look like it will stop anything. So what do you want?'

He didn't know himself what he wanted. He had talked to Bill Mackie about what they would do if the story came out. They had even talked about disappearing . . .

'So?' Jake looked at his watch again. 'Do you want me to get you a one way ticket to Bolivia?' He smiled. 'You could do a Lord Lucan, no sweat. But I'll tell you this, Foxy. A guy like you won't be able to hide anywhere for too long, so I think you can forget that.' He stood up.

Foxy got to his feet, too. His legs felt shaky. He straightened up.

'I don't know, Jake. I don't know what to do. That's why I came to see you. We're old friends. I thought you could help.'

Jake gave him a long look, and Foxy could see the smugness in his eyes. He stubbed out his cigar in the ashtray, and said, 'I can get you out of the country, you and Bill, but I can't make this go away. I'm well pissed off, Foxy. If I'd handled it my way, I'm sure this would never have got this far. There might have been a couple more stiffs, but not this much heat.'

Foxy said nothing as they walked towards the door.

'Look, we'll talk in the next couple of days,' Jake said. 'But when the shit hits the fan, Foxy, I won't be here. That much I can promise you. Keep me informed, we'll see what we can sort out.' He opened the door and gave Foxy a friendly pat on the shoulder as he ushered him out.

Humiliated, and by a fucking wide boy who can hardly write his name! Gavin Fox felt very small as he walked along the corridor and took the backstairs lift to the exit, where Bill Mackie was waiting in his car in the side street.

Jake watched from the window as Foxy came out of the building and onto the street. He shook his head. 'What a tit,' he said aloud. He knew that Foxy had no idea that two men were in a parked car fifty yards up the street, and one of them was taking pictures of him leaving the back door of the club.

If he had seen them, Foxy would have recognised DI Bob Fletcher of Internal Affairs, who had, in his inside jacket pocket, Mags Gillick's mobile phone, completely intact, with the message from Tracy Eadie – the one she left the last night she was seen alive. He was also in possession of a brown envelope with a photograph that would incriminate Fox, Prentice and Mackie. It had been Jake's parting gift to Fletcher – at a hastily arranged meeting yesterday – in return for the copper looking the other way while he got out of the country.

Jake saw Foxy get into the car, saw it drive off. Then he punched in a number on his mobile.

'Rab?' he said. 'Get me on a flight to Spain tonight.'

CHAPTER THIRTY-NINE

Everything was ready to roll. McGuire was strutting around the office, his sleeves rolled up. Nights like this were what you lived for, he told Rosie. It was already seven in the evening, and the plan was to run the Gavin Fox exposé in all of the editions of the newspaper.

The phone call to Rosie from DI Bob Fletcher, a trusted friend, had been a bolt from the blue in the morning.

'Rosie,' he'd said. 'Listen. You should know that I have, in my hot little hand, the mobile phone of one Mags Gillick, deceased. There's a message from Tracy Eadie. We believe it's her final phone call. You know if I'm telling you this, then it's a hundred per cent true.'

'Christ almighty, Bob,' was all she could say.

'Don't ask any questions, Rosie. And this phone call never happened. In the next twenty-four hours we will be all over this. Fox is finished. You have your scoop.'

'Thanks, Bob,' Rosie said.

'And Rosie: in about twenty minutes someone will arrive at the front door of your office and hand you an envelope. I'm sure you'll enjoy the photograph inside.'

'Thanks, Bob.' The line clicked off.

Her friendship with Bob Fletcher went back to the days when he was a uniformed desk sergeant and she was a young reporter. Their connection had lasted as he rose through the ranks. She knew there had been bad blood between Fletcher and Fox ever since the murder inquiry against one of Cox's boys, Dick Hamilton, had collapsed. Crucial evidence had gone missing from the police station where Fletcher had been working as a detective on the case, and Fox had been a DI. He had always suspected it was Foxy who'd made it disappear, but he knew it could never be proved.

When the envelope arrived Rosie tore it open, then rushed straight into McGuire's office. She told him that Fletcher had confirmed the message left by Tracy Eadie on Mags's mobile phone.

'Oh, fuck, Rosie! Holy shit! This is boots and saddles time. We were hanging them out to dry anyway with the confession and the one picture we had, but you know what the lawyers are like. Now we can just throw everything at this. Everything.' He buzzed Marion to get the lawyers in.

'It's down to you, Rosie. I know you can't tell me where you got the picture or the information, but if you have any doubt about your source, then tell me now.'

'No doubts, Mick. None. You have to trust me on that.' Rosie's stomach tweaked. The impact of getting this wrong didn't bear thinking about.

'Then let's do it.'

McGuire rubbed his hands as he looked down at the copies of all photographs he now had, scattered on the rough sketch page layout on his desk. The photograph Alison had given them was good because it placed Jake Cox on Fox's boat. But the picture Fletcher had sent Rosie showed Fox, Prentice and Mackie with hookers.

'Game on,' McGuire said.

Later, in McGuire's office, Tommy Hanlon sat sipping coffee as Rosie checked over the page proofs for the first day's exposure of the investigation. They looked fantastic. She could feel adrenalin pumping as she looked at the picture of Fox, with a big grin on his face, taking up most of the front page. The headline screamed 'TOP COPS' COKE AND TEEN HOOKER SHAME: World Exclusive by Rosie Gilmour'. The story was based on the Jack Prentice confession that Tracy Eadie died on Fox's boat, and it told how they had dumped her body in the water. Another headline blazed 'THE HEAD OF CID AND THE GODFATHER'.

Above was a picture of Foxy on his boat with his arm around Jake Cox. The inside story tracked Gavin Fox's career and gave a full account of a lifetime of corruption in the police. Another inside page gave details of the taped conversation of Mags Gillick talking to Rosie, of her claims that she had been with the three policemen on Fox's boat several times, and how it was she who organised for Tracy Eadie to go there the night she died. There was even a transcript of the frantic final mobile message Rosie had taped from Mags's phone that day they had met in the cafe.

McGuire was preparing to go on radio to talk about their exposé – revelations that would strike at the very heart of the establishment. On one of the inside pages was the facsimile text of Jack Prentice's suicide letter, and there was a rogue's gallery of colour pictures of Fox, Mackie and Prentice with prostitutes. The caption cheekily asked, 'Are you these girls? Contact us at the *Post.*'

'You're outrageous, McGuire.' Rosie laughed.

'Well,' he beamed. 'Can you imagine what stories these birds have to tell?'

The rest of the piece told of how Foxy and his cohorts had been involved with Jake Cox, the Big Man. It listed details of various convictions, where the men serving time in jail had always claimed they were innocent and had been fitted up by the cops. Prentice's confession revealed that they *had* been framed, making those convictions unsafe.

All they needed now was to doorstep Fox and Mackie. It had to be done simultaneously, and in the next half hour, so that their pictures and reaction could be used in the first edition. Rosie had asked for Matt to go along with her. They had already had a useful night on Friday, going back to the judge's house in Peebles a second time and witnessing the children arriving, driven by Quigley.

Rosie couldn't believe how well everything was going. She was nervous that the way the story was being presented hinged on that phone call from Bob Fletcher about the mobile, and also the damning photograph. But she knew in her gut it was true. She was eager to see the Foxy story in the paper, not just to bring him down, but for Mags's sake – for the shitty, horrible way she died, for Gemma, and for the other prostitutes used and abused by guys like Fox.

But even more, perhaps, than the Foxy exposé, Rosie wanted to get the judge's story published. It was even bigger, and would rock the entire system, from the social work department to the judges and lawyers at the very top of the legal establishment. And now that she had witnessed the kids going to Lord Dawson's house twice, *and* had the taped conversation with Woodbank's head from Quigley, she was certain the story was ready to go.

Tomorrow, first thing, she would write the paedophile ring copy.

'Okay,' she said, turning to McGuire. 'I can't wait to see the look on Foxy's face.'

'Go for it,' McGuire said.

'Mind you,' she said, 'it will be nothing to the look on the face of Lord Dawson when we knock on *his* door.'

McGuire smiled but said nothing. Rosie thought she saw him throw a fleeting glance at Hanlon, but perhaps it was her imagination. She left the office and met up with Matt at the lift. McGuire had arranged for one of his most trusted senior reporters, Joe Garret, to doorstep Bill Mackie. He had taken him into the office earlier in the afternoon and briefed him on the whole story, swearing him to secrecy. Joe had called to say he was already on his way.

'Is your tiny heart all aflutter?' Matt held open the door to the car park.

'Just a tad,' Rosie said, 'but it's a good flutter.'

They drove into the tree-lined avenue, where Gavin Fox lived at the end of a row of red sandstone houses. You needed money to live here. Some of it was old money, houses passed down the generations from when they had been occupied by industrialists and bankers. Others were owned by football stars and the nouveau riche. Foxy's house was a turreted mansion with a long driveway leading up to it.

'Christ,' Matt said, when they got to the huge pillars at the open gate. 'Look at this. Bastard must be minted. Crime pays, all right.'

But Rosie didn't feel like cracking jokes. Her insides were churning. 'Just drive right up, Matt. Get out and stand behind me, but don't take his picture until I tell him what the story is. I want to see his face fall.'

They drove up to the house and got out of the car. A soft light burned in one of the front rooms, but there was no sign of life. Two cars sat in the drive. One was Foxy's Jaguar and the other was a 4 x 4 which they presumed was his wife's. Rosie felt her palms sweaty as she got out of the car and went towards the huge oak door. She rang the brass bell, which made an echoing sound. A light came on in the hall, behind the stained glass door, and a figure approached. The door opened. It was Foxy. His face blanched when he saw her.

'Chief Superintendent Fox?' Rosie spoke almost chirpily but her mouth was dry. 'Rosie Gilmour, the *Post*.'

Foxy tried to smile, but Rosie saw his lip tremble. 'I know who you are, Rosie. But what on earth are you doing at my house?'

'Chief Superintendent Fox.' She would take her time, this was her show now. 'I'm here to ask for your reaction to a story we're running in the *Post* tomorrow. It concerns yourself, Detective Superintendent Bill Mackie and Detective

Chief Inspector Jack Prentice. The story is the result of a lengthy investigation into corruption inside Strathclyde Police. Corruption led by you, Mr Fox.' She raised her arm. Matt started taking pictures.

'Hold it,' Foxy said, his eyes blazing. 'Hold it right there, Miss Gilmour. I don't even know what you are talking about, but you're talking about a very good friend of mine who has died. Now could you please get away from my doorstep. I'm not having any of this.' He stepped back.

But Rosie persisted. 'Chief Superintendent, we have pictures of yourself, Mackie and Prentice with prostitutes on your boat. And we have a signed confession by Jack Prentice that the three of you have spent a lifetime taking bribes from Jake Cox and being involved in crime at every level. We have evidence that you fitted people up on cases, and that you used prostitutes and took drugs.'

She was longing to say that she had heard the message on Mags's mobile, and that the cops would be knocking on his door in the morning.

'Oh, for God's sake.' Foxy managed to look as if he was about to burst out laughing. 'What's this all about? Let me tell you, you're in serious trouble. I don't have a single clue what you're talking about, but rest assured there'll be legal action if you even embark on such absolute nonsense. For God's sake! Poor Jack wasn't well in the head before he died.'

'We're using the story tomorrow.' Rosie stood her ground. 'Is that all you want to say? Have you anything to add?'

'Get away from my doorstep.' He moved to close the door. 'I'm now about to phone your editor.'

'Fine.' Rosie stuck her foot in the door. 'But what can you tell us about the fourteen-year-old girl who died on your boat and was washed up on the beach at Troon? Tracy Eadie? And what about the murdered prostitute Mags Gillick, Chief Superintendent? What about that?'

Matt was able to get in one last frame as Fox closed the door. They got into the car and Matt made a swift turn before they sped out of the drive.

'Fuck me,' he said. 'I'm nearly wetting my pants here with excitement.'

Rosie laughed. 'Me too, Matt. Let's go.'

They raced back to the office.

CHAPTER FORTY

Rosie knew that she had to see TJ tonight and talk to him, or run the risk of losing him. She knew him well enough to understand that if his mind was set on leaving a place, then in his heart he had already left it. Trouble was, this was the only life she had known for the past sixteen years. She had never even considered packing up and leaving. She couldn't imagine her life without her work. Everything had been built around it, and it suited her. That way she didn't have time to think too deeply about life, but now TJ was forcing her to do that. The prospect of a leap in the dark was as terrifying as it was exciting. She could live without that. But then she would have to live without TJ . . .

She had called him when she got back to the office and was pleased to hear that he sounded his usual friendly and sarcastic self. Perhaps it wouldn't be too difficult.

Perhaps he would give her some more time to think. She hoped so.

McGuire had practically done cartwheels when she and Matt returned from Fox's house. Joe Garret was already in his office and told them that Bill Mackie just closed the door as soon as he got in the first line of his question. As the story was ready to go, the chief press officer from Strathclyde police was on the phone to McGuire. That was followed by one of the top lawyers who acted for the police force. Both were informed that the *Post* was running the story as planned. McGuire had put the call on a conference phone so they could all hear as he fended off their threat. Afterwards, as the paper was put to bed, he cracked open a bottle of champagne. When they were leaving, McGuire walked Rosie to the door. He shook her hand.

'Rosie, that was a fantastic job. Tomorrow's paper will be one of the best we've ever produced. And it's thanks to your hard work and perseverance.'

'Thanks, Mick.' Rosie couldn't handle McGuire being all sweetness. 'I'm spending the day at home tomorrow writing the paedophile, so it's ready to roll.'

McGuire agreed, and told her Garret would handle all the follow-up flak from the Foxy revelations. She walked out of the office into the crisp night air. She hadn't felt this good in weeks.

Outside TJ's flat, Rosie pressed the buzzer. She was

looking forward to a glass of wine and, she hoped, some understanding.

'On my way down.' TJ's voice came through the intercom.

'Okay.' Rosie looked at her watch. The paper would be coming off the press in two hours. She would be able to buy it at the late night paper shop, close to Giovanni's where she and TJ were headed.

'Hi, scoop.' He smiled as he opened the door. 'I take it you're about to ruin the lives of some of Glasgow's finest.' He kissed her on the lips and smiled.

'I'm afraid so.' She touched his face. 'And hopefully over the next two days, our top judge and a few cronies will bite the dust.'

TJ shook his head and put his arm around her shoulder as they walked towards the bistro.

'Successful day then?'

'And how. The paper will be out in a couple of hours and arses will be falling apart everywhere.'

TJ looked at her, then straight ahead. 'Good. Then what?'

Rosie knew what he meant, but she wanted to discuss things over a glass of wine.

'We'll see. Come on, I'm dying for a drink.'

They could see the lights of Giovanni's restaurant ahead, and Rosie hoped that TJ wouldn't say any more until they'd got to the table and had a drink in their hands. She needed to relax.

Rosie hadn't even noticed the man coming across the street towards her. All she was aware of was TJ grabbing hold of her and throwing her to the ground. Somewhere in that instant she heard a loud bang, like a car backfiring. But she had hit her head on the pavement and for a moment felt dazed and confused, with TJ lying on top of her. She thought she heard him groaning, followed by the sound of a car screeching off.

'Shit,' TJ said. 'I've been shot, Rosie.'

His face was close to hers and she wriggled out from under him.

'That bastard who crossed the street,' TJ said, his face contorted, 'he was going to shoot you. I saw the gun.'

'Jesus.' Rosie pulled out her mobile and dialled 999. Suddenly Giovanni and others appeared from the bistro and started running towards them. Rosie managed to pull herself up to a kneeling position. She could see blood pumping out of TJ's leg.

'Aw Jesus, TJ,' she said, shaking. 'You've been shot in the leg.' As Giovanni approached, she shouted, 'Quick. He's been shot. Somebody help. Please.'

'It's okay,' Giovanni said, out of breath. 'Someone is phoning the ambulance. Don't worry.' Then he noticed TJ. 'My God, TJ. It's you. My God. Don't worry, my friend. You'll be okay.' He knelt down beside him, and told one of his waiters to run to the restaurant and get a towel.

Rosie knelt by TJ, holding his head off the ground.

'Oh TJ . . .' She was sobbing. 'I'm so sorry. It's all my fault. You saved my life.'

'I'm okay, Rosie,' he said. 'It's not that bad. It's painful, but I'll be all right. It's okay.'

'I'm so sorry . . .' She held his hand as they waited for the ambulance. In a couple of minutes it was there, followed by two police cars. People came out of their houses to see the commotion, and cars stopped nearby. The paramedics came with a stretcher. It was like slow motion.

Rosie stood up slowly and unsteadily as a policewoman came towards her and took hold of her arm.

'He'll be fine,' she said. 'He's in good hands. Come this way.'

'No,' Rosie said. 'Please. I'm going with him. You can talk to me at the hospital.'

A burly police sergeant nodded to the policewoman, as the paramedics lifted TJ's stretcher. Rosie followed, trying to compose herself.

'This is a fine mess you've got me into, Gilmour,' TJ croaked, and forced a smile. His face was ashen.

She fought back tears. He had saved her life. She shook her head and he reached out for her hand.

'Now just relax,' the paramedic said, kneeling beside TJ in the ambulance. 'You'll be fine. There's a lot of blood, but it looks more like a flesh wound. You can tell your mates you were in the war or something.'

TJ laughed and squeezed Rosie's hand.

'Enough. Don't cry, sweetheart. I'm fine.'

She sniffed, wiped her tears.

'But,' he said, 'this is what I mean, Rosie. This is enough.'

She held his hand tightly. If ever she needed proof that enough was enough then this was it. If she could walk away right now and be with TJ for the rest of her life she would. But, even in the midst of this, she knew that she had better get on the phone to McGuire and tell him what had happened. And there was a part of her mind that was already thinking of how she was going to get through tomorrow writing all the copy on the paedophile ring.

TJ looked at her as though he were reading her thoughts. 'You'd better phone your boss,' he said. 'You'll be a big star in the morning.' He smiled.

Rosie felt a sharp stab of guilt.

CHAPTER FORTY-ONE

Rosie's eyes were stinging from lack of sleep. She sat drinking another mug of coffee and working at her screen. She had almost finished the first day's instalment of the paedophile story. It would reveal how kids from a Glasgow children's home were driven every Friday night to the home of one of Scotland's top High Court judges. Hanlon had warned her that the story had to be written ultra carefully. There had been arguments about that straight away. The kids were photographed in their underpants, she had told Hanlon. What more evidence did he need? But he still insisted that it had to be very carefully written. They had agreed on a form of words, but the pictures in themselves were damning enough.

She also knew that the information from Gemma and Trina about sexual assault could not be used because it had been obtained illegally. McGuire and the paper's lawyers had made a decision not even to touch that. In the tape of Duncan Davidson talking to Quigley there was no mention of sex. McGuire said it was one of these stories that didn't need acres of words. You just had to print pictures of these kids, saying they were being driven to Lord Dawson's home, and that would be enough. People would make up their own minds.

Rosie was frustrated, but she knew that the only way they could get any kind of story in the newspaper was not to spell out the obvious. McGuire had said that ultimately the safety of the kids was paramount, and that after the revelations there would be serious action taken to protect them. So, as she wrote, Rosie sailed as close to the wind, legally, as she dared.

She rubbed her eyes. She had spent half the night at the hospital being interviewed by police about what she saw at the shooting. By the middle of the night they had already seen the newspaper. Rosie told them that as far as she was concerned, the attempt to shoot her was connected to the exposé on Gavin Fox. The detectives had remained poker-faced when she said that, and arranged for another interview with her the following afternoon.

After the cops left, she sat with TJ while the doctors assessed the damage to his leg. He had laughed when they told him he was lucky. But they emphasised that the bullet had merely skimmed the top of his thigh and, miraculously, had not torn any muscle or bone. The wound was minor, despite the blood, and they stitched him up and suggested he remain overnight for observation. But TJ insisted on going home. Rosie helped him to hobble on crutches into the waiting taxi. Inside his flat she sat him down on the sofa and poured them both a glass of wine.

'I feel as though I'm in the wrong movie.' Rosie shook her head. She turned to TJ and hugged him. 'I'll never be able to thank you for what you did, TJ. Never.'

He smiled and kissed her.

'Jesus, I'm so tired, Rosie.' He lay back, his face pale. 'Too much excitement at my age. I need to crash out.'

'I know.' Rosie helped him to his feet. 'Come on. Let's go to bed.'

TJ grimaced as he tried to walk. He looked older, with dark shadows under his eyes. Rosie thought she could see fear beneath the bravado.

'Just don't be making any sexual demands on me,' he said, as he lay down on the bed. Rosie smiled and helped him off with his trousers. He put his head on the pillow, his eyes already closing. She took off her clothes and got into bed beside him. She put her arms around him and snuggled up close.

'I love you, TJ.' But TJ was asleep. Tears came to her eyes.

Now, as she burned a third disk of the paedophile story, Rosie just wanted to get through the next couple of days. Then, she promised herself, she would have a long hard think about her future. She reminded herself that she would have to phone Quigley to warn him the story was coming out. She would keep her promise so he could make himself scarce before the inquiry started. McGuire had expressly told her not to do that, but Rosie drew her own lines on how to deal with people. Regardless of whether or not he deserved to go to jail for his part in the paedo ring, Rosie was making her own decision. She would give him a break.

Her mobile rang. It was McGuire.

'Rosie?' His tone was businesslike. 'Can you get in here. Now.'

'Yeah, I'm actually about to leave. Copy's done. Is something wrong?'

'Talk to you when you get here.'

She pulled on her jacket, finished her coffee and headed for the office. She had taken a call earlier from Father Dunnachie to say that he had located the spot where her mother was buried, and she'd arranged to meet him later tomorrow, once she got the Lord Dawson story off her plate.

From the moment she entered the car park, she could see the waiting press pack and TV cameras. They turned towards her when she got out of her car. Photographers she'd known for years took pictures of her and reporters from other newspapers and television approached her for quotes about the shooting and about the Gavin Fox revelations. One asked her about the cocaine charges. She had been so busy over the past few hours it hadn't occurred to her that the press would be waiting for her. She couldn't understand why McGuire hadn't mentioned it. Rosie told everyone she had to speak to her editor and the company lawyers before giving any interviews. She waved them away and went through the swing doors.

All the way upstairs, other reporters and staff greeted her with handshakes, congratulating her on the exposé. She was too tired, and too keen to get on, to enjoy the moment. But she thanked each of them for their support, and made a few jokes on the way to the editor's office. She noticed that Reynolds sat smouldering at his desk and had picked up the phone as soon as she came onto the editorial floor.

McGuire's office door was open and his secretary nodded her in. As Rosie walked into the office, she met the newspaper's managing director, Gordon Thomson, on his way out. His face was grave, but he brightened when he saw Rosie. They had always got on well, and she knew Thomson had respect for her, despite his reputation of being a smiling assassin. He was top of the heap in management, but he had come from a working class background and applauded achievement against the odds. During a boozy lunch one time, when he was congratulating Rosie on a press award, he had told her he liked the way she stood her ground in the testosterone-fuelled editorial floor of a daily newspaper. And one time, when her life was being threatened, he told McGuire to spare no expense in sending her out of the country to a secret location for two weeks.

'Rosie,' Thomson said. 'Are you all right? We were all worried sick when we heard about what happened. Don't worry. You'll be protected from now on. Oh, well done, by the way. Fantastic stuff today. Award winning. Don't worry about the lawsuits.' He laughed and shook her hand.

'I never do,' Rosie said, as he breezed past her. But she was suspicious that he was in McGuire's office at all. She looked at the editor sitting behind his desk, his expression serious. Hanlon was on the sofa, along with Martin Brady, the boss of the legal firm. This was not good. Brady was only pulled in when there was a big problem. She knew how much credence had been given to her information about the mobile phone from Bob Fletcher. She prayed that nothing had happened to rubbish that. She knew the lengths the police were capable of going to cover up something that would bring this amount of shit on top of them.

'Hi,' she said. 'Howsit going? Why is everyone looking so glum? It was me they tried to shoot.'

Nobody reacted.

'Sit down, Rosie,' McGuire said.

She sat down, and glanced at Hanlon who gave her a sympathetic look.

McGuire took a deep breath. 'Rosie. Firstly, are you okay? I know it's been a long night for you. But straight off, you're going for a long holiday at the paper's expense. Promise.'

Rosie nodded. 'I'm fine.' She looked around. 'Well . . . I was fine until I came in here.'

'Look, Rosie . . . About the paedo story . . .'

She shifted in her seat. She could hear the sound of bottle crashing. She opened her mouth to speak.

McGuire put his hand up to stop her. 'Now just listen and hear me out.' The last twenty-four hours, well, a couple of days more, actually, I've been in constant talks with Gordon and the lawyers over this.' He took a deep breath. 'And the Lord President has been on the phone. There's also been discussion with the Lord Advocate.

'Why?' she asked, but she knew why. Someone had got to them. 'Why is management being brought in, Mick? I haven't even put the allegations to the judge yet. Or to the home. What's going on?'

'Listen, Rosie,' McGuire said. 'Obviously I had to inform the managing director that we were about to bring down one of the most powerful figures in the legal establishment. They had to know.'

'And?'

'Well,' McGuire said, 'on the advice of our lawyers, it was decided to approach the Lord President and tell him what we had. Obviously, he would have to talk to Lord Dawson himself and find out just what's going on.'

'What?' Rosie said, standing up. 'Why? In the name of Christ, why, Mick? Why would we tell Lord Dawson what we've got? Was he going to congratulate us? Jesus!' She shook her head. 'It was to give him an out. Give him the chance to resign on health grounds or something. Wasn't it? Christ, Mick! You're about to tell me he's going to stand down on health grounds, aren't you?'

McGuire looked at Hanlon who looked at his boss. Brady spoke.

'Now just calm down, Rosie. These things are a means to an end. Lord Dawson will be removed from his post, albeit officially at his own request. The entire paedophile ring will be tracked down and action taken. And the kids will be moved to a new home. There'll be a complete investigation. The most important thing is that the kids will be protected now and in the future.'

'So it's all done and dusted?' Rosie said, sitting back down. 'I can't believe this. No, I can, in fact. I don't know where I got the idea that I would actually get a story in the paper that would really shake the establishment.'

'But it will,' McGuire said. 'It already has, Rosie. Lord Dawson will be announcing his resignation tomorrow. He's finished.'

'But not prosecuted,' Rosie said. 'Not like the others who might face jail over this. Like the boss of the home or the janitor. Lord Dawson gets off scot-free, with his fat pension and his reputation intact.'

'Not quite,' Brady said. 'He might slip away quietly, but people will know. He's finished.'

'He should go to jail,' she protested. 'The bastard should go to jail. I can't believe we're part of this cover-up. Is that it?'

'It's not a cover-up, Rosie,' McGuire said. 'The job is done.'

'Our job is to tell the fucking story. To expose people like Lord Dawson.'

'But look what we've done today.' McGuire was on his feet. 'Look what you've done with Gavin Fox and the police force. That's a massive exposé.'

'That's not the point, Mick, and you know it. I take it that's why the MD was in here just now, making sure his knighthood was safe?' She was raging against Thomson now. They were cut from the same cloth, and she felt betrayed.

When nobody answered, Rosie stood up. 'Right. I understand. I see it all quite clearly now.' She turned to McGuire. 'Christ. Why did it take me so long?' She felt tears come to her eyes and bit her lip. The last thing she wanted to do was blub at a time like this.

'Rosie.' McGuire took a step towards her. 'You're shattered. You need a bit of a rest. Hanlon'll take you for lunch and you just relax for a while. Come on, you need a break. Try to understand that sometimes it happens like this. Sometimes we have to bend just a bit. But remember, the damage is done and it's all down to you. Dawson is finished. You did that, Rosie. Foxy is finished and so are a few others. You did all that. Enjoy the moment.'

Rosie stood for a moment and looked at each of them.

She tried to sound calm. 'Sorry. I understand. If you've got the shitty end of the stick in life, there is nothing to protect you, and you get away with nothing. But if you're from the top drawer, nothing can touch you. No matter what you do.'

Hanlon couldn't look her in the eye.

'I won't go for lunch if you don't mind. I'm tired, and I have to go and visit my friend who nearly got killed for me last night. You've made your decisions, so let's just leave it at that before I say any more.' As she turned to walk away, she looked at McGuire.

'I'll take the rest of the day off, if that's all right.'

'Sure, Rosie. I'll call you later. We'll go for a drink.'

CHAPTER FORTY-TWO

Rosie was back in the cafe in the East End where she first met Mags Gillick. She didn't know why she drove there when she left the office. She just found herself going in that direction.

Everything had changed on that rainy morning when Mags walked into her life. As Rosie sat at the window, the girl she remembered serving them the last time came towards her. Rosie ordered a coffee and looked out of the window. So much had happened over these past few weeks. So much had changed. In places like this everything stayed the same, no matter how many lives unravelled at its greasy tables.

She was trying hard to be objective about the Lord Dawson debacle. McGuire was right. The Gavin Fox story was crucial and would go down in history. So what if the next big story didn't make it? That was life. She remembered an old reporter telling her never to take it too seriously. That's just how it was, it would all be chip-shop paper tomorrow, he used to say. Or lining the budgie's cage. So why sit here, making so much of something over which she had no control? As long as she worked for a newspaper, she could never actually control anything. The only thing she was able to control was herself. By working flat out and making her job the centre of her life, she needed nothing else. But now it was different. She wanted TJ – she just didn't know how she was going to do it. The thought of upping sticks and moving out was just something she didn't do. Perhaps now that he'd been injured he would take some time out to think about things himself.

Rosie decided to phone Quigley and let him know it was time to get out. She didn't give a damn about what McGuire or anyone else thought. Why should Lord Dawson and the others get off the hook while Quigley would be thrown to the wolves? She dialled his number.

'Paddy? It's Rosie.'

'Hallo.' Paddy's voice was shaking. 'I'm at work. Something's happening. Davidson got summoned to head-quarters and there's social workers all over here. What's going on?'

'Get yourself out of there, Paddy.' She didn't want to engage in any conversation with him. 'That's all I'm saying. Get yourself away. Now.' She hung up.

Her next call was to Alison Prentice.

'How are you, Alison? Are you bearing up?'

'I'm all right,' Alison said. 'It was a shock seeing it all in the paper, even though I knew it was coming, but my best friend is with me, and I will get through this.'

'You did the right thing,' Rosie said. 'But it's a lot for you to deal with.'

Silence. Then Alison spoke. 'Rosie? Could we meet some time for a coffee or something, once this is all over?'

'Of course we can.' Rosie was relieved that Alison wasn't full of regret. 'Give yourself a couple of weeks, and come to Glasgow. Call me and we'll meet.'

'I'd like that.' The line went dead.

Rosie drank her coffee and left the cafe. A biting wind had sprung up. She felt weak and angry and tired all at the same time. She wished she could lie down somewhere and wake up and everything would be clear cut. She got into her car and drove to TJ's.

'Up you come.' His voice on the intercom sounded a little distracted.

The hall door was open when she got to his flat, and she walked towards the living room. A Chet Baker CD was playing, and Rosie remembered TJ telling her it was that music which had made him take up the sax when he was a teenager. He said it was the background music to his life. The bedroom door was open and TJ called her to come through. An open suitcase lay on the bed with folded clothes piled around. TJ turned from the bed and hobbled across to her.

'You're packing?' Rosie said.

'Well spotted. They don't call you intrepid for nothing.' He smiled. Then his face was serious. 'I told you, Rosie, I'm leaving. I've been sitting here all day thinking and I just made my mind up. It's now or never, Rosie.'

She was stunned. 'But where are you going? I mean your leg and stuff. I thought you would be waiting for a little while.'

He moved closer to her and took both her hands.

'No. I don't want to wait, Rosie. I just want to get out of here.' He looked into her eyes. 'I want you to come.'

Rosie sighed and looked away. She wasn't ready for this.

'But TJ . . . Jesus!' She rubbed her face with her hands. 'Listen. I've just come from McGuire's office. They're not publishing the paedophile story. My head's all over the place. I can't make a decision right now.'

'Why not, Rosie?' He shrugged. 'If ever there was a better time to realise that you've had enough, then it's right now. The fact that they're not publishing the story speaks volumes. Is that what you want? To be a part of that? Do you want that for the rest of your life? Look at the state of you. You're wrecked.'

Rosie burst into tears. He took her in his arms and held her.

'I'm sorry, TJ.' She tried to smile. 'This is getting to be a habit, crying like an eejit.' She sniffed and composed herself. 'I'm just so tired and frustrated. I can't believe they won't use the story. It's criminal.'

'It's crap, Rosie.' TJ wiped her tears away with his hand. 'It's just a game to these people. You don't belong there any more. I don't even know if you ever did.'

'I don't know where I belong. I don't know anything any more.'

He let her go and went back to a rucksack on the bed. He pulled out an envelope with two airline tickets. 'I was going to show you these last night.' He handed one to Rosie and she opened it.

'New York?' She almost laughed. 'I've never been to New York.'

'So now's your chance.' His arms went around her and he kissed her on the lips. 'Come with me, Rosie. Just leave it all behind. Who knows what will happen. Take a chance.'

She stood still, gazing at the ticket. 'It's tomorrow morning,' she said, surprised. 'It's too quick, TJ. Come on . . . Tomorrow morning?'

He turned away and continued putting clothes into the case.

'That's how it's done, Rosie. Just cut loose.'

'I don't know, TJ.' Rosie sighed. 'Christ. I don't know.'

'Neither do I.' He turned to her. 'That's the whole point. We don't know, but maybe it's worth finding out. I'll be on that plane tomorrow anyway. Seven-thirty. You don't want to come, it's up to you, but you've got your ticket.' He shrugged. 'Come on. Turn off the control switch. See what happens.'

Rosie watched him packing. How could she do that? Just get up and leave it all behind?

'TJ,' she said, 'I'm going home to sleep for a couple of hours. I'll call you later. I just don't know . . . Please understand.'

He kissed her again and hugged her close.

'I do understand, Rosie. Whatever you decide, I'll understand.' He went on speaking into her hair. 'But I do love you, Rosie, no matter what. It's up to you.' He eased himself away from her and looked into her eyes. 'Listen. I won't be calling you. If you decide to come, phone me, and I'll pick you up. Or just be at the airport. If not, don't phone to say goodbye. I hate goodbyes.' He smiled wistfully. 'I'll send you a postcard.'

She kissed him on the cheek, and left.

CHAPTER FORTY-THREE

On the way home, Rosie drove to Woodbank Children's Home. She had to see Gemma – just in case it was for the last time. She glanced at the airline ticket lying on the passenger seat of her car. This would be the biggest decision she had taken in her life. She would make her mind up tonight over a long hot bath in her flat. She would switch all her phones off and consult nobody but herself. Whatever she'd decided by the time she went to bed, she told herself she wouldn't ever go back on it.

There was more supervision than before at the reception in the children's home. When Rosie asked to see Gemma Gillick, a second woman, whom Rosie assumed was a social worker, asked her who she was; she decided to tell the truth. She explained that she had known the girl's mother and that she had written the story in the newspaper. The woman said she had seen the story and congratulated her on exposing the corruption. But she went on to say it may have cost Gemma's mother her life. Rosie couldn't bring herself to disagree.

'I understand what you're saying,' she replied, 'but all I can say is that it was Mags who came to me. I never sought her out. She was determined to tell her story, and if it hadn't been me, it would have been somebody else.'

'Doesn't make it right,' the woman said.

'It's hard to make anything right, in these circumstances,' Rosie said.

The woman didn't look convinced. Rosie said she just wanted to see Gemma. The woman told her she could only talk to the kid if she was with her.

'Rosie!' Gemma spotted her coming into the cafe area. 'Rosie! I knew you would come. I told them.' She nearly knocked Rosie over as she hurled herself into her arms.

'Gemma.' Rosie hugged her tight. The woman watched. 'How are you, darling? I heard you went on a bus run.'

Gemma looked at the social worker and made a sheepish face. 'I know,' she said. 'I was bad. But I won't do it again.'

Rosie took her by the hand and led her to a table where they sat down. She bought Cokes for all three of them, and chocolate for Gemma.

'Rosie.' Gemma drank down the Coke, then stretched her arm across the table to squeeze Rosie's hand. 'They said we're going to another place to live. Loads of us. They might even find foster mums and dads for us. That would be great.' Her eyes lit up. 'Is that why you're here, Rosie? I'd love you to be my foster mum.'

Rosie's heart sank. 'But I haven't even got a husband, Gemma,' she said. 'I'd be no use as a mum. Sure, I'm never in.' She smiled and swallowed hard.

'You would, Rosie. You would so. We could go everywhere, and I wouldn't run away and I'd do everything you said.' She leaned towards Rosie and whispered. 'And I won't wet the bed. I haven't done it for nearly two weeks.'

'Good for you.' Rosie ruffled her hair, then asked about the bus run and what happened. She listened while Gemma told them everything they had seen. Then she spoke about the big house and how all these different people were asking questions now and getting her to draw pictures, which was a good laugh. But sometimes the people were very serious when they were asking questions, and Gemma said she was a bit fed up with it. She just wanted to get back to a normal house again.

The social worker nudged Rosie and suggested it was time to go now. Rosie got to her feet.

'Right, Gemma,' she said. 'I'll have to get back to my work. But we'll not lose touch, even if you're away from here. I'll write you a letter. Would you like that?'

Gemma's face fell. Her bottom lip trembled and tears welled in her eyes.

'You're going away and you'll never see me again. I might be going far away. How will you know where I am?'

'I'll find out.' Rosie choked. 'Don't you worry, you'll not be that far.'

'We never got the pizza at your house,' Gemma said. 'You promised.'

'I know.' Rosie rolled her eyes. 'I was awful busy. But we will one day, Gemma, I promise.' She went towards her. 'Now give me a big hug.'

Gemma threw her arms around her and held her tight. Rosie almost had to prise herself away from her.

'Now you be good,' she said.

'I will. Will you always be my friend, Rosie? Will you?'

'Of course, Gemma. Always.'

The social worker took Gemma's hand and told her they had to go. She wiped the child's cheeks with a tissue.

Rosie stood for a moment and watched as Gemma left the cafe, holding the social worker's hand. She could see she was sobbing, and the woman stroked her hair. At the door, she turned around. Rosie waved weakly as she saw Gemma's flushed face.

'Bye, Rosie,' Gemma called, trying to smile.

'Bye, Gemma.' Rosie turned so she wouldn't see her own tears.

Her mobile rang. It was McGuire. He told her to meet him in O'Brien's.

Now.

CHAPTER FORTY-FOUR

In O'Brien's bar, Rosie sat in a booth with a glass of iced water, waiting for McGuire who was already ten minutes late. She felt irritated and decided she would give him ten more minutes then she would go. Stuff him. Rosie knew what the meeting was all about anyway, and the way she felt right now, she couldn't be bothered with the bullshit. She knew McGuire meant well and that he thought the world of her. But this one time, a bit of soft soaping and back slapping from him wouldn't be enough. She looked at her watch again. She wanted to get home and think. If she was going with TJ, she needed to do practical things, like get packed. Jesus! He was really going. It hadn't sunk in yet.

She knew if she didn't go, she would be creating the easiest way out for herself. Tomorrow, she would have another story to get her teeth into. Life would go on. But it might be for the best. No risk. Walk away while you still can.

'Sorry I'm late, Rosie,' McGuire said. 'Big legal meeting. Lord Dawson's resigned. Oh, and Gavin Fox has been suspended; Bill Mackie too. They're finished. All of them. Word is, they'll throw the book at them. Disposing of a body, sex with a minor if they could prove it, perverting the course of justice. They'll get banged up for years.' He slid into the booth.

'It's the jail Dawson should be in,' Rosie said, flatly. 'If people around me had any balls.'

McGuire said nothing. Rosie knew he would take some snash from her, but she also knew he wouldn't take too much.

'Anyway,' McGuire said, turning to the waiter and ordering a mineral water, 'we just have to live with what's happened, Rosie. Understand that, please, will you?' His tone was friendly but firm.

She nodded.

'Listen,' McGuire said. 'I want us to draw a line under this and that's one of the reasons why I'm here. It's time to move on.'

Rosie swallowed a mouthful of water. For a moment she thought he was going to fire her. Perhaps she had pushed things too far yesterday in front of the lawyers . . .

'Move on?'

'Yeah, Rosie. You did a fantastic job on Fox. And the paedophile ring. You excelled yourself and I don't know how I could ever replace you.'

Rosie raised her eyebrows. The bastard was going to sack her. She was ready for him.

'But,' McGuire said, 'it's time to replace you.'

Rosie moved to speak, but he put his hand up to silence her.

'No, wait. Let me finish. I think, Rosie, that there's only so much of this kind of stuff you want to do in your life, and I really value you as a journalist. But I want you to move on. I want to make you assistant editor, with special responsibility for investigations. The big exposés. You'll be in charge. So you see, you'd still be involved, but not getting your hands dirty. And you'd be inside, knocking heads around at the editorial conference. You'd be influential in all the decision making.'

She didn't know what to say. She hadn't been expecting this. Assistant editor would be a perfect job for her in many ways. It would take her off the road, give her more money, more clout, and she would still be at the heart of the investigations. She could change things. She could make things happen.

'Interested?' McGuire sipped his water. 'I hope so. There's another eight grand on your salary and the expenses will stay about the same. I'd obviously have to watch my back in case you want my chair.' He grinned.

'If you thought I was capable of getting your chair,' Rosie said, 'there's no way you would make me assistant editor, Mick. Don't bullshit a bullshitter.'

'Well,' he smiled wryly, 'that's not quite true. But anyway, do you fancy it, Rosie? Please say yes. I've more or less told them you would.'

Rosie drank some more water and looked around the bar as it filled up with lunchtime diners. All the suits were there. The usual movers and shakers and executives. Now she could be one of them. All she had to do was say the word. She thought about TJ. He would be at the airport tomorrow, watching for her. She wished she could call him for advice. She had always imagined what it would be like to have a real say in what was in the newspaper every day. To have a real influence on how stories were presented, and a role in the decision-making. She had longed for that most of her career, but she could never bring herself to play the political game with some of the tossers she would have to deal with at management level. Still, if she *were* ever in a position of power, perhaps stories like the paedophile ring would actually make it into the paper . . .

'Yes,' Rosie heard herself saying. 'Okay, Mick, I'll take it. But don't expect me to toe the line with you every day, because I won't. I'm my own woman.'

'Of course,' McGuire said. 'If you were to toe the line with me every day, I'd be nervous. I want your spirit, Rosie. I want your fire around me. Let's rattle a few more cages.' He reached out and shook her hand. 'Have we got a deal?'

'Deal,' Rosie said, flatly. This was a new beginning. She could throw herself into the job and put all the emotional turmoil of the last few weeks behind her. She had been turning into an emotional wreck. Maybe she just imagined she was in love with TJ. It was crazy to think about running away with him. Now she could get wrapped up in her new job, it would be a perfect way to forget.

They got up and walked out of the bar together. McGuire told her what office she would get, and how they would have a big celebration dinner tomorrow night, with just a few handpicked people. Gordon Thomson would be there, and a few executives. McGuire told her to take the rest of the day off. He laughed as she said she would shop for a power suit so she could look the part in the new job. He waved from the back of the black taxi as it sped away.

Rosie stood at the traffic lights and looked around at the bustle in the city centre. Everyone going somewhere. Everyone with a different story to tell. She would miss being on the streets, miss the buzz of meeting people and getting involved with their stories. Too involved sometimes. But deep down she knew she couldn't go on like that, and now was the best time to move on. But nothing stirred inside her, the way it had over the past few weeks. She got into her car and drove towards her flat. She needed to be alone – to be lonely. She did lonely very well. She drove towards the West End, thinking how predictable the future was now that she had accepted the job. At least she would get home every night. But then what? She imagined the long nights in her flat by herself, and the sameness of the days. And no TJ . . . Not even as a friend . . . She glanced at the airline ticket. There was a niggling feeling in her stomach. Tonight she would decide.

She slowed down the car and pulled into the side of the road. She took her mobile from the dashboard, and punched in the number Father Dunnachie had given her.

'Hallo, Father,' she said. 'It's Rosie . . . Any chance you could meet me at the graveyard now? Something's come up tomorrow and I'll be tied up . . . okay . . . That's brilliant. I'm on my way.'

The rusty gates to the old cemetery were hanging off the crumbling sandstone wall, and the road in was overgrown with weeds and grass. The graveyard was built on a hill at the edge of the city's East End. Rosie remembered how, as a child, she was spooked by the eerie shadows of the headstones if she passed by on a bus in the dark. It was even more eerie now, in the stillness of a damp, chilly afternoon. She stopped her car on a path just inside and got out to wait for the priest. She sighed, looking out at the hundreds of graves, most of them overgrown with grass and weeds climbing up the grey headstones. Beloved. The word was everywhere, barely readable on some of the older, more weathered stones. But it was still there. She felt a tightness in her throat. Her mother was beloved too. By her. All her life. She turned when she heard the car scrunch on the gravel behind her.

'Hi, Father,' she said, when the priest got out. 'Sorry it's such short notice, but I've got something on tomorrow.'

The priest shook her hand. 'Not a worry, Rosie.' He motioned her to walk up the hill with him. 'I saw your name on the big police story today,' he said, as they walked. 'My, my, but you've really set some cats among the pigeons there, all right.' He smiled. 'I'd say you'd better not drop a bus ticket from now on or they'll be after you.' He patted her arm.

'They were rotten, Father,' Rosie said. 'Rotten from the core.'

They walked to the top of the hill, then further and deeper into the cemetery, until the gravestones were few and far between. They came to a spot that was about fifty square feet of overgrown grass with no headstones at all. The odd little cross, stuck into the ground, poked out of the grass. The priest stopped and looked at Rosie.

'This is the spot, Rosie.' He spread his hand out and sighed. 'It's a pauper's grave. All of this.' He clasped his hands together. 'There are many poor souls buried here. That's how it was then. They don't use it nowadays.' He stopped. 'When your mother died, and there was nobody, this would be the only place to lay her to rest. Sometimes, years later, somebody would be in a position to put up an old cross or a stone, just to mark it.' He took Rosie's arm. 'But if you come over here, I want to show you something.'

She followed him, trying to keep herself together. He walked a few steps, and crouched down.

He pulled away some grass and looked up at her. 'There's a cross here. It's old and worn, obviously been here a while, but you can still make it out. It's got your mother's name on it. Come closer. See?'

Rosie stepped forward and crouched down beside him.

'Annie Gilmour. Died September 9, 1969. Aged 37. Beloved.' It was barely legible, but it was there.

Rosie closed her eyes. She could see her mother in the kitchen, her welcoming smile when she turned around as Rosie burst in from school. The tears came and she stood up. The priest put his arms around her.

'Somebody cared enough, Rosie.' He patted her back. 'Somebody put the cross. I have no idea who, and we have no way of checking.' He laid a hand on Rosie's hair. 'We will probably never know.'

Rosie composed herself. 'Thanks, Father. It means such

a lot to me. I never forgot her, Father. I never forgot her for a day.'

'I know.' He touched her arm, and looked at the grass. 'And she knows too, Rosie.' He smiled. 'She's always known. She still knows.' They stood in silence. Then he looked at her, and at his watch.

'I'm just going to leave you here now. Have some time alone. To reflect.'

Rosie nodded.

He shook her hand. 'And now, at last, you have somewhere.'

'Thank you, Father.'

'I hope we'll still see you at St Gregory's, Rosie. Even if it is only on All Souls' Day.' He turned and walked away.

'You will, Father. Thanks,' she called after him.

When she heard the car drive off, Rosie shivered as the greyness of the late afternoon grew darker. Soon the gravestones would be eerie shadows again.

She crouched down and her fingers lightly caressed the words etched on the cross.

'Oh, Mum,' Rosie said softly. 'I missed you. Every single day. I have missed you so much.'

CHAPTER FORTY-FIVE

Rosie closed the door of her flat behind her and stood with her back resting against it. For a moment, she closed her eyes and took a deep breath, relishing the peace of being in her own home, away from everything. She could clear her mind of the last few days and think about nothing but her future. She switched off her mobile phone, then went down the hall and into the living room to turn off her house phone. She looked at the television and picked up the remote control. She was tempted to put the news on, just to see what they were saying about Fox, and about Lord Dawson's resignation. No. Forget it. She tossed the remote on the sofa and kicked off her shoes.

She went into the kitchen and poured herself a glass of red wine and drank a delicious mouthful. She felt better already. She padded into the bedroom, threw open the curtains and stood sipping her wine, watching the people in the driving rain on the street below. It was already dark.

'Bitch.' The arm was around her neck before she was even sure if she'd heard the voice. Her glass dropped to the floor. 'Bitch.' The hand went over her mouth and strong arms dragged her backwards. She heard herself making muffled sounds through the hand that was squeezing her mouth and nose. She couldn't breathe. Panic. She was going to pass out. Suddenly the hand was away from her mouth and she gasped. Then she felt the coldness of the metal against the side of her head. A gun. She groaned in pain as a hand jerked her backwards by the hair. She was face to face with him, the gun still at her temple. There was a moment when she thought she recognised the face. Then she crumpled, dizzy, as the fist hit her face. Her cheek made a shattering sound. Blood poured from her nose.

'Please,' she managed to say. 'Please, don't hurt me. Please.' The face in front of her was a blur.

'Hallo again.' The voice sounded in the distance. 'Thought you'd seen the last of me, ya fucking bitch.'

Rosie blinked. She was seeing double. She blinked again. It was the fat man whom Adrian had stabbed. Her legs gave way. He grabbed her with his other hand and dragged her across to the sofa. He threw her down and she lay there, blood gushing from her nose. Her whole body was shaking.

'The Big Man's no happy with his picture in the paper.' The fat man sat beside her, leaning over her. She could hear him breathing. He smelled of sweat and alcohol. His eyes scanned Rosie from top to bottom. He traced her with the barrel of the gun, from her chest to her groin. He grinned.

'He said I could do what I want with you before I finished you.' He licked his lips. 'But I just like hurting people.' He wiped his nose with the back of his hand, then dug in his pocket and took out a small wrap. Rosie knew without looking it would be cocaine. He opened it with one hand, stuck a finger in it and shoved some up his nose. He sniffed hard, then sat back on the sofa with the gun still aimed at Rosie.

'Your big pal shouldn't have knifed me, you know,' he said. 'That was downright cheek.'

Rosie swallowed. She tasted blood and felt sick. Her stomach retched.

'Hey.' He moved back from her. 'Mind the suit, bitch. If you're gonnae boak, do it on your couch.'

Rosie tried to breathe deeply. Keep calm. Just breathe slowly.

Silence.

Then he turned to her. He started shouting.

'Where's he from? That big guy? Your mate.' He pushed the gun onto Rosie's forehead. 'Where can I find him? Tell me his fucking name.'

Rosie shook her head. He slapped her face. The pain brought tears.

'Please,' she said. 'I don't know. I don't know where he lives. I hardly know him.'

'Fucking liar.' He stood up. He walked to the window and looked outside. He turned around. 'Nice view, bitch. Ever seen it from mid-air?'

Rosie shook her head. Her fingers trembled as she touched her cheek. One of her eyes was almost closed.

He came back towards her.

'Listen.' He sat down. Then he started shouting again into her face. 'Tell me where I can get that big fucker. Nobody stabs me and lives to brag about it, it just doesn't happen.' He moved closer to her. 'So just tell me where I can get him, and maybe I'll not hurt you any more.'

A mobile phone rang. Rosie automatically looked for hers. Then she remembered she'd switched it off. Shit. She never did that. He took his mobile out of his trouser pocket.

'Aye. She's here, boss. How's the weather over there?' He stood up while he spoke. 'No, not really . . . No much. She's got a wee bit of a sore face, but that's all . . . She won't tell me where that big bastard who stabbed me is . . . I want him, Jake. You said I could get him myself . . .'

He stood in silence. Rosie watched. He turned to her. 'The Big Man says hallo,' he said, grinning. Then he put the phone to his ear again and listened. 'Can I throw her out the window, boss? We're three up . . .'

Rosie glanced at the window and closed her eyes. Jesus. A psycho. She wiped blood from her nose and tried to breathe.

He was silent while he listened on his phone.

'Aye . . . Yep, right . . . Okay, boss, that's fine.' He put the phone in his pocket and looked at Rosie. 'He says I've to take you for a swim.' He chuckled, shaking his head. 'He's some fucking man.'

He walked out of the living room, and Rosie could see him in the kitchen through the serving hatch. He opened her fridge and drank from a bottle of lemonade, then opened one of the cupboards and came into the living room eating from a packet of crisps.

'I'm starving,' he said, sitting on the couch. He took another handful of crisps and threw the packet over his shoulder. He switched on the television. 'Might as well settle down. It's better to wait till first thing in the morning for a swim. Do you not agree?' He smiled and turned back towards the television. 'But if you can remember an address between now and then, let me know.'

Rosie eased herself up so she was sitting. She wanted to ask if she could have a drink of water, but she was terrified. She looked around the room for ideas of how she could escape. How she could possibly take him on. She knew she had a hammer under the sink. But she could never get near it. And even if she could, she wouldn't know what to do with it.

He stood up and went towards the window. Rosie sat forward, watching. He opened the doors and went out onto the balcony and stood staring. Rosie saw him take the bag out of his pocket again and dip his finger in. He rubbed some on his gums, and stuck some up his nose. She looked around the room, and her eyes fell on the brass candlestick on the dining table. She stood up, her legs shaking, and she was across the room in a second. She crept up to the balcony. Please don't turn around. He lit a cigarette. Then, as hard as she could, she brought the candlestick down on the back of his head. But he didn't fall. He turned around, his eyes blazing. He roared.

'Bitch. Fucking bitch. Look!' He ran his hand across his bald head and felt the blood. 'Look what you've done!'

Rosie backed away, but he grabbed her and threw her against the wall. She slid down. He lifted her up and slammed her head several times against the wall. She could see him. Then she couldn't. She tried to scream. Then blackness.

She could feel the movement of the car and hear the voices. Maybe it was a dream, but the pain shooting through her face was real. She opened her eyes. Pitch black. She pushed her hands up and they hit the metal. She was in the boot of a car. Jesus Christ! She could hear laughing and loud voices somewhere. The car was moving and she winced every time it went over a bump. Then it stopped. She held her breath. The voices were quieter. She closed her eyes as she heard the boot opening.

'Get her out. Hurry. In case someone comes down here.' She recognised it as the fat man's voice.

'There's never anybody down here,' another voice said. 'Maybe the odd whore with a punter, but that's all.'

'Hurry up. Just get her to fuck. I need to get my head fixed. It's fucking killing me.' The fat man's voice.

Rosie opened her eyes as two men reached into the boot and grabbed her by the legs. Pain seared through her body. The fat man lifted her arm and they hauled her out. They tried to stand her up, but her legs gave way.

'Please.' Rosie's voice was weak. She blinked, and from one eye she could make out where she was. She could see the railings on the River Clyde walkway. The lights across the river were Kinning Park. They dragged her towards the railings.

'Please,' Rosie said. 'Please don't do this.' She felt sick rising in her stomach. Her head was spinning. They pushed her against the railings and she could see the blackness of the water. Hail Mary, full of grace. She saw her mother's face. Beloved.

Bang! The gunshot echoed in the darkness. One of the men who was holding her collapsed. Bang! The fat man was down. She slumped onto the railing. The other man who was holding her let go. He turned around long enough to see the gunman pointing the gun at his stomach and firing. He fell to the ground. Rosie covered her head with her hands, waiting to be shot. She lay against the railing.

'Rosie?' The voice was unmistakable.

'Adrian . . .' She could feel him lifting her, carrying her, running away from the quayside.

'We must hurry,' Adrian said. 'We must hurry, my friend.' He took her towards a car and sat her in the back. The light, as he opened the door, stung her eye.

'You are hurt, Rosie. Oh Rosie, I am so sorry you are hurt.' He jumped into the driving seat. 'I will take you to hospital. The Royal. It is close by.' He switched on the engine, reversed and screeched off the quayside onto the road. Rosie was sobbing with shock and pain.

'Don't cry, Rosie. You will be all right, I promise.' He sped through the city. She passed out.

When Rosie woke up she could only see out of one eye. She squinted, trying to make out where she was. She turned her head, and through the glass partition she saw nurses in a corridor. She strained her eyes, trying to make out the figure at the edge of the bed. It was Adrian. He smiled as he touched her hand. It began to come back to her.

'Oh Adrian.' The tears hurt her face. 'Adrian.' She squeezed his hand.

'Ssssh, it's finish now, Rosie. They are gone.' He gently touched her head.

'How?' Rosie was confused. She tried to remember what had happened. It was coming back. 'Adrian, how come you were there? I don't understand.'

Adrian moved close and pulled up a chair so he was sitting beside her. His voice was almost a whisper.

'I came to your flat, Rosie,' he said. 'I get no answer on your mobile, and I wanted to talk to you, to see if you were all right after last week. I saw the story about the policemen in the newspaper and on the television, so I think, okay, I will visit my old friend. And I had something to tell you. But that's not for now.'

Rosie couldn't believe it. She shook her head. 'But how did you know what was happening?'

'Well, when I came near your house, I was first of all in the street and I look up and see the fat man on the balcony. To make sure, I came into the building when somebody opened the front door, and when I come to your door, I hear shouting inside, and I recognise his voice. From last week. I never forget things like that. I listen very hard, and he was asking for me, where he could find me. I think that is what he is saying, yes?'

She nodded.

'But you did not tell him.'

'No.'

'Very brave,' he said. 'So, I waited outside and I watch, and I see them bring you out and put you in the boot of the car. I could not believe it.'

He told her he stole a car parked outside and drove after them. 'I had the gun. I knew I can shoot them all in the street at your house, but I didn't want to in case the cops come. Then they would send me back to Bosnia. So I followed.'

'Jesus, Adrian! They would have killed both of us.' Rosie lifted her head, but the pain shot through her.

Adrian shrugged. 'But they did not. They won't kill anybody any more.' He stood up. 'Listen, Rosie, I have to go. I must go away from Glasgow for a little time now in case somebody comes to look for me. And also because I have something I must do. I told the nurses that I found you in the street. I give them a false name. I have to go before the police come, but I will be in touch, Rosie, I will see you again some day. I promise.' He squeezed her hand, then turned and left.

Rosie sank back into the pillow. If it hadn't been for the pain in her cheek she would think she was dreaming. Two nurses came in, smiling.

'Hallo, Rosie,' one of them said. 'Back in the land of the living. You have a visitor.'

She saw McGuire appearing behind them. When he saw her, his expression changed.

'Gilmour, for Christ's sake! Look at the state of you.' He came towards her. 'Jesus. I wouldn't like to see the other guy.'

Rosie tried to smile. The other guy. If only he knew.

He sat down and she told him what had happened. He cursed himself for allowing her to go back to the flat by herself after the story appeared. He looked genuinely upset.

Rosie suddenly thought of TJ.

'What time is it?'

'Eight-thirty,' McGuire said, looking at his watch. 'Not going somewhere, are you?'

Rosie turned her head away. Tears came to her eyes. She asked for her mobile and rang TJ's number. It rang and rang. She looked at her missed calls. One was from TJ at seven this morning. She tried his number again. It rang and rang, but there was nobody to answer it.

It lay in the rubbish bin where TJ had dropped it, as he made his way to the departure gate at Glasgow Airport.

ACKNOWLEDGEMENTS

A word of gratitude to a whole bunch of people I'm so fortunate to have around me. Firstly, my sister Sadie, who listens to all my moans and always finds a way forward, and my family – including all my fantastic cousins – for their love and support; my friend Carole Malone who introduced me to the redoubtable Ali Gunn – thank you, Ali, for loving the book and having such a big heart; my closest friends who laugh with me in the good times and cry with me in the bad – especially Mags McGowan and Betty Gillick, whose names I shamelessly hijacked for one of my characters; my friend Franco Rey, for his encouragement; my brilliant editor Jane Wood, who keeps me on my toes, and the top team at Quercus.

Thanks, also, to Dr Marjorie Black, Consultant Forensic Pathologist at Glasgow University for her expert advice. And finally, my mum, who was my heart, who didn't live to see this, but who will be forever on my shoulder, inspiring me.